"I am not the kind of guy you want to get experience with."

Nicole stood on tiptoe, stretching a little to make a better fit. "How will we know if we don't even try?"

She was going to kiss him. And, God forgive him, he was going to let her.

He stood there like a dummy, like a stone, with his heart doing a hundred and forty in his chest while Nicole kissed him. Her soft mouth caressed his upper lip and tugged gently at his lower one. He angled his head and kissed her back, sucked on her soft, plump lips and explored her mouth.

She separated from him by a breath and smiled into his eyes. "Well," she said. "That was different."

"Yeah," he said hoarsely. "The first time I kissed you, I was trying to scare you off."

She blinked. "And now?"

"Now you're scaring *me*," he said.

Dear Reader,

This month we have something really special in store for you. We open with *Letters to Kelly* by award-winning author Suzanne Brockmann. In it, a couple of young lovers, separated for years, are suddenly reunited. But she has no idea that he's spent many of their years apart in a Central American prison. And now that he's home again, he's determined to win back the girl whose memory kept him going all this time. What a wonderful treat from this bestselling author!

And the excitement doesn't stop there. In *The Impossible Alliance* by Candace Irvin, the last of our three FAMILY SECRETS prequels, the search for missing agent Dr. Alex Morrow is finally over. And coming next month in the FAMILY SECRETS series: *Broken Silence,* our anthology, which will lead directly to a 12-book stand-alone FAMILY SECRETS continuity, beginning in June. In Virginia Kantra's *All a Man Can Be*, TROUBLE IN EDEN continues as a rough-around-the-edges ex-military man inherits a surprise son—and seeks help in the daddy department from his beautiful boss. Ingrid Weaver continues her military miniseries, EAGLE SQUADRON, in *Seven Days to Forever*, in which an innocent schoolteacher seeks protection—for starters— from a handsome soldier when she mistakenly picks up a ransom on a school trip. In *Clint's Wild Ride* by Linda Winstead Jones, a female FBI agent going undercover in the rodeo relies on a sinfully sexy cowboy as her teacher. And in *The Quiet Storm* by RaeAnne Thayne, a beautiful speech-disabled heiress has to force herself to speak up to seek help from a devastatingly attractive detective in order to solve a murder.

So enjoy, and of course we hope to see you next month, when Silhouette Intimate Moments once again brings you six of the best and most exciting romance novels around.

Leslie J. Wainger
Executive Senior Editor

Please address questions and book requests to:
Silhouette Reader Service
U.S.: 3010 Walden Ave., P.O. Box 1325, Buffalo, NY 14269
Canadian: P.O. Box 609, Fort Erie, Ont. L2A 5X3

All a Man Can Be

VIRGINIA KANTRA

Silhouette®

INTIMATE MOMENTS™

Published by Silhouette Books

America's Publisher of Contemporary Romance

SILHOUETTE BOOKS

ISBN 0-373-27285-5

ALL A MAN CAN BE

Visit Silhouette at www.eHarlequin.com

Printed in U.S.A.

Books by Virginia Kantra

Silhouette Intimate Moments

VIRGINIA KANTRA

credits her enthusiasm for strong heroes and courageous heroines to a childhood spent devouring fairy tales. A three-time Romance Writers of America RITA® Award finalist, she has won numerous writing awards, including the Golden Heart, Maggie Award, Holt Medallion and *Romantic Times* W.I.S.H. Hero Award.

Virginia is married to her college sweetheart, a musician disguised as the owner of a coffeehouse. They live in Raleigh, North Carolina, with three teenagers, two cats, a dog and various blue-tailed lizards that live under the siding of their home. Her favorite thing to make for dinner? Reservations.

She loves to hear from readers. You can reach her at VirginiaKantra@aol.com or c/o Silhouette Books, 300 East 42nd Street, New York, NY 10017.

To Jean, Andrew and Mark,
who taught me a lot about unconditional love,
and to Michael, who knows everything.

Special thanks to Jane Langdell
for insights on the law and losers;
and to Colleen Blake-Calvert of the DNA Testing Centre.

Chapter 1

Both the babe and her ride gleamed, high maintenance and fully loaded.

Bartender Mark DeLucca stepped closer to the window to get a better look. *Yeah.*

The ride was a Lexus SUV, a cashmere-beige LX470.

The woman had to be Nicole Reed. The new owner of the Blue Moon wore a you-can't-afford-this tailored shirt and a you-can't-touch-me attitude.

Rich, Mark judged. Blond, to match the car. And late.

Three strikes, sweetheart, and you're out.

He gave the bar a last swipe with a rag and crossed the planked floor to let her in. She was sorting through the keys in her hand when he unlocked the door.

"Looking for someone?" he asked.

She blushed. In embarrassment? Nah. Irritation. Recovering, she offered him a polished smile and a smooth hand. She wore thin gold rings on her fingers and neat pearl studs in her ears. Classy. Feminine. Very sexy. A pale, tiny scar on her upper lip emphasized the perfection of her face.

It was his rotten luck she turned him on.

"How do you do?" she said. "I'm Nicole Reed."

"Mark DeLucca."

Her hand was cool and firm. He held it a heartbeat too long, just to see if he could make her blush again. She didn't. She looked…blank, Mark decided. Not disapproving or flirtatious. Not hopeful. Not intrigued. Not any of the things a woman usually put on her face when she thought she had his attention.

He was annoyed to find his ego was pricked.

"It was nice of you to meet me like this," Nicole said politely.

Mark shrugged. "Not really. You're paying for my time."

She met his gaze straight-on. "Yes. I am."

It was a line drawn in the sand. Mark almost smiled. He ate girls like little Miss Michigan Avenue for breakfast.

He opened the door wider. "Then I better offer you a drink."

She frowned. "It's only ten o'clock."

"Ten-twenty," he said.

Her composure flickered. "Yes, I…I know. I'm sorry."

"Traffic?" he asked easily.

She lifted her chin. "No."

No more explanation than that.

"You are late," he said.

"But still too early for a drink," she countered.

Great. Carry Nation had just bought herself a bar.

Mark walked toward the gleaming wooden length of it, saying over his shoulder, "I've got seltzer. Soda. Orange juice. Or I could make you coffee, if you want."

"Oh. I would like a diet cola. Please." She followed him, her tasteful leather pumps clicking on his hardwood floor.

Her hardwood floor, Mark reminded himself. He grabbed her Pepsi and shoveled ice into a glass. She didn't strike him as the kind of girl who drank from a can.

He put the drink on a napkin and slid it across the bar. "You want me to ring that up?"

A gleam appeared in her cool blue eyes. So maybe she had a sense of humor after all. But all she said was, "That won't be necessary, thank you."

She sipped her drink and looked around the bar. He knew it all already: the dark booths, the clustered tables, the stuffed pike and the lineup of neon signs on the walls. So he watched her instead.

She swiveled gently back and forth on her stool, back straight, long slim legs in tailored khakis crossed. "Isn't it a little dark in here?"

It was a bright, clear September morning. The sun, slanting through the shutters, glinted off the bottles behind the bar and the glassy eyes of the stag's head mounted above the pool table.

Mark raised an eyebrow. "This can't be the first time you've seen the place."

"No," she acknowledged. "Kathy Webber showed me the plans."

Kathy Webber was the real estate agent who had handled the sale of the bar. Mark had met her. New in town, red-haired and hungry. She'd offered to show him the plans, too. Along with some other things.

"She give you the tour, too?"

"Yes. But it's not the same as actually sitting here like a customer."

"Most of our customers come at night."

"It just seems a shame to shut out that wonderful lake view."

"There is no view at night."

"The lights from the hotel? The moonlight on the water?"

Mark shrugged and didn't answer. If she wanted to romanticize the place, that was her business. But the bar's patrons didn't come for the view.

She set her drink on the center of her napkin. "We'll have to do a use study, tracking our sales by the hour."

A use study, hell. He'd just told her the bar did most of its business at night.

"I'm surprised you didn't do one already," he said.

She twisted the pretty gold rings on her fingers. "I should have. I would have. But the owner was in a hurry to sell."

"Yeah, I heard that."

If Heather Brown hadn't been so anxious to sell up and leave town after her husband went to prison, Mark might have had time to scrape up more money.

Nicole left off fiddling with her rings and smiled at him. "I guess I was impulsive."

She sounded almost pleased, as if "impulsive" was a big deal for her. It made him almost like her.

"I guess you got lucky," he said.

"That, too. Fortunately, the only other offer for the bar wasn't serious."

Mark felt his shoulders tense. "How do you know that?"

"Insufficient capital." She sipped her diet soda, unaware she'd said anything to offend him. "And from what I understand, the prospective buyer had an inadequate business plan and no background to obtain the necessary bank funding."

"And you do," he said flatly.

"Well, yes. I was chief financial officer for Connections.com."

She didn't look old enough to be CFO of her own lemonade stand. "Which is what? A dating service?"

"Internet service provider," she corrected him. "Connections provided immediate hookups and excellent customer service for a low basic rate."

"Why aren't you still doing that, then?"

Her gaze dropped back to her rings. "The founder sold the company to a larger provider."

Mark leaned against the bar. "You agreed with his decision?"

"I profited from it."

"And decided to sink your profits into running a bar."

"I decided to invest in providing real goods and services to people with whom I would have a warm, live, human connection, yes."

Mark thought of inviting Blondie up to his place for some one-on-one, warm, live, human connection and then dismissed the idea. He was past the point where he got off being anybody's walk on the wild side.

Besides, he didn't want to get fired that fast.

"You got any experience running a bar?" he asked.

"I've read extensively."

"But you don't have experience."

Her lips tightened. "I have a strong work ethic, a business degree from the University of Chicago, sufficient working capital and excellent ideas. I can hire people with experience."

She sounded like a walking textbook. *Small Business Management for Dummies,* maybe. Resentment licked along his nerves like a match set to brandy. He lifted an eyebrow. "People like me."

"It *was* my understanding you came with the Blue Moon."

"You mean, like the tables and chairs or the leftover scotch?" He shook his head. "Sorry, babe. I agreed to manage this place while they found a buyer, but I'm not for sale. Whether I stick around or not depends."

"On what?"

"On you."

She leaned forward earnestly. "I'm more than willing to keep you on while I complete a needs assessment and determine what changes should be made."

The flicker of resentment flared into a blaze. He wanted to shock her. He wanted to shake her privileged poise, her cool self-possession. He wanted…a lot of things he could never have.

Awareness of those unattainable things kindled his temper. And his judgment went up in smoke.

Deliberately he let his gaze drift down her slender throat to the first button of her blouse, where the pale-blue silk parted to reveal pale, smooth skin. She stiffened. He looked back at her face, enjoying the flush that stained her cheeks and the widening of her clear blue eyes.

"Big of you," he said. "But I wasn't talking about whether you can stomach me. I haven't decided yet whether I'll work for you."

Nicole flipped the dead bolt closed behind lean, dark and dangerous Mark DeLucca and then sagged against the cool, varnished panel of the door. Her heart thudded. Her head pounded.

Things could be worse, she told herself. Things had been worse and she had survived. But clearly, her luck with men wasn't about to change anytime soon.

And even if her luck did change—if the Fates smiled or her fairy godmother waved her magic wand or the bluebird of happiness decided to poop on Nicole's head—even then it sure wasn't going to start with the man who'd just walked out her door.

She closed her eyes. That was the old, bad thinking, she told herself. This was the new, improved Nicole. Her life wasn't subject to luck. It was about control. She was in control here.

Sure she was. Except her heart still hammered. Her face was flushed.

Sighing, she threaded her way through the empty tables. The problem was she'd always been susceptible to sexy, self-absorbed men. It was a curse.

Nicole shook her head. No, it wasn't. It was bad judgment and the need for approval.

But all that was about to change.

She was about to change.

After Connections was sold out from under her three months ago, Nicole had decided she wasn't going to let her need to be needed or her yearning for affection betray her into bad choices anymore. When Kathy called to tell her about her new commercial property, it seemed like a sign. It felt like a second chance.

Nicole made a face at the dark shutters that covered the windows. Okay, maybe a fourth or fifth chance. But she was going to make the most of it. She'd read up on bartending. She'd studied retail business. She'd bought an entire shelf of self-help and psychology guides and highlighted her copy of *Losing the Losers in Your Life* until half the pages were brilliant yellow. Finally she sank her severance package into buying the Blue Moon, put her furniture into storage and moved in with Kathy until the space over the bar could be converted into a snug apartment of her own.

Maybe the last decision had been a little precipitous, Nicole acknowledged. But she hadn't wanted to waste her capital on a short-term lease, and Kathy was eager to clinch the sale. The two women had roomed together their freshman year at college. Really, the situation was ideal. The Blue Moon was perfect.

Until this morning, when Nicole had run smack into the snake in her personal paradise. Mark DeLucca.

She unlocked the shutters over the first set of windows and folded them back. Dust grimed her fingers and tickled her nose.

She sniffed. *Lead us not into temptation…*

Tempting, yes. DeLucca had the brooding appeal of a Real Man fantasy who wore riding boots and an open-necked white shirt. Or motorcycle boots and a black leather jacket. He had flat black eyes and wavy dark hair and a face so hard and perfect it belonged on a coin. He looked like every mistake she'd ever made...only better.

She crossed the tiny square dance floor to the bar, her low heels echoing in the empty room. Maybe she had managed to get through this first meeting without throwing herself at his feet and begging him to use her. But she was pretty sure that continued exposure to Mark DeLucca's lethal good looks would be bad for her nerves, wearing on her resolution and dangerous to her heart.

She wiped her hands on a bar rag and reached for the phone. Riffling through her day planner, she found Kathy's work number and dialed. She stood, staring out the window, as the line rang on the other end. Behind the cold, dusty glass, the ruffled lake threw shards of light.

"Paradise Commercial Realtors. This is Kathy."

Nicole wedged the phone between her shoulder and jaw and said, "Tell me again why I need Mark DeLucca."

Kathy—clever, confident, divorced—laughed. "You weren't impressed with our local heartthrob?"

Nicole scrubbed at the faint black streaks on her fingers. "I was impressed all right. Is he like that with customers?"

"Like what?"

Arrogant. Intimidating. Sexy.

"Rude," Nicole said.

"We-ell, I'm fairly new in town myself, but the real estate office hasn't had any complaints. He knows his drinks. He knows the regulars. He seems pretty popular with the summer people." Kathy gave another knowing laugh. "Especially the teenage daughters of the summer people."

Nicole frowned. "He doesn't serve drinks to minors, does he?"

"Not that I'm aware of." Kathy paused before adding, "Of course, his sister's engaged to the chief of police, so I don't think you're in danger of losing your license. But I think DeLucca just flirts with them."

"Wonderful. Does his future brother-in-law, the police

chief, bend the laws about sexual harassment and statutory rape, too?''

"From what I saw last Saturday night, I'd say your bartender's on the receiving end of the harassment.'' Kathy sounded amused.

"So you don't blame him,'' Nicole said.

"I don't blame him or them. I've been tempted to harass the man myself. He can handle it. And he can handle the Monday-night football crowd, which is saying something around here. That's why we kept him, really, despite his background. He did a good job for the previous owner. She couldn't run the place, and she needed the income.''

Nicole might be a dupe where men were concerned, but she wasn't that naive about business. "Not to mention that an active operation is more attractive to purchasers than a closed one,'' she said dryly.

"That, too,'' Kathy admitted. "I showed you the numbers. So, what did DeLucca do to upset your apple cart?''

Nicole couldn't say. Didn't want to say, not when her confession would make it painfully clear how susceptible she was to the wrong kind of guy.

"Nothing much. He was a little aggressive. And I was late,'' she added, trying to keep the accusation from her tone.

"Oh, I forgot to wake you, didn't I?''

"That's all right,'' Nicole said, although it wasn't, really. "I should buy myself a new alarm clock.''

"Put your old one in storage?''

No. Her clock had been missing ever since Kevin had packed his things and a selection of hers and moved out of her apartment—right before he fired her. And in the three months since, Nicole had kept an irregular schedule, reading until all hours of the morning and then sleeping through the day. But she didn't feel like confiding that to Kathy, either.

"Something like that,'' she said.

"Well, another good thing about Mark DeLucca is he shows up when he says he will. He's reliable."

Nicole eased her death grip on the receiver. Reliable was good.

And then Kathy went and spoiled it all by adding, "It's remarkable, really, given his background."

"What background?" Nicole asked.

"Well, remember, I'm not a local, so I can't tell you everything," the real estate agent said. Though she seemed to be doing a mighty thorough job to Nicole. "But that whole family has issues. I know the mother has a drinking problem."

Nicole closed her eyes. No new business owner wanted to hear that her key employee came from a dysfunctional family with an alcoholic gene pool.

In Nicole's own personal rogues gallery, that résumé put Mark DeLucca somewhere between Charles the self-absorbed graduate student and Yuri the vodka-prone cellist. Some women fell for tall, dark and handsome. She was a sucker for tall, dark and misunderstood.

Not anymore, she reminded herself. She opened her eyes to the light streaking through the window.

Never again.

She would not allow herself to be used, and she would keep Mark DeLucca around only as long as he was useful to her.

The memory of his smooth, flat voice mocked her resolution.

I haven't decided yet whether I'll work for you.

There was a woman waiting upstairs in Mark's apartment.

He recognized the signs: the car parked in the marina's lot below, a light in the window above. But this car, a battered compact, belonged to his sister. And since his sister was also the only woman who currently possessed a key to his apartment, it was a good bet she was the one waiting inside.

Too bad. Mark pulled his Jeep into a space by the boat-house steps. He wondered what Tess wanted this time.

Or—since this was Tess, after all, who had bullied and mothered him since they were both old enough to stand—what it was she thought he needed now.

He smiled as he climbed the stairs. He was sure she would tell him.

She was already in his kitchen when he opened his door, a pretty dark-haired woman in tight jeans and a red sweater, standing in front of his refrigerator.

"You've got cold pizza and three different kinds of mustard in here," she said without turning around. "What kind of a diet is that?"

Mark grinned. "Jarek got you on some kind of health food kick now?"

Jarek Denko, Eden's chief of police, was Tess's fiancé. They were getting married in three weeks.

Tess snorted. "Hardly. I brought hazelnut crescents." She pulled a white bakery box from the fridge, dangling it by its string. "From Palermo's. I thought I'd have to leave them for you."

Mark raised his eyebrows. "Palermo's, huh? That's some kind of bribe. What do you want, Tess?"

"Aren't you home early?"

Ah, hell. As if being his big sister wasn't bad enough, Tess was also a reporter. She was both perceptive and dam-nably hard to shake. "Joe's opening the bar today," Mark said. "My shift doesn't start till four."

"Which hasn't stopped you from being there at eleven every other day this week."

He shrugged, not denying it.

"It didn't go well, did it?" Tess's golden gaze was con-cerned. "Your meeting with the new owner."

Not well. Now, there was an understatement.

Mark cut the string on the bakery box. "She hasn't fired me yet, if that's what you're asking."

"Of course she didn't fire you," Tess said. "She'd be a fool to fire you. You're all that's kept that place running."

His sister's quick loyalty was both touching and more than he could bear right now.

"I don't know if I want the job."

Tess frowned. "What else would you do?"

That was the problem, Mark acknowledged. Despite his stint in the marines, he didn't like taking orders. He had enjoyed running the bar. Calling the shots. But Nicole Reed, with her silk blouses and dot-com fortune, had nixed his dream of making the place his own.

Since he came back to Eden a year ago, he was just drifting through civilian life. So far he'd avoided repeating his old mistakes. He wasn't drinking, and he hadn't been arrested. Not yet, anyway. He'd come close a couple of months ago. But he couldn't blame his sister for looking at him like a loose boat cruising toward an accident.

He regarded her with affection. "Is that why you're here? To stand over my shoulder like you did when I had that paper due in Mrs. Williams's English class?"

"Of course not," Tess said. But her cheeks turned dull red. "I came to tell you you've got a tux fitting tomorrow at ten-thirty."

"You could have called."

"And to bring you dessert."

"You could have waited."

"And to deliver your mail."

She must have collected it from his mat when she let herself into his apartment.

He stuck out his palm. "Fine. Hand it over."

She marched around him, scooped a sheaf of envelopes and circulars from the mess on the coffee table, and thrust it at him. "There. Special delivery."

"Gee, thanks. But you shouldn't have." He started to

thumb through the stack. "There's nothing here that can't—"

A heavy cream envelope with an embossed return address snagged his attention. Johnson, Neil and Younger. Since when did high-priced Gold Coast law firms troll for business in tiny Eden?

"What?" Tess said. "What is it?"

Mark slit the flap and unfolded the letter inside.

Dear Mr. Delucca, I am writing to you, blah blah, *guardian ad litem*— What the hell was that? —*for Daniel Wainscott.* More blah, *inform you of the passing of Elizabeth Jane Wainscott*—

His eye caught. His mind stumbled. Betsy? Betsy was dead?

—*will suggested that you are Daniel's father and requested that you become his guardian.*

The news slammed his chest like a swinging boom. The air left his lungs. The room tilted.

"Mark? What's the matter?"

He couldn't speak. He couldn't think. He could only read while his world capsized around him.

Phrases leaped off the page. The words were jumbled and his vision blurred, but the meaning seemed horribly clear.

…*no legally binding effect.*

Daniel's grandparents, Robert and Helen Wainscott, have expressed interest in adopting Daniel and appear ready to pursue all legal avenues to do so.

…*advise you…*

…*choose to prove paternity…*

…*seek custody of Daniel…*

"Mark!" Tess touched his arm.

The letter in his grip quivered like the edge of a sail. Mark folded it and tucked it back into the stack. But the words still burned and swirled in his brain.

…*possibility that you are, indeed, Daniel's father…*

…*act quickly to avoid losing your rights…*

"It's nothing," he lied. "A mistake. Want a pastry?"

Chapter 2

She was pretty when she smiled.

Mark paused in the dark entryway. Behind the bar, chubby Joe Scholz was trying to explain the idiosyncrasies of the Blue Moon's cash register to Nicole Reed. Her blond head was bowed. Her pink lips curved in a secret smile. And with the suddenness of a squall, swift, blind, animal lust took Mark by the throat and shook him at the root.

He sucked in his breath and waited in the dark, his blood roaring, until his eyes adjusted fully to the dim room and his body recovered from the impact of that smile.

Nicole glanced toward the entrance and saw him. Just for a second, surprise and relief shone in those blue eyes. And then her slim shoulders squared, and her smile disappeared as if it had never been.

Mark took another breath. Good.

"I didn't expect to see you here," she said in her precise, private school voice.

He forced himself to move forward; summoned a shrug. "Then I guess you didn't look at the work schedule."

Her lips firmed. "I looked."

"Then you should have known I was on at four."

"I thought you hadn't decided yet whether you would continue to work here."

He liked the way she took the battle to him, instead of dithering around. But he couldn't afford to like her too much. He couldn't afford to say too much, either.

The problem was, he hadn't decided what to do yet. Nobody in town would believe it—the Delucca men weren't exactly known for sticking around—but Mark's pride wouldn't let him walk away without at least giving notice.

Not to mention that as long as there was the slightest chance there was a kid out there somewhere with the Wainscott name and Delucca genes, this could be a really bad time for Mark to find himself unemployed.

Mark's jaw tightened. No, he wouldn't mention that.

He wouldn't even think about it.

Much.

He lifted up a section of the counter and slid behind the bar. "You need a bartender."

Nicole slipped out of his way, watching him with her too-cool, too-perceptive blue eyes. In the cigarette-and-beer-tinged air, her scent lingered, expensive and out of place. "Joe is here."

Joe was doing his best to fade into the bottles behind the bar. "Joe's off now."

"I would have managed."

"They teach you how to mix drinks in business school?"

"No," she admitted. "But I pour a mean glass of chardonnay."

Mark stopped inventorying the glassware for the evening rush to stare at her. Little Miss Michigan Avenue wasn't actually poking fun at herself, was she?

She offered him a small smile. It didn't transform her face the way the other one did, but it was still very, very nice. "Thank you for coming in," she said. Like she meant it.

He lifted one shoulder. "Don't thank me. That's what you pay me for."

"Is there anything I can do to help?"

Uh-oh. Another minute, and he might start liking this chick. And that would be as big a mistake as mixing beer and brandy.

"Try staying out of my way," he suggested, not caring if he sounded like a jerk. Hell, hoping he sounded like a jerk, like somebody she wouldn't in a million years want to get to know better. The last thing he needed was another sweet-smelling, spoiled blonde complicating his life.

…need to consider the possibility that you are, indeed, Daniel's father.

Damn.

A couple of regulars dragged in—the eight-to-four shift was ending at the nearby paper plant—and Mark greeted them with smiles and relief.

"Hey, Tom, Ed. How's it going?" He moved smoothly to pull a beer and pour a whiskey, comfortable with the demands of his job, easy in the world he'd created.

A world where he knew almost everybody by name and could give them what they wanted without having to think about it too much.

Okay, he was good, Nicole admitted several hours into Mark's shift.

Good to look at, too, she thought as he turned to set a drink at the other end of the bar and she had the chance to admire his hard, lean back and the fit of his Rough Rider jeans.

Not that his appearance mattered, she reminded herself. She was here to evaluate his job performance, not his butt. She stole another surreptitious glance. Although at the moment she had no complaint with either one.

He didn't spin or flip or juggle bottles. Unlike Joe, who had kept up an unthreatening stream of jokes and small talk through the afternoon, he didn't try to entertain the customers. Surely he could offer them more than, "What can I get you?" and "Be with you in a sec."

But he never got an order wrong, Nicole noticed. He never asked a customer to repeat one, either. His memory—and his patience—astounded her.

It wavered only once, when an older man in a well-cut suit and ill-fitting hairpiece gulped half his drink and then demanded a new one.

Mark raised an eyebrow. "Can I ask you what's wrong with what you've got?"

The older man scowled. "I ordered a Manhattan, damn it. I can't even taste the scotch in this."

Mark whisked the offending drink away. "Let me take care of that for you."

Nicole shifted on her stool at the other end of the bar. Maybe the University of Chicago didn't offer courses in mixology, but…

"What's in a Manhattan?" she asked as Mark approached her perch.

"Vermouth, bourbon. Bitters." He barely glanced at her. His eyes and hands were busy on his bottles. Below his turned-back sleeves, he had long, lean hands and muscled forearms and—heavens, was that a tattoo riding the curve of his biceps, peeking below the cuff? "But our guy doesn't want that," he continued. "He wants a Rob Roy."

Nicole tore her attention from his arm. Liquor was expensive. She wasn't giving away free drinks because Mr. Hairpiece didn't know his ingredients. "I'm sure if you explained to him that he ordered the wrong drink—"

"—I'd be wasting my breath." Mark added a twist of lemon peel to the fresh drink. "The customer's always right, boss. I'm surprised they didn't teach you that in business school," he added over his shoulder.

Cocky, conceited, know-it-all *jerk*. Nicole twisted her rings in her lap.

"Well, hel-lo, pretty lady." A warm, male, lookee-what-we-got-here voice swam up on her other side. "I haven't seen you here before."

Nicole squeezed her eyes briefly shut. She was a loser magnet, that's what she was. She took a quick peek through her lashes at the man crowding her bar stool. Not quite young, not exactly good-looking, and married. She would bet on it. She sighed.

"That's because I haven't been here before."

He laughed as if she'd said something funny. "Guess it's up to me to make you feel welcome, then."

"No, thank you, I—"

He leaned into her, his stomach nudging the back of her arm, his face earnest and too close. "What'll you have?"

"Miss Reed doesn't need you to buy her a drink, Carl." Mark DeLucca's voice was edged with amusement and something else. "She owns the bar."

The pressure on her arm eased as the man—Carl—took a step back. "*This* bar?"

"This very one. And if you want to come back, I suggest you take your beer and go join your pals."

"Well, excuse me," Carl blustered.

"You bet," Mark said.

Nicole was grateful. Embarrassed. Defensive. The author of *Losing the Losers in Your Life* was adamant that a successful life plan did not include waiting for rescue.

As soon as her new admirer was out of earshot, Nicole snapped, "I could have handled him."

Mark removed a couple of glasses from the bar and gave the surface a quick wipe down. "Old Carl would have liked that."

Her face flamed. "I meant, I can look after myself."

Mark paused in the act of emptying an ashtray. He gave her a quick, black, unreadable look that scanned her from the top of her smooth blond head to the glittering rings on her fingers and nodded once. "Yeah, I can see that. My mistake."

And after that he pretty much treated her as if she wasn't there.

Nicole squirmed on her wooden bar stool. Well, she squirmed on the inside. On the outside, she sat with perfect poise, her spine straight, her knees crossed, typing her observations into the slim-line laptop she'd set up on the bar.

Men and women on their way home from work were replaced by young people out to have a good time. Couples pressed together in the booths in the back. Singles hooked up at tables or swayed by the jukebox. Nicole sipped her Diet Pepsi and let it all wash over her, the raucous music and the flickering TV, the drifts of cigarette smoke, the bursts of laughter. It was louder, looser, more exciting than she'd imagined.

Thrilling, because now it was hers.

She typed a note about the music. The jukebox selection needed updating. She couldn't imagine her clientele playing "Takin' Care of Business" that often if they had an adequate choice.

Mark greeted most of his customers—*her* customers— by name, took their orders, poured their drinks. No one had to wait more than forty-five seconds. No one was neglected.

Well, except for Nicole. Mark kept her supplied with Pepsi and otherwise ignored her.

He did a good job for the previous owner.

Maybe. He certainly collected his fair share of tips, Nicole thought, with an eye on the beer mug beside the register. And more than his fair share of interested glances.

A sultry brunette in big hoop earrings leaned her cleavage on the bar. A giggling group of teenage girls, shrink-wrapped in skinny tops and hip-hugging jeans, bumped and nudged each other by the pool table.

Nicole watched as Mark filled their drinks and returned

their smiles. The brunette licked salt from the rim of her glass. The gum-snapping cocktail waitress—Diana? Debbie?—unloaded a tray of diet sodas by the giggling girls.

Nicole's shoulders relaxed slightly. At least her liquor license was safe for another night. Her investment was safe. Everything was going to be fine. She hadn't made another monumental life mistake, the way her mother said and her father feared.

Nicole glanced again from the hair-flipping teenagers to the brunette laying it all out on the bar. Right. Everything was fine. Unless, of course, a fight broke out over her bartender.

Or he stole from the till.

Nicole watched Mark DeLucca unload a stack of bills from the cash register and start riffling through them. It was late. She consulted her Givenchy watch. After midnight. The front lights were out, the front door was locked, and she was alone with a man who made every tiny hair on her body stand at attention.

"What are you doing?" She hated the way her voice sounded, sharp with suspicion.

He barely glanced at her. "Daily register report."

That sounded reassuring. He was the bar manager, she reminded herself. He had a responsibility to count the cash and figure the day's net sales.

Correction. *Had* had the responsibility.

She shifted on her perch. "I can do that. Since I'm here."

His lean back stiffened. And then he shrugged and moved away easily from the register. So easily she wondered if she'd imagined that moment of resistance.

"Be my guest," he said.

She wasn't his guest. She was his employer, a fact she didn't need to remind him of. Or apologize for.

Nicole raised her chin and slid off her bar stool.

At least he could take orders, she thought, as she checked

his total for the day. And he could add. Apparently he wasn't dipping into the cash register, either. There was no reason for her to feel so gosh darn uncomfortable around the man.

No reason except he looked like an invitation to be bad.

She watched him prowl around the room, collecting glasses, emptying ashtrays. Maybe it was the hard, long body, the jet-black hair, the take-no-prisoners face. Maybe it was the wicked dark brows over those I've-got-a-secret eyes. Maybe it was—

—her problem. She rubbed the space between her eyebrows, as if she could massage her tension away. Her fault. The man couldn't help the way he looked, for goodness's sake.

He swung a chair up onto a table, the muscles flexing in his back and arms, and her stomach actually fluttered.

She frowned.

"You want to lock up, too?" Mark asked, his voice flat.

Oh, dear. She didn't want him to think she didn't trust him.

Although that had been one of Zack's favorite ploys, pretending injury at her lack of trust. *Don't you trust me?* he'd demanded, making her feel horrible, while he boinked every film student and wannabe actress who would lie down for his camera.

She swallowed hard. That was personal, she told herself. This was business.

She looked at Mark's hard, expressionless face.

"You can do it," she said, hoping she didn't sound as strained as she felt. "I'll see you in the morning, and we can talk about procedures then. Eight o'clock."

"Nine," he said. At least he didn't make a crack about her being late. "Let me walk you to your car."

"That's not necessary, thanks."

He strolled closer. Her pulse jumped. She made an effort not to retreat. "Because you can take care of yourself."

"I can, you know." Suddenly it was important that he see her as a competent, confident individual, and not another bar bunny. "I've taken self-defense classes."

"Great. So you don't need an escort. Maybe I need to see you to your car anyway."

That was clever of him, Nicole decided. And rather sweet. As they walked to the entrance, she tried to find a way to say so that wouldn't sound like a come-on.

"I appreciate your concern for security."

He slanted a look at her as he opened the door. "Security, hell. I can't afford to let anything happen to you."

She was immediately flattered. And suspicious. "Why not?"

"Didn't you ever ask why the owners were in such a hurry to sell?"

The parking lot was very dark. And isolated. The wind rustled the trees and ruffled the water. High overhead, the pale moon rode the cloudy sky. At this hour all the other Front Street businesses were closed. The other buildings were dark and faraway. The only light came from a bait-and-convenience store at the far end of the marina.

Nicole took a deep breath. She would have to investigate the cost of more lights. "I—no. Kathy never said."

"Never mind, then."

She dug her heels into the gravel of the parking lot. "Tell me."

He shrugged. "Last spring three women were followed or attacked after leaving the Blue Moon. One of them was murdered. The police chief, Denko, finally figured it was the owner who did it. Tim Brown. He was convicted, and his wife put the bar up for sale."

Nicole was shaken. "That's terrible. But if the man who did it is locked up—"

"Yeah, *if.* Some folks still think the police got the wrong guy."

He slouched beside her car. She couldn't read his expression in the dark. There was just this general impression of black hair, broad shoulders and male menace.

Her heart pounded. "Who do they think did it?"

His smile gleamed like a knife in the shadows. "Me."

Chapter 3

He had pulled some boneheaded, shortsighted stunts in the past, Mark thought as he polished off the last Palermo's crescent for breakfast. School fights. Petty vandalism.

He snagged a quart of milk from the fridge, sniffed and drank from the carton.

Scaring his new boss in the parking lot didn't rank up there with the time he'd liberated a powerboat to go joyriding at the age of twenty or his career-ending screwup in punching out an officer. But it was still dumb.

He'd be lucky if Blondie didn't fire him.

Unless… He lowered the milk carton. Unless that had been his aim all along. Piss her off enough, and he wouldn't even have to take responsibility for quitting.

Self-sabotage, his sister would call it, with the authority of a woman who had gotten her start editing the "Ask Irma" column in the *Eden Town Gazette*. Mark didn't believe in that psychobabble self-help bull. He replaced the empty carton in the fridge and closed the door. Anyway, he took responsibility.

When he had to.

Which, admittedly, wasn't very often.

He shuffled through the bright stack of advertising flyers until he uncovered the cream-colored letterhead from the lawyer.

''Jane Gilbert'' was typed below the nearly illegible signature. The phone number was printed above. His gut tightened.

He glanced at his watch. Eight-twenty. He wasn't due to meet Blondie at the bar for another forty minutes. Plenty of time to call this Gilbert broad and find out what the hell she expected him to do about the bombshell she'd lobbed into his life.

Hell. He picked up the phone.

She had let him intimidate her, Nicole thought grimly, meeting her own serious blue gaze in the bathroom mirror. She knew it.

And she knew better.

It was all covered in chapter six of *Losing the Losers in Your Life.* You couldn't always control the people around you, but you could control your reactions to them. And her pulse-pounding, breath-catching reaction to Mark De-Lucca—which had to be apprehension, it would just be too awful it if were lust—well, anyway, that would have to stop.

She nodded decisively at her reflection and got an encouraging nod in reply. Yanking open the bathroom door, she marched into the hall and collided with her exquisitely turned-out roommate.

''Ouch,'' the redhead said. ''You're in a hurry this morning.''

Nicole felt the hot sweep of blood in her cheeks. She didn't care what the author of *Losers* said, it was impossible to control a blush. ''Sorry. I don't want to be late.''

Kathy lifted a penciled eyebrow. "Got a hot date with Delicious DeLucca?"

"Yes. No. Sort of. I don't want to be at a disadvantage when I see him again."

"Sweetie, a guy that gorgeous puts every woman at a disadvantage." Kathy peered past her at the mirror, tweaking at her hair. "Well, almost every woman. The man's a menace."

"Yes," Nicole said dryly. "So I heard."

Kathy's hand froze. "Who told you?"

"He did." Nicole swallowed the lump of betrayal that burned in her windpipe. "You should have said something."

Her roommate continued to fuss at her reflection in the mirror, still not quite meeting Nicole's eyes. "What was I supposed to say? It happened months ago. Before I came to town. Besides, the paper said he didn't do it."

"I know." She had checked the on-line archives of the McHenry County papers last night. "I also noticed that at least two of the articles were written by someone named DeLucca. Any relation, would you guess?"

"His sister," Kathy said. "But that doesn't change the fact that the guy is innocent."

"How can you be so sure?"

"Because they locked up somebody else."

Nicole drew a deep breath. She hated confrontation. Which was one of the reasons her boyfriends had a tendency to wipe their feet on her before they walked away. But all that was changing now. *She* was changing. "That's another thing. Why didn't you tell me the former owner of the bar was convicted of murder?"

"Why should I? His wife was handling the sale."

Okay. Still…

"You should have told me," Nicole said stubbornly. "I might have been interested to learn that I was buying the business of a convicted killer and employing the other main suspect in the case.''

''See? That's exactly why I didn't say anything. I knew you'd blow things out of proportion. This was a good deal, Nicole.''

Kathy's voice awoke the echo of other voices, other accusations. Her mother's. Charles's. Kevin's.

Don't make a fuss, Nicole.

I only kissed her. You're overreacting.

Why do you always have to make such a big deal out of everything?

''A good deal for you,'' Nicole said.

Kathy rolled her eyes. ''Well, sure. This was my first big commercial property sale on the new job. What do you want me to say? I appreciate your business?''

Nicole was shaken. ''No. I just—''

''Fine. Because I do. And thank you. But you were the one who couldn't wait to get out of Chicago.''

''Yes,'' Nicole said. ''You're right.''

But Kathy was on a roll. ''You were the one who lost your job.''

''The owner sold the company,'' Nicole corrected her.

''After he broke up with you.''

Nicole flinched. ''Yes.''

''And didn't you say you wanted to move further away from your parents?''

Nicole felt herself visibly shrinking, like Alice at the bottom of the rabbit hole, drinking from a bottle she never should have opened. ''You're right,'' she said again. ''I'm sorry.''

Kathy shrugged. ''I just don't like you thinking you're doing me any favors. You were as eager to clinch that sale as I was. An established business in a great location with available living space doesn't come along every day.''

''It's a wonderful property,'' Nicole said truthfully.

And wondered, as she drove carefully to work along unfamiliar streets, how soon she could renovate the upstairs apartment and move in.

With a sigh, she saw that Mark DeLucca had managed to get to the Blue Moon before her. His black Jeep Cherokee occupied the parking space closest to the entrance.

Nicole wasn't upset. Really. It wasn't like the space had a big sign on it that read Owner.

She tugged on the door. Locked.

Well, of course he *would* lock it while he was alone inside. Hadn't she told him last night that she appreciated his concern for security?

She fished in her bag for her new keys, trying not to twitch with irritation. Her hand closed on her keyring just as the door opened, and Mark DeLucca stood framed against the shadows, every bit as lean, dark and dangerous as he'd looked last night.

He wore a navy work shirt with the cuffs rolled back, exposing his muscled forearms. His hair clung damply to his temples. A tiny bead of sweat streaked the harsh plane of his face.

Oh, my.

She wanted him the way a nicotine addict craves a last cigarette, wanted to breathe him in and hold him inside her.

Bad idea. Get with the program, Nicole.

He frowned. "Sorry I didn't answer right away. I was in back cleaning up."

"Oh." Because that didn't seem to be sufficient response, she added, "Thank you. I noticed last night that the place could use a thorough cleaning."

His expression became shuttered. "I can get you a mop and bucket from the closet, if you want."

Nicole blinked. Was he teasing? "I thought I would hire a cleaning service."

He shrugged, already moving away from her toward the bar. "It's your money."

It was her *bar*. Still, she expected to operate it at a profit.

She nibbled her lip. "Do you think that would be too expensive?"

"Depends on what you call expensive." He began to restock his work station with coasters and napkins, his movements so quick and practiced she had to wonder if he were even aware of what his hands were doing. "Commercial cleaning a place this size, including the degreasing, will run about fifteen hundred dollars. More, if you don't want to close for the day and have to pay the crew to come in at night."

She nodded. She would check his figures later, but what he said sounded reasonable. "I'd rather not close if I can help it. There will be enough disruptions with the remodel."

"Hold the train. What remodel?"

Oh, dear. This was not how she had planned to introduce the topic.

"Well…" She would talk about her plans for the lunch room later, she decided. "There's that empty storage space upstairs. That could be converted into an apartment."

"Sure it could. If you could find somebody willing to rent rooms over a bar."

"I wasn't planning on renting. I want to live there."

"What about the noise?"

She shifted on her stool. "Soundproofing would of course be part of the renovation." God, she sounded stuffy.

"What about the inconvenience?"

"What inconvenience? I'm used to immersing myself in my work. I've had enough of hour-long commutes. And this way I'd always be available to keep an eye on things."

"Swell. The next time I have to break up a bar fight at one in the morning, it'll be a real comfort to me, knowing you're on hand to keep an eye on things."

She stuck out her chin. "I'm not really concerned about your comfort level."

He muttered something that sounded like, "No kidding."

"This is a business decision," she said firmly.

Which was a lie. It was intensely personal, this need to have a place that was wholly hers. She was tired of making room in her heart and her life and her closets for men who moved in, made a mess and moved on. The Blue Moon was hers.

"Anyway, it's my decision," she said, which was true and made her feel better.

"Well, that puts me in my place."

Heat swept her cheeks. "I didn't mean—"

His lips twisted in a smile. If he hadn't looked like Lucifer rejoicing over the fall of mankind, she might have thought he was teasing. Or even sympathetic.

"Forget it," he said. "If you don't see any problem with a young, single, attractive woman living alone over a bar, it's not my job to educate you."

Pleasure spurted through her. He thought she was attractive.

No. He thought she was dumb as a rock.

Keeping her voice cool, she said, "Actually, it is your job. To educate me, I mean."

He leaned against the bar. "Now that could get interesting."

She ignored the little jump of her pulse. "Why don't we start with a review of the employee schedules," she suggested.

He went very still. And then he nodded once, in a brief gesture of…acquiescence? Respect? "You're the boss."

Or was he mocking her?

For over an hour, they discussed schedules and procedures and suppliers. Nicole took notes on her laptop. Mark showed her the work schedule pinned to a bulletin board in the back and the contact numbers taped by the phone, but most of the information he seemed to keep in his head.

It was inefficient, she decided. And intimidating.

"Deanna's the only waitress with the hours to get benefits,'' he was saying. ''Then you've got Joe on days, and me on nights. Both full-time. And Louis, who runs the kitchen. You meet Louis yet?''

A slightly built, softly spoken black man with a bald head and a dry handshake. She nodded.

''Everybody else is part-time,'' Mark continued. ''You'll meet them all eventually.''

She wanted to hold a staff meeting and meet them all at once. ''Actually—''

''Payroll's done by a service,'' he went on. ''I'll give you—''

Nicole cleared her throat. She was getting tired of interruptions. It was time to take control. ''Wouldn't it be cheaper to calculate the deductions and write the checks ourselves?''

''Yeah. If you have time for that kind of thing. Which I don't.''

She smiled, pleased to have discovered an area where she could make an immediate and positive difference. ''But I do. Have the time. And the software.''

''You want me to give you a gold star?''

He didn't sound jeering, she decided. More…amused.

''How about a cherry in my drink?''

He grinned suddenly, and the shock of it ran through her system like a computer virus. ''You don't strike me as the fruit-and-paper-umbrella type.''

''I don't?''

''Nope.''

Drop it, her new, improved self ordered. *You are not a healthy woman. You are a relationship addict. You cannot indulge in a flirtation, even a tiny one, without going on a love binge.*

She moistened her lips with her tongue. ''What type am I?'' she asked.

Her better self groaned and threatened to call their mother.

Mark DeLucca studied her with his flat, black eyes. "Hard to say. Yesterday I had you pegged as a chardonnay girl."

"And...today?"

"Today I think that's too ordinary."

He thought she wasn't ordinary. Excitement licked along her nerves like flame set to paper.

The phone behind the bar rang.

They both reached for it.

Mark's hand, hard and lean, closed over Nicole's. She felt her cheeks color, but held on. This was her establishment. It was her phone.

After a moment he let go.

"Good morning, Blue Moon," she said breathlessly into the receiver.

"Good morning." The woman's voice was pure Gold Coast, warm and rich as melted butter over lobster. "Is Mark DeLucca in?"

Nicole's insides congealed. "One moment, please." She thrust the phone at Mark. "It's for you."

He took the receiver from her cold hand. "Thanks. Mind if I—"

"Please, take the call. I think we're done here."

She was looking at him funny, like he'd said or done something on purpose to upset her, instead of just flirting with her a little.

But Mark didn't have time to figure it out.

He didn't have time to figure her out, not if this was the call he was expecting.

He held the receiver to his ear. "DeLucca here."

"Mr. DeLucca, this is Jane Gilbert. What can I do for you?"

He turned his back on Nicole Reed, with her too-blue, too-interested eyes. "Isn't that supposed to be my line? You wrote to me."

"Yes."

"So, what do you want?"

"I want whatever is in the best interests of six-year-old Daniel Wainscott. It remains to be seen if you can help me there."

He didn't bother to take offense at her tone. Hell, he agreed with her.

"Have you—" His heart was beating harder than it had on the airstrip at Kabul. His palm was sweaty on the receiver. "Have you said anything to him about me?"

"No. I see no point in raising the child's hopes unless and until it is established that you are indeed his father. Are you?"

He was dimly aware of Nicole behind him, moving away to the other end of the bar. To give him more privacy?

"I don't know," he said.

He sure hadn't thought about becoming a father seven years ago when he was making it with shy blond Betsy every chance they could both sneak away. Or when her mother figured out what they were up to and her daddy put a stop to it. Or at the end of that summer, when he'd joined up and shipped out, or in any of the intervening years since. But he'd given it plenty of thought in the last twenty-four hours.

"I could be," he said.

"Then your first step should be a paternity test," Jane Gilbert said briskly. "There are home kits, of course, but it would be better if you had the test done at a collection center, to establish a proper chain of custody. In case your claim to Daniel were to be questioned in court."

His only previous court experience had been as a defendant. He wondered what her lawyership, this Gilbert woman, would make of that.

Daniel's grandparents have expressed interest in adopting Daniel and appear ready to pursue all legal avenues to do so.

Hell.

"What do you need?" he asked. "Blood?"

"No. The technician will take a buccal swab—a sample of skin cells from the inside of your cheek."

"How much?"

"How large a sample? I'm afraid I—"

"No. How much is this going to set me back?"

The lawyer's voice chilled like vodka over ice. "The cost can probably be recovered from Elizabeth Wainscott's estate. However, a test of the child and alleged father can run anywhere from $450 to nearly $800."

"Why the difference?"

"I haven't decided yet whether to subject Danny to the normal testing procedure or to collect a special sample."

It was too much to take in.

He should have suggested he call her back, this afternoon, maybe, when he had more time to think.

And fewer distractions. Even with the length of the bar between them, he could still smell the light, expensive scent of Nicole's perfume, could still hear the soft click of her computer keyboard, *rappity-tap-tap* behind him. He *so* did not want her getting the drift of this conversation. Which was dumb, since it wasn't like he was going to make it with her anyway.

He pulled his mind back. "What kind of sample?"

"Chewing gum," Jane Gilbert said simply and unexpectedly. "The lab can extract Danny's DNA from well-chewed chewing gum. I'm told Wrigley's Juicy Fruit works best."

"So then he wouldn't know what was going on."

There was a little pause. "In a case such as this, when a child may already be feeling upset or abandoned by one parent's death—"

Mark didn't need a lawyer to tell him about children's feelings of abandonment.

"Do it," he ordered.

"Excuse me?"

"Get the special thing. I'll pay for it."

"It will take a week longer to process," the lawyer warned.

Mark had already spent—what, six years? seven?—without knowing that he was a father. *If* he was a father.

"I can wait," he said.

"Very well." Did he imagine it, or had the lawyer's voice warmed ever so slightly? "There's probably a lab or doctor's office near you that could take the sample. However, if you choose to have the test done in Chicago, we could meet. To discuss Daniel."

To see if getting him mixed up in the kid's life would be in the best interests of the child, she meant.

"Yeah," he said. *Rappity-tap-tap,* went Nicole's fingers behind him. "Yeah, that would be good. When?"

"Next week sometime?"

"Sure."

"Thursday? Four o'clock?"

"Fine."

He hung up the receiver, annoyed to note that his hand wasn't steady. When he turned, Nicole was watching him with narrowed blue eyes.

"You got a problem?" he asked.

Swell, DeLucca. Make it a perfect day. Pick a fight with the boss.

Her slim shoulders squared. "Not necessarily. Do you?"

He could almost like the way she didn't back down. Almost.

"Not necessarily," he said, mocking her. "I need next Thursday off."

"All right. I—did you say Thursday?"

"Yeah."

"I'm sorry. I have a previous commitment that night."

Mark shrugged. "It doesn't matter. I'll switch hours with Joe."

"And if he's not available?"

"I'll work something out."

"I need someone who can close the register."

He was unwillingly pleased that she trusted him with her money. But that didn't give her the right to command his time.

"So, you do it."

"I told you, I have plans for that evening."

He might have just dismissed her as a spoiled rich girl. But her voice was stiff with distress. Her shoulders were rigid.

He frowned. "What kind of plans?"

"If you must know, I'm attending a party with my parents."

Any temptation to feel sorry for her died. "A party is that important to you?"

She sighed. Some of the starch left her shoulders, like the wind abandoning a sail. "No. My parents are important to me. Their good opinion is important to me."

Betsy had cared about her parents' opinion, too, Mark remembered.

More than she'd cared about him.

More than she'd cared about…their son?

Pain stabbed an old wound, making him snarl. "Sorry. I'm not going to give up my plans so you can make nice with your parents."

Nicole glared. "Well, I'm not giving up my evening so you can make time with your married lover!"

Chapter 4

She was wacko.

"What are you talking about?" Mark demanded.

Nicole's face turned fiery red. He could almost—*almost*—feel sorry for her.

"I'm not judging you," she said painfully. "But it's unwise to form a relationship with someone who isn't free to commit to you fully."

Mark lifted an eyebrow. She was so earnest it was funny. "You speaking from experience here?"

Her face got even redder. He wouldn't have believed it.

"I'm not trying to get personal," she said. "I'm simply saying it's a mistake."

He could go for the direct approach. Sometimes that worked. "He really did a number on you, huh? What was his name?"

"Ted," she said, surprised into a reply. She looked down at her rings. "He had three children. Boys."

Her lips pressed closed, as if she'd let something precious escape. Interesting.

"You got a problem with boys?"

She didn't smile. "No. I liked them. I liked spending time with them. I never minded going over on the weekends so that he could meet with customers or go into the office. Only—" She broke off.

"Let me guess. It wasn't only customers he was meeting."

Her blue eyes widened. "How did you know?"

"I hear it all the time, babe. It happens all the time."

"He wasn't even divorced," she said. "Only separated."

He heard that, too. But it didn't make sense. She was rich. Blond. A looker. "Why'd you put up with it?"

"I don't want to talk about it."

He shrugged. Her love life wasn't his problem. "Okay."

"And you don't have any right to sound so superior."

"Hey," he said, genuinely startled. "You don't need to get so defensive."

But she went on as if she hadn't heard him. "You can't tell me you've never gotten involved with a married woman."

"No. I can't tell you that," Mark said grimly. "But I can tell you that's one mistake I don't plan on repeating."

Nicole sniffed. "Why did you agree to meet with her, then?"

"Meet who?"

"The woman on the phone."

He almost goggled at her. The lawyer?

He turned to check the liquor levels in the bottles behind the bar. Not that anyone in Eden was likely to order a lunchtime grappa, but it bought him some time to figure out how to deal with her accusation.

"You shouldn't jump to conclusions," he said.

Nicole lowered her voice to a wickedly deep imitation of his. "'Have you told him about me?'" She shook her head and said in her normal voice, "Big leap."

He wanted to shake her. He wanted to laugh. She was funny and concerned and totally wrong.

Mark was getting pretty damn tired of being accused of things he hadn't done.

"You don't know the situation," he said.

You don't know me.

"So tell me." Her voice was bright and sympathetic. So were her eyes.

"No."

She stiffened. "I can't let you have Thursday night off without some kind of explanation. Staffing is a problem."

"Your problem," he said. "You're the boss."

"Yes, I am. And since I am—" she took a deep breath and straightened on her bar stool "—I want you back by eleven that night to close the register."

She was drawing her line in the sand.

He could do what he wanted. Let her call the shots. His business with the Gilbert woman would be over by five. Six, tops.

Or he could tell her to go to hell.

Yeah, and then he could explain to the guardian-ad-whatever, at their first meeting, that not only was he the kind of loser scum who lost track of a seventeen-year-old girl and their baby, he was an *unemployed* loser scum incapable of supporting said child.

Oh, yeah. That would go over well.

He looked at Nicole, sitting at the end of his bar in her don't-touch-me blouse with her don't-mess-with-me face, nervously twisting those pretty gold rings on her fingers. What would she do if he walked on her? She'd be screwed. They both knew it.

"Eleven?" he asked.

She tried hard to keep the hope from her expression, but it shone in those incredible blue eyes.

"In time to close," she said.

"Fine. I can manage that."

He didn't know what he expected. Not gratitude, exactly, but… Well, okay, gratitude would have been nice.

Instead she nodded, like his capitulation was never in doubt, and started grilling him about the menu.

Okey-damn-dokey. He wasn't trying to make points with her. From now on, he would just do his job and hope she didn't interfere too much.

She was taking him line by line through the appetizer listing, with him explaining which items Louis prepared in the kitchen and what he purchased from their wholesaler in Chicago, when a horn blared in the parking lot.

Nicole jumped. "What's that?"

Mark shrugged. "Beats me."

The horn sounded again, a quick, impatient tattoo.

Nicole nibbled her lip. "Well, don't you want to go see?"

"Nope. It's probably some kid with a new car."

Whoever it was decided hitting the horn wasn't working and starting banging on the door instead. Nicole slid from her seat.

"Or a drunk," Mark added, "who can't wait for opening hour." In which case he couldn't very well let Blondie answer the door alone now, could he? He strolled from behind the bar. "Or it could be—"

Nicole threw the bolt and opened the door on a very attractive, very ticked-off brunette wearing gold jewelry and sunglasses.

His sister, Tess.

Oh, hell.

He had a tux fitting at ten-thirty which he had just totally blown off.

Of the two women, Tess looked more surprised. But she also recovered faster. Growing up with an alcoholic mother and an abusive father did that for you. Both DeLucca kids had plenty of practice in hiding their feelings and thinking fast on their feet.

His sister stuck out her hand. "You must be Nicole. I'm Tess. Is Mark here?"

Nicole froze like one of those ice sculptures they set on the buffet tables in the Algonquin Hotel dining room. "Yes, he is. Is he expecting you?"

"He should be," Tess said. "The rat." She looked over Nicole's shoulder at Mark. "You are not getting out of this. I don't care how uncomfortable it makes you or what you think of this marriage. If you hurry, they can still squeeze us in."

Oh, yeah. Tess was one tough cookie, all right. Only he knew what a softie, what a sucker she was.

He owed her. Always had.

And maybe now was a good time to prove to his blond boss—hell, to prove to himself—that he could walk away at any time.

"Okay," he said to his sister. "I'm gone," he told Nicole.

"But—"

Looking into those wide blue eyes, he felt a very unfamiliar and totally unwelcome need to explain. To apologize. To reassure.

He squashed it.

Nicole Reed didn't need him or his explanations.

Besides, Joe would be along in a few minutes to help her open.

"I work four until close," he said. "Maybe I'll see you then."

"It was nice meeting you," Tess added.

He followed her out to her car.

Nicole folded back the grimy shutters, watching through the window as Mark drove off with the gorgeous brunette with red nails and attitude.

Things could be worse. At least this time she knew what kind of man he was before her heart got involved.

Mark DeLucca was not the type of guy who could make her happy. He was a player. Like Charles. Like Zack. Like every other guy who had ever strung her along and used her. Only this guy wasn't even bothering to string her along. He had enough women on his line already. That Kathleen Turner wannabe on the phone. The exotic-looking brunette in the car.

Nicole couldn't compete.

She shouldn't want to compete.

Her relationship with Mark was strictly professional, employer to employee.

She slid into a booth, kneeling on the bench seat to unlatch the heavy shutters.

Employee. *Right.*

Only she hadn't been in the kitchen flirting with *Louis.* She hadn't quizzed *Joe* about his personal life or blurted out the pathetic story of married-Ted-the-insurance-salesman-and-his-three-children to *Deanna.*

Oh, no. Nicole tugged at the dirty shutters. Because that wouldn't be humiliating enough. No, she had to go and expose herself to Mark DeLucca instead.

Outside the windows, the sky was overcast. The lake reflected shards of light like an open drawer of tarnished flatware. Nicole closed her eyes and rested her forehead against the cool glass.

She was such a loser.

"Miss Reed? Nicole?" It was Joe, coming through the open front door. She'd forgotten to lock up. "Is Mark here?"

Strictly professional, Nicole reminded herself. She scrambled around on the seat.

"No, he, um, left." Oh, that was smooth.

Joe's cheerful, chubby face creased. "His car's our front."

"Yes. He got a ride." She gritted her teeth. "From Tess somebody."

"Oh, yeah?" Joe grinned. "Wonder if she roped him into helping with the wedding."

Oh, God. It hurt. Nicole hadn't expected it to hurt. Not this soon. Not this much. She barely knew the man. She didn't even like him.

"I think so. Yes," she said stiffly.

Joe moved behind the bar. "Hard to believe they're getting married in just three weeks."

"Very hard," Nicole agreed.

Mark didn't look like a soon-to-be-married man. He didn't act like an engaged man.

All her instincts rejected the possibility that he belonged to another woman.

Of course, her instincts generally sucked.

"I'm sure they'll be very happy together," she said. "They seem very—" sexy, careless, confident, all the things she was not and never would be "—well suited."

"You know Chief Denko?"

Nicole blinked. "Who?"

"Jarek Denko. The chief of police. Tess's fiancé."

"Wait. I thought—" she took a careful breath "—I thought Mark was her fiancé."

Joe laughed. "Mark? Nah. Mark is Tess's brother. She's making him give her away at the wedding."

Relief bloomed in Nicole's chest. She was almost dizzy with it.

The brunette was Mark's sister. Mark wasn't engaged.

Maybe just this once her instincts weren't entirely wrong.

Tess pulled into the lot beside Mark's Jeep Cherokee. Her wiper blades shuddered and streaked against the windshield.

"Thanks," she said. "I hope your boss isn't going to be too upset with you for taking off."

Mark grinned. "Maybe you should write me a note."

"It wouldn't be the first time," Tess said tartly. "When

are you going to get married and let some other woman take care of you?''

His last experience with a married woman hadn't left him feeling cared for at all. But Mark didn't tell his sister that. He never talked to anybody about that.

He teased, instead. ''Don't you love me anymore?''

But she replied seriously, ''I love you. That's why I want you to be happy.''

''Uh-huh. And tying myself down to one woman is going to make me happy.''

''It would. If she were the right woman.''

This was what came of being disgustingly crazy in love. Tess was a bright girl. But her engagement to Jarek Denko had obviously shorted out a few brain cells.

''Yeah, well, the right woman isn't going to want to have anything to do with me. Not if she's in her right mind.''

Tess rolled her eyes. But he noticed she didn't argue with him. She gave him a kiss on the cheek and told him to stay out of trouble.

Yeah, like that had ever worked.

He hunched his shoulders against the rain and stomped up the plank walk to the entrance, vaguely surprised to see Nicole's gold-toned Lexus still in the parking lot. The new owner was putting in some long hours. Either she was really conscientious, or she'd decided to stick around long enough to bust his butt.

But when Mark opened the door, it wasn't his butt that occupied his attention.

It was hers.

Nicole was leaning over a table in one of the booths, her knees on the seat and her khaki-covered behind in the air. And she had, without question, one of the finest female rear ends he had seen in his life. Lush. Heart-shaped. Hot.

It wiggled. She turned. And—oh, jeez—caught him staring.

Only she didn't seem to notice.

At least, she didn't seem to mind.

She smiled, her face all sunshine despite the gray day outside, and asked cheerfully, "Like it?"

Surprise almost made him laugh.

"Love it," he told her solemnly.

"Good. I know you can't see it too well now, but you'll have a much better view tomorrow."

Okay, he was confused. Or she was. Not that he would object or anything, but it didn't seem real likely that she was inviting him to ogle her butt.

"Why tomorrow?" he asked.

"Well, obviously clean windows are more noticeable on a clear day."

Windows. She was talking about windows. And now that he didn't have her cute rear end burning into his eyeballs like the sun at noon, he could see that the glass behind her shone. Even the wooden shutters gleamed, free of their usual coat of crud. A pile of crumpled rags lay on the floor beside a bucket. Nicole's sleeves were pushed back, water spotted her left breast, and a smudge decorated her forehead.

She looked damp and untidy and very pleased with herself.

"Looks...good," Mark said.

She beamed. "Thank you. Do you want to move those chairs, and I'll get the windows by the—"

He hated to snuff her enthusiasm. But—

"No," he said.

Her shoulders squared. "Is this the part where you tell me you don't do windows? Moving furniture is not in your job description?"

He had to admire her spunk, even if she was wrong. "No. This is when I tell you the eight-to-four shift just ended at the plant and the four-to-seven rush is starting here. You need me behind the bar pushing drinks right now. Not out front pushing tables."

"All right. I can do it myself."

"Bad idea."

Her voice rose in frustration. "For heaven's sake, why? I won't be in the way. The tables don't fill up that quickly."

"Because, babe, the guys who stop in here for a beer after work don't care about clean windows. They don't want to be reminded that they have chores and wives waiting at home. They want to relax, not watch you rearrange the furniture."

To his surprise she nodded. "Selling atmosphere."

"What?"

"It's in one of my books on restaurant management. We're not simply providing drinks, we are selling a total ambiance."

"You aren't going to be selling much of anything if I don't get behind the bar."

She wiped her hands on a rag and folded it in precise quarters. "Well then, you'd better get started, hadn't you?"

He didn't know whether to laugh or go smack his head with a bottle.

He did neither. It wouldn't be cool, and cool was something Mark had cultivated since he was a scabby six-year-old trying desperately to find his place in the first-grade pecking order. He'd never been smart like Tess. He wasn't well dressed like the kids from the big houses across the lake. He didn't have the kind of mother who baked cupcakes for the class on his birthday or the kind of home you invited friends to after school. But he was cool. Man, was he cool.

He got behind the bar and pulled a draft for one of the regulars. Jimmy Greene was just off his shift at the paper plant, looking for a beer to wash away the taste of wood pulp and his general dissatisfaction with his life.

Right there with you, Jimmy boy.

When Nicole bent over to pick up her bucket and rags,

Mark let himself look. She was just a hot body with a snotty attitude, no different from any other blonde who'd done a hit-and-run on his life.

He didn't want her to be any different, because then he would want her, and wanting her wouldn't get him anywhere.

Jimmy nudged him. "Nice, huh?"

The son of a bitch was leering at Nicole's butt.

"Watch it," Mark warned. "That's my boss."

"Oh, I'm watching," Jimmy said. "And I bet you're doing more than that, you lucky bastard. She any good?"

"She's my boss, Jimmy," Mark said quietly. "So put your eyes in your head and your tongue in your mouth before I have to knock your teeth down your throat."

Jimmy slumped on his bar stool and sulked in his beer. So much for selling atmosphere.

But over the next week, Mark was forced to watch as Nicole did her damnedest to create ambiance—whatever the hell that was—in his bar. She attacked dirt like it was her personal enemy, coming in, Joe had reported, before the bar opened and working sometimes through the quiet hours of early afternoon.

Her ideas weren't bad. Not all bad, anyway. Mark had had some ideas himself, back when he'd thought he had a chance of buying the place. But…

"What are these? Handkerchiefs? Doilies?" Mark asked on Thursday, brandishing a little white square with a stylized cobalt moon rocking over a purple wave.

Nicole didn't miss a beat. "New cocktail napkins. They match the new menus," she explained, and went out to plant flowers in the tub outside the front door.

New menus?

Strange sandwiches appeared from the kitchen and on the chalkboard that listed the daily specials, grilled sandwiches with tasty ingredients and stupid names.

"What the hell is a Tuscany Twosome?" Mark grumbled to Louis.

Nicole overheard. "Capicolla and provolone with pesto aioli on focaccia," she said. "And before you start getting negative, you might as well know I'm not adding them to the permanent menu. They haven't sold very well."

"There's a surprise," Mark said.

"When I want your opinion, DeLucca, I'll ask for it," Nicole snapped, but she didn't sound so tough. Just tired.

And there was that sad baby droop to her lip when she thought no one was looking that made him long to...do something for her.

Mark rubbed his jaw. It was kind of too bad about the sandwiches. The one he'd wolfed down when he came to work today had actually tasted pretty good. And Louis seemed okay with the idea of occasionally cooking something besides chicken wings and loaded fries.

Maybe Mark didn't know food. Dinner in the DeLucca household had mostly been a matter of Tess opening cans. And neither the chow at the mess or the MREs he'd bolted down in the field were exactly dining at the Algonquin.

But he did know the Blue Moon's clientele.

"Try changing the name," he suggested.

"Excuse me?"

"Call it Italian ham-and-cheese," he said.

"Thank you. I'll consider that," she said stiffly.

Like she didn't gave a rat's ass for him or his opinions or anything. But then he walked into the kitchen at the end of the night and caught her packing the unused sandwiches into a big white box.

"What are you doing?"

Nicole blushed like he'd spotted her adding water to the vodka bottles over the bar. "I'm packing a carton for the interfaith food shuttle."

He raised an eyebrow. "Are you giving food away?"

She tossed her blond hair over her shoulders. "Better than throwing it away."

But he wasn't fooled by her snippy attitude this time.

"Yeah," he agreed slowly. "I guess you're right."

And when some of the guys wandered in after league night at the Thunder Bowl, he gave out a couple of the new sandwiches for them to try.

"We sold out of ham-and-cheese," Nicole announced three nights later. "And it's not even seven o'clock."

Mark set up the drink order for table five—two Millers and a seven-and-seven—and slid it over the counter for Deanna.

"Congratulations."

But Nicole didn't look very happy. "Do you think Palermo's is still open? Because I need to pick up more focaccia, and—"

"Hey," he interrupted her. "Relax. This place isn't going to close down because we ran out of one sandwich."

"But—"

"Erase the specials board, and increase the bakery order for tomorrow."

"Yes. All right." She flushed. "I suppose you think I'm pretty silly, getting all worked up over a sandwich."

"I think you're—"

Sweet. Special. And trying too hard.

Uh-huh. Like he could say any of those things to his boss.

"—anxious to see things succeed."

Nicole beamed at him as if he'd said something really deep. "I am." She laid her slim hand gleaming with golden rings on his arm and squeezed gently. His tongue dried to the roof of his mouth. "I want you to know I realize it wouldn't have happened without your support. I really need you here."

He almost fell for it. Staring into her baby blues, feeling

the warmth that stole through him at her words, he almost fell for her.

Was anything more seductive than those whispers?

Betsy, her eyes swimming with easy tears. *I need you, Mark.*

Hayley, her voice trembling with well-assumed anguish. *Mark, I need you.*

Was anything more painful than those memories?

Mark's jaw clenched. He *so* did not need this. Not again. Not with her. Not ever.

And so he did the one thing guaranteed to end it, made the one move sure to drive her away. Or get him fired.

"Not here, babe." He turned to set up the drinks for another ticket, checking to make sure no one was near enough to overhear. Grateful he wouldn't have to watch her face as he said the words. "We're kind of busy, you know? But after we close, maybe we can get naked."

Chapter 5

She should have slapped him.

There simply were no words to describe how awful he had been. There were no words to describe how terrible he made her feel.

Nicole bent over the sink in the ladies' room, feeling as if she was going to throw up. Her face burned. Her eyes burned. Her throat burned.

But of course she wouldn't throw up. Any more than she could have slapped him. She could not show—not by the flicker of an eyelash—how devastated she was by Mark DeLucca taking her sincere overture of friendship and turning it into something casual and dirty.

And so she had pulled her totally shaken self together enough to say, "You are a jackass. And I am your boss. So our 'getting naked,' as you so charmingly put it, here, now or ever, would be as wildly inappropriate as it is unlikely."

Inappropriate was good. She'd managed all five syllables without a stammer.

And then she'd retreated to the ladies' room to bawl her eyes out.

Nicole pulled her hands out from under the cold water and pressed her fingers to her face. She was not going out there with puffy eyes. Hadn't she humiliated herself enough already?

She'd told him she appreciated his help at the bar.

And he'd thought...

He'd said...

She blotted the mascara from her lower lids with the tips of her fingers. He was worse than a jackass. He was a snake. A pig. A wolf.

And she was a fool.

She ought to fire his butt.

But what if his stupid, cruel, crass remark was somehow her fault? Nicole raised her head and stared into the mirror. The author of *Losing the Losers in Your Life* made it clear that the actions of those around us were often reactions to our own signals, spoken and unspoken.

Had she inadvertently said the wrong thing? Sent the wrong message?

Her teeth dug into her lower lip. She had touched him, she remembered. Only on his arm, but...

He had nice arms. Lean and muscled, with strong wrists and warm skin under a dusting of dark hair. She had pressed his arm and looked up into those black, amused eyes and said—and said—oh, God. Her cheeks, her face, her whole body burned. *I really need you here.*

He probably thought she was coming on to him. Women did. All the time. She watched them. He probably thought that she was one of them.

And she knew what he was. She ought to know. If the University of Chicago had offered a degree in Men Behaving Badly, she would have graduated magna cum laude.

Nicole tore off a piece of toilet paper and blew her nose vigorously. Okay. She was an adult woman, fully responsible for how she felt. Mark was a typical unevolved clueless male. So wasn't it up to her to set the tone of their relationship?

Of course it was.

This was all her fault, really, she thought, lashing herself with the old arguments. She had let things get out of hand. She had overreacted.

She balled up the tissue and threw it away. Tomorrow, she promised herself, she would do better.

If he didn't think about her, he didn't feel too bad.

Mark sent four glasses of house white to the ladies' booth in the corner and slapped a couple of coasters on the bar for the next round of drafts.

The problem was it was hard not to think about her. The woman left evidence behind her everywhere, like a messy picnicker littering an unspoiled beach. Her menus on the tables. Her music on the jukebox. Her perfume in the air.

Even the damn coasters, with their fancy stylized logo, were her idea.

Three days had passed since he had brutally rejected her tentative thanks. She should be over it. So should he. Hell, this wasn't the first time he'd been called a jackass. Or worse.

The real problem was, this time he felt like a jackass.

Mark filled two mugs, took another order, wiped the counter clean. As long as he was working, it was still his bar. Behind it, he was in control.

Until Nicole appeared from the kitchen, wearing one of those buttoned-down blouses and an I'm-going-to-be-nice-to-this-jerk-if-it-kills-me smile. He wanted to rip off the blouse. He wanted to dig behind that defensive smile and find…what, exactly?

Whatever she'd hidden away from him since he'd slapped her down the other night. The warm, vulnerable, hopeful woman under the ice boss routine.

She hovered just out of arm's reach. "How's it going out here?"

He could be nice, too, he decided. It wouldn't kill him. Say something nice, he ordered himself.

But what came out of his mouth was, "We need a basket of cheese fries and one of those fancy sandwiches down at the end of the bar."

He could have passed the ticket to the kitchen himself. He wasn't that busy. Weekday lunchtime traffic was light: a couple of boat heads, an office birthday party, three or four suits looking to escape for an hour. Nothing he couldn't handle.

He expected Nicole to point that out. But she nodded. "I'll tell Louis."

Fine. Good. Save him some steps.

But instead of letting it go, instead of letting her go, he put out a hand to stop her.

"What is it with you?" he asked.

Her brows arched. "Excuse me?"

"There you go again. 'Excuse me,'" he mimicked savagely, keeping his voice low so that the suit at the end of the bar couldn't hear. "You don't have to be so polite all the time. This is a bar, not a damn tea party."

"This is a bar," she agreed steadily. Her pulse thrummed under his hand. "It is also a workplace. My workplace. Which requires a certain level of professional behavior from me."

God, she was a trip. "So you're just being…professional?"

Color stained her cheeks, but she didn't back down. "I think it's best."

"Better than, say, hauling off and slugging me one?"

She blinked rapidly. Aha, so she'd thought about it.

But she had a reply. Of course she did. She was the professional. "Aggressive behavior is never appropriate."

"It is if somebody has it coming."

There. It was the closest he could come to an apology. And he thought—well, he hoped—anyway, for a minute there he thought she was going to smile.

But she shook her head and said, like she was quoting or some damn thing, "I am responsible for my own actions." Her shoulders squared. With painful earnestness she said, "And it occurred to me after you…after I— It's quite possible I did something to mislead you."

Sure it was. Just like it was possible Little Bo Peep was head of a vast international crime syndicate and the Big Bad Wolf had gotten a bum rap.

"Forget it," Mark said. "You didn't do anything."

"Yes, I did," she insisted. "I—well, I touched you."

This was too heavy. She was too sincere. "Yeah? What did you do? Make a grab for my butt?"

"Your arm. I touched your arm."

He ran his thumb over the smooth skin of her inner wrist, where the blood beat wildly. "You mean, like I'm doing right now?"

Her brows drew together. "Is this some kind of trick?"

"Nah. Call it a test. Maybe I'm trying to see how far this responsibility thing of yours goes. Because here I am, touching you, and so far you're doing a real good job of not taking that to mean I think we should have sex. Although, you know, I do."

He watched in satisfaction as her blue eyes widened. Hey, he'd never claimed to be that nice a guy. But he couldn't let her keep taking the blame for his fear and bad temper.

He cleared his throat. "What I'm saying is, whether I'm making a move or not, you seem to be controlling yourself pretty well. So just because you thank me for helping you sell a sandwich doesn't mean I'm entitled to jump your bones."

This time she did smile, a real one, and cracked something in his chest wide open.

"What you're saying is that you are as responsible for your actions as I am for mine."

It sounded like something Tess would say. Or their mother, after one of her A.A. meetings.

Way too heavy.

He didn't "do" sincere.

He for damn sure wasn't sensitive.

And the distance he'd been so careful to set between them was shrinking much too fast.

He leered at her. "Maybe. Although, like I said, if you're inclined that way, I'm available."

Only instead of getting all offended and running away, Nicole treated him to another of those melt-your-bones smiles.

"No, you're not," she said. "At least, not now. Aren't you leaving for your—appointment—soon?"

The reminder caught him like a loose boom, smack across the chest.

He let go of her wrist to look at his watch.

"Twenty minutes," he said. "Joe's coming on at two, and then I'll be back tonight to close."

"I appreciate it," Nicole said.

She'd insisted on it, Mark thought wryly, but it didn't grate the way it had a week ago.

"It's no big deal."

She hesitated. "It must be fairly important. You look dressed up."

He'd pulled on khakis in place of his usual jeans, and a long-sleeved shirt with a collar.

"Yeah, I'm doing my responsible citizen impersonation today."

No point confirming the lawyer's worst fears right off the bat.

"You look very nice."

He shrugged to hide his discomfort and his pleasure.

"Hey, if it works for you, babe, I'll go get my jacket out of the car."

Nicole placed a hand on her chest. "I'm not sure my heart can take the excitement."

He grinned. She could be pretty cute. "Too bad I don't have a tie."

"Do you want one?" she asked. Like it was a real offer.

"Do you have one?" he asked, amused.

"Oh." She twiddled the rings on her fingers. "Probably."

She had a tie. Her boyfriend's?

He didn't ask. It wasn't any of his business.

Although married-Ted-with-children should have been enough to put her off men for life.

He said lightly, "You thinking of requiring ties in the bar now? With loaners on hand for the slobs?"

She shook her head. "No. I bought it for my—" Her lips closed.

Do not ask.

It's none of your business.

"Boyfriend?" he inquired.

"My boss." She colored, in the sudden, painful way that blondes—real blondes—could do. "Well, actually—"

Ah, jeez, it was coming, another of those earnest revelations that made him feel like he should apologize for being male.

"He was sort of both. At least, I thought he was. Anyway, about three months ago, he had a big meeting, with some investors, he said, and I bought him the tie as a gesture. You know, welcome to the big leagues, Mr. Executive?"

Mark didn't know, but he nodded.

"Anyway, Kevin got back from this meeting, and—"

"He flopped?"

"No." She smiled, without humor and without joy.

"He'd sold the company. Leaving me with a nice fat payout on my stock options and no job."

"He didn't need his chief financial officer to explain the books to the new boss?"

"He didn't need me. In any capacity," she added with painful precision.

What a jerk.

"So you kept the tie."

"It's in my car." He must have showed his surprise, because she added defensively, "Well, we didn't have any children or pets. And he took my alarm clock. It only seemed fair to keep custody of the tie."

Mark stiffened. If he stopped to think about it, he knew Nicole didn't mean anything by her comment. But with the lawyer's visit looming, any custody reference hit a little too close to the bone.

"You drive around with it? Like some sort of—" Scalp, he thought. Trophy. "—souvenir?"

Nicole reached for the reassurance of her rings. Mark was doing that narrow-eyed-squint thing again. Sexy. Dangerous. Effective. She wondered if he practiced it in the mirror, or if it came naturally.

"Does it matter?" she asked. "I mean, I have a tie. You need one. Just take it."

He shook his head. "No. Thanks, though," he said, and drifted away like smoke along the bar.

Frustrated, she stared at his lean back as he cleared the businessman's empty glass.

He'd done it again.

She had made an overture, an offering, and he had rejected her. What in heaven's name had she said or done wrong this time?

Unless…had she offended him by suggesting, perhaps, that he didn't own a tie? Or didn't know how to dress? Or…?

Oh, God, *she* was doing it again.

What Mark thought, what he felt, was none of her business. How he acted was not her responsibility. He'd come right out and told her so.

He pulled another beer, his strong, tanned hands easy on the tap.

Resentment churned in her stomach. She was an intelligent woman, a good person, with a degree from the University of Chicago and her own business. She had recently read her way through an entire shelf of experts—educated, insightful, positive people who talked on *Oprah* and had strings of letters after their names, and her reactions were being questioned by Lucifer the Bartender.

What made it worse was he was right.

She could barely forgive him.

Nicole was right. He should have taken the tie.

Mark slouched deeper into one of the leather armchairs provided by the Chicago law firm of Johnson, Neil and Younger for their waiting clients. The armchair was deep and comfortable, the walls were paneled wood, the plants were stiff and glossy, and the receptionist was stiff, glossy and suspicious.

The fourth time she stopped clicking away on her computer to glare at him—what did she think he was going to do, walk off with the lobby copies of *Modern Maturity?*— he deliberately caught her eye and grinned. She turned pink under her powder and dropped her gaze to her computer. She didn't look up again.

Which left him with nothing to do but stare at the portraits of dead white guys on the walls. All of *them* wore ties.

"Mr. DeLucca? Thank you for waiting. I'm Jane Gilbert."

He stood. Turned.

No tie, was his first thought. She was female, she was young—well, forty—and the look in her eye was sharp and very much alive. Nicole had the assured veneer of education, beauty and privilege. This woman was hard as oak all the way through.

She raised her brows. "Oh, my."

He scowled. She wasn't *hitting* on him, was she?

And then she held out her hand and smiled. "You look just like him."

Him. The kid. *Daniel.*

All of a sudden it was hard to breathe the refrigerated air of the lobby. If he'd been wearing a tie he would have tugged on it.

"I wouldn't know," he said flatly.

She nodded once and released his hand. "I can show you his picture."

So then he had to follow her, down several hallways carpeted in deep gray to her office. Her desk was cluttered. A narrow window in the corner sealed in the air and admitted a little light.

"Do you want something to drink?" Jane Gilbert asked. "Coffee?"

Maybe she wanted to see if he dribbled. "No, thanks."

She inserted herself into the narrow space behind her desk and sat. And waited…like he was going to open his mouth and hand her a topic to flog him with.

Mark had a CO once who used the same tactic, so he sat back and kept his yap shut. Lawyers billed by the hour, didn't they? So she'd talk soon enough.

She did. She leaned forward and said, "Tell me why Elizabeth Wainscott would not have told you there was a possibility you had a child together."

His pulse jumped. That was getting to the point. But he didn't mind. Not really. It wasn't as if he hadn't spent the past week and a half asking himself the same question. By now he'd even thought up some answers.

"How much do you know about Betsy and me?"

"Why don't you tell me what you want me to know?"

Right. He struggled for words that would describe what it had been like, what they had been like, without being too damning.

"Well…we were really young."

Jane Gilbert nodded.

"I was nineteen. Fresh out of high school. No idea what to do with myself except get into trouble. Which I was good at. Do you want details?"

"Do you feel they're necessary?"

"Not really. Anyway, Betsy was younger than I was, just as clueless but with a lot more opportunities. Her folks rented a big house right on the Pines Golf Course for the summer. Only Betsy wasn't into golf."

"What was she into?" the lawyer asked quietly.

"That summer?" He smiled, remembering. Little blond Betsy Wainscott, so pretty and so sweet and so young. Young and dumb, both of them. "Me."

Jane Gilbert nodded again. "All right. That explains the pregnancy. It doesn't explain why Elizabeth wouldn't tell you about it."

Mark rolled his shoulders to relieve the tension there. "Her parents found out about me. About us. Which was not that hard, since Betsy had been sneaking out of the house for weeks. Her daddy told her I was no good, which was mostly true, and they all went back to Chicago. End of story."

"Except for the child."

His gut tightened. "Yeah. Except for that."

"Did you ever make any attempt to keep in contact with her?"

"I called. Every day for the first week, a couple of times after that." The memories now were just as sharp and much more bitter. "I even wrote her a letter."

"And received no response?"

"I got the letter back. Unopened. And a visit from our local law enforcement telling me to stop hassling her or the

Wainscotts would file charges. Since I wasn't a juvie anymore, that could have been big trouble. So I rolled over.''

"And Elizabeth never made any attempt to contact
you?"

Ah, hell. The bitch of it was, he didn't know.

"If she did—" He stopped.

Jane Gilbert waited. He couldn't tell what she wanted
him to say, so he went with the truth.

"If she tried to reach me anytime after that September,
I might not have known. I was in the Marines."

"A patriotic choice," the lawyer remarked.

Mark smiled thinly. "No choice at all. It was that or
jail."

His sister would have snapped at him to shut up. Jane
Gilbert raised her penciled brows and said, "Please continue."

"I got arrested for liberating some old guy's boat and
taking it for a joyride. He offered to drop the charges if I
enlisted."

Jane Gilbert glanced down at the open folder on her desk.
"Because, as I understand the story, he was impressed that
you were apprehended only after you went to the rescue of
another boat in distress."

Mark shrugged. "Sunday sailors. They—" He stopped
as realization struck. "You knew."

"I *am* Daniel's court-appointed guardian, Mr. DeLucca."

Swell. "So you had me investigated."

She sat back, comfortable with her decision and confident
of her power. "You should know that Robert Wainscott
will do everything in his power to prevent you from getting
custody of his grandson. The fact that you didn't know
about Daniel's existence is in your favor, but if there is
anything else in your past that could give Mr. Wainscott
ammunition—"

"Tell you now and you can shoot me for him?" Mark
suggested tightly.

"—it would be better to get it out in the open now," Jane said.

"Better for who?"

He didn't want—he wasn't ready for—the responsibility of a kid. And he was no great prize as a father. Hell, he didn't even know for sure he was the father yet.

Jane Gilbert rested her fingertips on her desk. "What is it exactly you're hoping for regarding Daniel, Mr. De-Lucca?"

Like he would tell her. Like he even knew.

He held her gaze. "Why don't we hold off on the heart-to-hearts till the lab tests come back, okay?"

The Gilbert woman inclined her head. "That seems reasonable. Have you had a DNA sample taken yet?"

"I've got an appointment at five."

"I won't keep you, then." She stood.

He was being dismissed. Fine. Mark stood, too, wiping his sweaty palms on his thighs. He needed to leave anyway. He needed—

What is it exactly you're hoping for?

"Can I see it?" The words felt dragged from his throat.

"See…?"

"The picture. You said you had a picture of the kid."

The lawyer's facade cracked into a smile. "Of course." She flipped to the front of the file on her desk and turned it around so he could see. "That's Daniel," she said quietly.

He didn't know what he expected.

You look just like him.

But staring at the photograph of the boy who might be his son, Mark didn't feel that jolt of recognition he had seen in the lawyer's eyes. He felt…nothing, he decided, ignoring the rapid beating of his heart.

It was just the face of a kid he didn't know, with the soft, unused look most kids' faces had.

It didn't match Mark's memories of Betsy.

Maybe he looked like Tess, a little: the same dark,

straight hair and dark, arched brows and the sensitive pout of the mouth. Only the boy's eyes were dark, too.

Like Mark's.

Mark realized he had been staring too long at the picture and broke it off to glare at the lawyer.

"How's he doing? With his mother—" Dead, Mark thought. "—gone?"

Jane Gilbert hesitated. "I believe Daniel is adjusting as well as can be expected. The Wainscotts arranged for him to see a grief counselor."

"How did she…?" Mark chopped the air with his hand.

"A car accident," Jane said gently.

What a waste. What a fricking waste. His own mother, Dizzy DeLucca, might have done every other dumb thing she could think of to screw up her life, but at least she'd never gone and gotten herself killed.

"How long ago?" Mark asked.

"Two months."

"Took you long enough to find me," he said.

Jane Gilbert met his accusation coolly. "You're the one who stipulated any 'heart-to-heart' discussion of the situation would be premature."

"Okay, cute," he said. "Why don't I come back after they scrape the inside of my cheek or whatever and you can convince me of the error of my ways?"

She smiled. But she said, "Unfortunately, I'm busy for the rest of the afternoon."

He thought of Nicole. He'd promised to close. But—

"Tonight, then. I'll buy you dinner."

She shook her head. "Tonight I have to attend a very boring fund-raiser on behalf of my firm. Although…"

He grinned at her, experienced enough to gauge when a woman was falling. "You reconsidering?"

"I might be. Yes. Seven o'clock, Mr. DeLucca. We can talk about Daniel at seven."

"Great. Okay. I'll see you at seven."

"And Mr. DeLucca?"

He turned in the doorway.

"Wear a tie."

Chapter 6

In the Palmer House ballroom, a jazz quintet played. Nicole's temples pulsed in rhythm to the snare drum. Her feet, pinched in ice-blue Charles David sandals, throbbed, too. Miserable from head to toe, she clutched her glass like a lifeline and listened to a recital of her sins and her mother's grievances. Since the two lists were nearly identical, Nicole had hoped the recitation would be short.

But Margaret Reed, fueled by her second martini, was eager to explain the connections between Nicole's most recent transgressions and her own deep disappointment.

"I still don't understand why you have to go back tonight," Margaret said plaintively.

"It's my business, Mother," Nicole said stiffly. *Not yours.* "I have to be there."

Only she didn't. She *wanted* to be there.

Nicole sipped her white wine, trying to ignore the mocking memory of Mark's voice. *I had you pegged as a chardonnay girl.*

She longed to be anywhere but here.

''Can't you pay someone to take care of things for you for a few hours?'' Margaret asked.

She had. She paid Mark. Only— ''It's not that simple, Mother.''

''Why? Can't you trust them?''

The cello scraped along Nicole's nerves. Her ex-lover Yuri had played the cello. When he could find work, which was not often. ''Of course, I can trust—''

Him.

Mark.

Here.

Mark DeLucca was standing on the other side of the dance floor, lounging between a potted palm and a marble column. His height and his sharp, predatory profile made him stand out among Chicago's elite in their suits and cocktail dresses like a crow in a flock of pigeons.

Nicole's first, clenching thought was that something was wrong and he'd come to find her. But he didn't look worried. In fact, he didn't look at her at all. He was chatting up a frosted brunette in last year's Ann Taylor who was sophisticated enough and certainly old enough to know better.

Mark's head thrust forward to listen. When he raised it, he saw her.

Nicole was too far away to read his expression. She thought glumly that most of the time, he kept his face too closely guarded for her to guess what he was feeling anyway. But he murmured something to Mrs. Robinson and started across the room.

Her heart beat faster. She shifted her weight in her strappy sandals, in an agony of discomfort.

''Who is that...extraordinary-looking young man?'' Margaret whispered in her ear.

Nicole barely heard, all her attention on Mark negotiating the dance floor. She tightened her grip on her glass, grateful the hotel's thick stemware was unlikely to break in her grasp.

"What man, Mother?"

"That jacket is all wrong for a function like this. Although there's something about him…" Margaret mused. "Do you suppose he works for the D.A.'s office?"

Oh, God. She meant Mark.

And he was definitely heading toward them.

"Actually," Nicole said faintly, "he works for me."

He stopped in front of them. Compared to the expensive tailored suits all around them, his off-the-rack navy blazer was a cheap imitation. But the tough, lean man inside was the real thing. His dark, straight gaze made her insides melt. Nicole pressed her knees together so she wouldn't dissolve into a puddle on the floor.

He nodded. "Nicole."

She inhaled. "Mark."

"He works for you at that bar?" Her mother sounded scandalized.

Mark's gaze cut to Margaret.

Nicole wished the floor would open and swallow them up. In the background, the jazz group swung into another number, like the band playing on the deck of the *Titanic* as it went down.

"This is Mark DeLucca, who works with me at the Blue Moon. Mark, this is my mother, Margaret Reed."

"Nice to meet you," Mark said blandly.

"What are you doing here?" Margaret asked.

Nicole burned in embarrassment.

"I'm with a friend," Mark said.

Margaret sniffed. "Well, your 'friend' should have told you this was a semiformal affair. The invitation—"

"Mom," Nicole said. "Stop it. I don't like it when you talk this way."

Margaret turned on her, glittering with diamonds and dislike. "Don't let's get into a discussion of what we don't like about each other, dear. Because I have a *lot* to say."

Nicole's breath caught. The remark jabbed into her like a needle: first the shock and then the pain and then the welling blood.

"Seems to me you've said enough already." Mark pried the wineglass from Nicole's hand and set it on a tray. "Let's dance."

Gripping her cold hand, he pulled her into his arms and onto the dance floor. She grabbed at his shoulder in surprise, steadying herself. It took her two steps to find her balance, six strides to catch his rhythm. He didn't do anything difficult or funky—one, two, step, step—nothing beyond the ability of her dancing partners in cotillion. But none of the boys she'd danced with at thirteen had strong, dry hands and solid shoulders and muscled thighs. Heck, at thirteen Nicole had been lucky to find a partner whose eyes weren't on a direct line with her breasts.

She wanted to ask what he was doing here, except then she would sound like her mother. So what she said, stupidly, staring at his throat, was, "You can dance."

"Surprised?"

She lied. "No."

He bared his teeth in a smile. "Bet you had dancing lessons when you were a kid."

"My mother insisted. Also art, tennis and horseback riding." She stumbled slightly as he pulled her in to avoid another couple. "I'm not very good at any of them."

He didn't seem to mind. His hand was warm against her back. "Family responsibility sucks," he said, so sympathetically she forgot she had ever been mad at him.

"Your mother made you learn to dance, too?" She tried hard to wrap her mind around the image: Lucifer before the fall, with a mother and half hours devoted to the fox-trot.

"No. My sister."

The exotic brunette with the killer nails. A little of Nicole's headache floated away on the music. "I met her, didn't I? She seemed very nice."

Mark slanted a look down at her. "She's a sucker. But she's getting married in a couple of weeks, and the dance-with-the-bride thing matters to her, so…"

So he'd learned to dance to please his sister. Nicole's heart melted.

"That's so sweet."

Mark looked revolted. "It's not sweet. It's self-preservation. When my sister decides she wants something, it's easier to give up and go along."

"And she wants to dance with you at her wedding. I think it's nice."

"It's not like she's got a lot of choices. Jarek—her fiancé—has family crawling out of the woodwork. Tess needs somebody on her side, and I'm it."

"Your father?" Nicole asked delicately.

He clenched his jaw. He had a nice jaw. He didn't need to shave, exactly, but there was a subtle suggestion of beard that tempted her to test it with her fingers.

"Gone," he said.

She jerked her mind back from the texture of his chin. "Oh, I'm so sorry."

His mouth relaxed. His eyes were amused. "Not dead, Blondie. Gone. He took off when we were kids."

"It still must have been hard on you."

"Not as hard as when he was around."

"Your parents argued?" She could relate to that.

"My parents drank," Mark said flatly. "When they drank, they argued. When they argued, my dad liked to knock my mom around. It was better when he left."

She stumbled. "I didn't mean to pry."

He steadied her, tightening his grip on her hand until she found the rhythm again. "Sure you did. It's okay."

Chapter Two, "Who Is a Loser?", cautioned about the seeds of alcoholism and the pattern of domestic violence.

Everything Mark told her confirmed he was a bad relationship risk. Everything he did made her like him more.

"Sometimes when I was growing up I wished my father would move out," she confided.

Mark didn't falter, but the arms around her tensed. "He hit you?"

"Oh, no," she said quickly. "Nothing like that…. He and Mother liked to let me know that since they were staying together for my sake, the least I could do was show some appreciation by making them proud."

"Well, you did, didn't you? CFO at the age of— What are you?—twenty-four?"

"Twenty-seven. And I haven't done anything with my life that they wanted me to."

"What did they want?"

"My father wanted me to go to law school and join the firm." Mark looked unimpressed. "He's the Reed in Reed, Davis," she explained.

He looked as if he'd never heard of them. It was…nice. "And your mom?"

My mother wants me to stop sleeping with men like you.

Heat flooded her face. "Oh, you know," she said airily. "The usual. She wants me to stay in Chicago, get married and join the Junior League. Not buy a bar and move out of town."

"And you have a problem because they disapprove."

No. She had a problem because she was afraid they were right.

She tripped over his feet again. "Sorry."

He raised an eyebrow. "You want to sit this one out?"

She didn't. She could have danced with his arms around her forever. Besides, if they stopped, she would have to go talk with her mother again.

"It's these shoes," she said. "They pinch, and the heels are too high."

"Then why did you buy them?"

"They matched my dress."

He shook his head. "Take them off."

"Oh, I couldn't," she said automatically.

"Why not?"

"Well, I— Well, they— It would ruin my stockings, for one thing."

He gave her a warm look and a slow smile. "So peel off the stockings. I'll watch."

She managed a breathless laugh. "Go without hose at a legal fund-raiser attended by all my mother's friends and half my father's firm? I don't think so."

"Do you always do what's expected of you?"

"Since the expectation is that I will screw up... Gee, I hope not." She couldn't quite meet his eyes. It seemed safer to concentrate on his jaw and the smooth, tanned column of his throat above his collar. He smelled good, all animal male and some ordinary, guys' cologne. She opened her mouth to breathe. "I like your tie."

"Is that a polite way of telling me to butt out?"

"No." She risked a glance at his face. He was still smiling, and her heart did a little two-step all on its own. "It's a polite way of telling you I'm not about to start taking my clothes off for you here."

"I'm okay with it if you want to go someplace else."

She wanted to shock him. To tease him. To tempt him. She wanted to say yes. *Do you always do what's expected of you?*

She sighed. "Not a good idea. Tell me about your tie."

"It's blue."

"Thank you, I'd noticed that. Is it new?"

"What if it is?"

"I was just wondering if—" she had to ask, she couldn't bear not to know "—it was a gift or something."

She felt his withdrawal. He was still moving with her, moving to the music, but he withdrew from her all the same.

''You think I don't know how to pick out my own clothes?''

Oh, dear.

She tried again. ''Well, you weren't wearing a tie this morning. You can't have had many opportunities to go shopping today, so I wondered if—''

''If I had a tie-producing girlfriend on the side?''

She winced. Yes. Their thighs brushed. He felt so good, she was tempted to let it go. Wasn't it enough that he was here and hard and warm against her?

No.

She straightened her spine, conscious of his hand on her back. ''Do you have a girlfriend?''

He stopped at the edge of the dance floor. ''Not last time I checked.''

Could she believe him? She wanted to. And that alone made her suspect her judgment.

''Then that woman you were with—''

''Sorry to keep you waiting.''

It was her. Mrs. Robinson, sleek and stunning in her power suit and feminine blouse. She looked at Nicole. ''Hello.''

Nicole was glad she hadn't taken off her shoes. She needed every inch of confidence she could buy.

''Hi. I'm Nicole. A friend of Mark's.''

''Jane Gilbert,'' Mark said. ''A friend of…the family.''

Jane Gilbert raised her eyebrows. ''Nice to meet you. Do you have a minute?'' she asked Mark.

''Yeah. I'll see you,'' he said to Nicole.

She nodded, trying not to look as if she minded being abandoned like an empty glass on a busboy's tray. ''Don't forget to lock up when you get in tonight,'' she said.

He gave her a brief, hard glance. And then he grinned. ''I'll do that.''

She watched him go, his head bent to listen to the

other woman, leaving her with nothing but her blistered feet and bruised pride.

"'A friend of the family?'" Jane repeated.

Mark shrugged. Nicole's scent, her warmth, her softness, were messing with his head. "It's not like I could introduce you as my son's lawyer. I don't even know for sure yet if the kid's mine."

"Would it cramp your style too much?"

Cramp his style to have a six-year-old running around calling him Daddy? Looking to him to provide hot meals and discipline and support? Living with him in his three rooms over the boathouse, expecting him to be home—alone—at regular hours?

Panic struck. His stomach cramped. The boathouse. Could the kid even swim?

He took a deep breath. "Would it matter?" he asked coolly.

"To the court? It might," Jane said. "Would it matter to your girlfriend?"

In his mind he was still measuring the distance from the bottom of his apartment steps to the water. It took him a minute to realize she was talking about Nicole.

"She's not my girlfriend. She's my boss."

"A live-in boss? How convenient."

Maybe later he would feel glad the Wainscott kid had somebody sharp and tough on his side. But right now she was pissing him off.

"We don't live together. I have responsibility for closing the bar tonight."

"And do you take all your responsibilities seriously?"

Did he?

"I guess we'll find out," he said grimly.

To his surprise Jane smiled. "I might like you," she said. "I certainly trust you more than I would if you told me this was the best thing to ever happen to you."

"I thought you were supposed to want what was best."

"What is in the best interests of the child, yes. In most cases the court considers those interests are served by uniting the child with his natural parent."

"And you? What do you think?"

"I think Elizabeth Wainscott may have known what she was doing when she named you Daniel's guardian."

Pleasure at the compliment pricked him. Shocked him.

He shook his head in quick denial. "Maybe. Or maybe she was just using me to get back at her father."

"Get back at him for…?"

"They didn't get along. And he hated my guts. Then I was too young and dumb to get that she was sleeping with me partly out of spite. Or maybe I was too grateful. But I'd buy it now."

"Bitter, Mr. DeLucca?"

"Experienced. And as long as we're discussing my sex life, you might as well call me Mark."

She gave a slight smile. "Mark. Would Elizabeth have claimed Daniel was your son simply to frustrate her father?"

"Is that what he says?"

"The argument might have been made."

"Son of a bitch."

She didn't correct him. "He's here tonight," she said. "He wants to see you."

"Why?"

"You could ask him that yourself."

He narrowed his eyes. "You setting me up, Jane?"

"Let's say I'm providing you with an opportunity to see what you make of it."

He had a medal in his drawer and a reprimand on his service record for leading his squad against orders out of the line of friendly fire. Whatever land mines lay ahead at this high-toned legal shindig, he wasn't gaining any ground by sitting still and getting shot at.

"Let's roll," he said.

Jane led the way around the ballroom as if she'd mapped their destination from the beginning. Following, Mark wondered where in the shifting, glittering crowd Nicole was hiding. She wasn't his ally. She wasn't his girlfriend. She was his boss. But venturing across enemy territory with only his legal guide, Mark caught himself watching for her.

He didn't get it.

He had always lived solitary. He had always felt alone. This was a bad time to be imagining a connection with a blue-blood blonde in designer shoes.

He should have followed the lawyer.

He remembered Betsy's father was built like a whiskey bottle, tall and narrow, capped by shiny black hair. Seven years hadn't changed him much.

He looked at Mark in dislike. "You know this is preposterous. We were shocked Elizabeth even remembered you."

Mark rocked back on his heels. "Yeah. It was a surprise to me, too."

"You're not Daniel's father."

There were two cotton swabs loaded with his DNA on their way to a testing center in Texas that could prove the older man wrong. But Mark didn't say anything.

"Daniel has a good home with us," Robert Wainscott insisted. "There's no need for you to get involved."

"Your daughter thought different."

He scowled. "I'll give you twenty thousand dollars to walk away right now."

Damn. Twenty thousand. Hell, he could have bought the bar with another twenty thousand.

"Is that legal?" Mark asked Jane.

She pursed her lips. "Private adoptions often include costs and fees. Although typically the children in those cases are younger."

Private adoption? This was a sale, pure and simple. Anger kindled in him as he glanced from Wainscott's stubborn face to Gilbert's impassive one. How could they do this, reduce a kid to a commodity? Any kid? His son or not, it was obscene.

"No dice," he said. "No sale."

And he turned on his heel and walked away. Blind with anger, he barely noticed the crowd that parted for him like waves before a prow.

"Mark?"

Dear God, it was Nicole, tottering toward him on her stupid blue shoes, her curvy body in that flowing blue dress like something out of a sailor's fantasy. She looked like every woman he'd ever wanted and most of all like the two he couldn't keep: polished, privileged, perfect, blond.

Exactly his type.

Not his kind.

She reached him and put her hand on his arm. His mind was messed up, his gut was on fire, but his body still took notice of the feel of her fingers through his jacket sleeve.

"Is everything all right?" she asked, concern shining in her beautiful eyes.

"Everything's swell," he said roughly. "Look, I've got to go."

"But…it's still early."

"It's nine o'clock. I've got to close."

"Wait," she said. "I could come with you."

Oh, yeah. Wouldn't that be a trip? Him out of his skin with temper and lust and her sitting beside him like the ultimate do-over all the way to Eden.

"No," he said.

"I don't mind."

"But I do." He stepped away from her. Away from temptation. "Excuse me, princess. My pumpkin is waiting, and I have work to do."

Chapter 7

It was a good night for getting drunk and howling at the moon. But a curtain of rain hid the moon. Mark's howling days were over. And the memory of Paul DeLucca, with his hands like hams and his breath rank and cutting as a broken bottle, took a lot of the appeal out of getting drunk.

It was Nicole's fault for making him remember.

It was the lawyer's fault for making him think he had a son.

Mark locked the Blue Moon's front door and dimmed the lights. He'd never wanted to end up like his old man, a broken-down, abusive drunk. But tonight he wouldn't have minded taking a swing at something. He'd half hoped Jimmy Greene would give him an argument at closing time, just so he could throw a punch or two and let off steam. But Jimmy went off mild as a lamb, leaving Mark alone with the stuffed pike over the bar, the flickering shadows of a ball game on ESPN and his own thoughts.

None of them was particularly good company.

He punched open the cash drawer and started counting.

The drops on the window blazed. Headlights, Mark thought. From the parking lot. He twisted a rubber band around a stack of twenties. Somebody was going to be disappointed; he wasn't opening up for one late customer.

Outside, an engine cut off. The twin lights died.

He didn't bother glancing up from the piles of bills. He'd turned off the neon Open sign fifteen minutes ago. If this guy was moron enough to run through the rain and yank on a locked door, that was his problem.

The lock clicked. The door opened.

Nicole Reed stood in the entryway, her damp dress clinging to all her curves and the rain in her hair like diamonds. She was wet. She was gorgeous. Lust punched him in the stomach. And the hair rose on the back of his neck like the scruff on a dog scenting disaster.

Nicole's heart thumped. Mark wasn't very happy to see her.

He was…wary, she decided, studying his closed expression, the tension in his lean arms and broad shoulders. Wary and maybe a little pissed off.

"Are you looking for trouble?" he demanded.

She shivered, damp and apprehensive. "I'm looking for you."

"Same thing. Go away, Nicole."

She stood her ground, shaking in her uncomfortable shoes. "I came to see how you were doing."

He leaned against the bar and crossed his arms against his chest. "To check up on me."

She resisted the urge to apologize. "Yes."

"It's after hours, boss. I don't have to report to you."

Frustration made her bold. "Well, you're still on the clock, bozo. So talk to me."

He raised his eyebrows. "What do you want me to say?"

She wanted his anger. She wanted his laughter. Anything

would be preferable to this brick wall of silence. "Tell me why you ran out tonight."

He didn't even hesitate, the liar. "I had to close."

"Something else," she insisted. "You looked upset."

"If I did, it's none of your business. In fact, it's not business at all."

She drew a painful breath. What was she doing? What good could she hope to accomplish by forcing a conversation on a man whose idea of intimacy was "Take it off and I'll watch"? Better for him, safer for her, if she admitted defeat and fled.

But she didn't. He drew her.

It wasn't because he could pose on a billboard and thousands of women would drive to their deaths craning to get a look at that face. That body. Okay, that was part of it. Once a sucker for drop-dead sexy, always a sucker for drop-dead sexy.

But that wasn't why she was standing here in her wet dress courting rejection. Something in her recognized and responded to something in him. It was there in the defensive set of his shoulders, the twist of his mouth, the confusion darkening his eyes.

Earlier that evening, when he brushed by her in the ballroom, she had seen—she had felt—the same tremors that shook her the afternoon she'd come home to find Zack and his latest wannabe starlet making it on her grandmother's quilt. The same shock. The same hurt and anger.

She hadn't had the wit or the tools, then, to stand up for herself.

But she was learning.

"I'm not talking about the business. I'm not here as your employer, Mark. I'm here as your friend."

"I don't have friends. I don't need friends."

"What do you need?" she said softly.

His eyes were hot, his tone insulting. "You're so smart, you figure it out."

"I think you do need a friend."

And she needed to have her head examined. Was she really offering to be pals with tall, dark, disturbed Mark DeLucca?

He gave her a slow once-over. "And you're volunteering."

His open skepticism scorched her pride—and touched her heart. "I'm here, aren't I?"

"Yeah." He seemed surprised by that. Maybe almost as surprised as she was. "I guess you are. So tell me, *friend,* exactly what does this kind of relationship involve?"

She took a cautious step forward. "Well…friends talk to each other."

He shrugged. "We're talking."

She sighed. Men were from Mars, women were from Venus, and Mark existed in his own solitary orbit. "And they do things together."

He lifted one dark eyebrow. "What kinds of things? Hot tubbing? Naked back rubs?"

She blushed. Smiled. "Not usually. When things go right, friends celebrate together. And when things go wrong, they comfort each other."

"Comfort." His voice was without expression.

She nodded, her heart beating wildly.

"Okay." He uncrossed his arms and straightened away from the bar. "Let's go with that. This is the only comfort I want."

His hands closed on her shoulders, and his mouth crashed down on hers.

This was no hello-getting-to-know-you kiss, no thanks-for-caring embrace.

This was a we're-all-grown-ups-here, full-body contact with tongues. His hands were hard and urgent. His mouth was hot and avid. And she welcomed it, welcomed him, glorying in the raw need she felt in his kiss.

If this was all the solace he could understand, all the comfort he could accept, then she gave it gladly.

He kissed her to shut her up.

He kissed her to scare her off.

He kissed her because she was breathing and available and he couldn't bear not to kiss her any longer.

So, it wasn't smart. He'd done a lot of dumb things in his life, and most of them hadn't felt this good.

And Nicole felt really, really good, soft and smooth and firm against him. She smelled like very expensive sin and kissed like an angel. A very hot angel. Her curves mashed nicely against his planes. Her recesses fit his angles. Her damp silk warmed and wrinkled under his hands.

He reached for her breast, figuring what the hell, any second now she was going to haul off and slap him, so it wasn't like there was going to be any permanent harm done. Except instead of clobbering him, she made this accepting noise deep in her throat—very sexy—and pushed her nipple more firmly against his palm.

A definite turn-on. A guy would have to be dead or a saint not to respond to that invitation. Mark was no saint, and he felt more alive at this moment than he had since he'd hunkered down under fire on an airstrip in Kabul.

He kissed her, tasted her, licked her, devoured her.

And she met him, matched him, her tongue dueling with his, her hands clutching his shoulders and grabbing his hair. Good. He wanted her grasping. He needed her greedy. Never mind if all she was after was hot kicks or a quick fix. Never mind if she was slumming, screwing the help to get back at her awful mother. Because as long as she was using him, he could use her, too.

Only it didn't—God help him—it didn't feel like she was using him.

When he broke their kiss to reverse their positions, to shove her back against the bar and grind into her, he saw that her eyes were open. She looked honest and trusting and maybe a little scared.

She wasn't pretending to be anything else.

She wasn't pretending to be with anyone else.

And her hand, when she raised it between them to stroke his cheek, trembled slightly.

Hell.

He leveraged his weight off her. "We—" He had to clear his throat. "You better go now."

She blinked once, slowly. "Why?"

He fumbled for words. For reasons. *Because I like you? Because you're a nice girl? Because you deserve better than to get nailed against a bar by a guy with a grudge looking to let off some steam?*

"Because friends don't let friends do this drunk."

"I thought that was driving."

"Any dangerous activity," he said firmly.

She smiled, but her eyes were serious. Her mouth was soft and red-lipped and wet from kissing. God, he wanted to kiss her again.

"Then…we're friends?" she said.

Friends. A week ago he would have said he didn't even like her. Not to mention the major reminder pushing at his fly that insisted he had feelings for her that didn't exactly fall into the "friendly" category.

She waited for his answer, her smile slowly fading.

Ah, jeez. She was killing him.

"Yeah," he said. "Friends. Why not?"

She relaxed just a little bit. "We could probably come up with a list. If we tried."

Hell, he didn't even have to try. He could already think of a million reasons why any kind of relationship between them would never work. But he said, "Let's not go there. It's been a long night."

"Yes." She pushed her slippery blond hair behind her

ear and sneaked a look at him sideways. "I'm not really drunk," she offered.

He couldn't afford to think of that. Couldn't think about what else she might be offering. Drunk or sober, he'd be taking advantage.

"Yeah," he said. "Whatever."

She touched his arm with her warm, light fingers. "Are you still upset?"

"No," he said, surprised to discover it was true. Turned on, yes. Frustrated, absolutely. But he was no longer in the grip of the blind, black anger that had seized him when Wainscott offered to buy him off. Thanks to Nicole. "No, I'm okay."

At least, he was okay until the following afternoon, when he came on shift to discover that in her zeal to transform the bar into an upper-class watering hole, Nicole had taken down the deer trophy that hung—that had always hung—above the pool table.

Mark looked from the empty space on the wall to the bar, where Joe, Louis and Deanna were waiting to see how he would take this latest change. Hoping for a show.

Well, he wouldn't give it to them. He was a master, after all, at disappointing people.

He set his jaw. And maybe it was no big deal. Probably Nicole didn't realize the significance of what she had done.

A faint, unfamiliar hope nudged him. She had said they were friends. Friends talked to each other, she said. So he would talk to her, would point out to her, in a perfectly friendly way, that she was out of line and out to lunch on this one, and everything would go back to the way it was.

Yeah, right.

He relieved Joe at the bar, sent Louis back to the kitchens and asked Deanna to bus table nine.

And when Nicole buzzed by with a fresh supply of fancy little cocktail napkins, he cleared his throat. "I'd like to talk to you a minute."

She turned, and her face brightened and warmed at the sight of him, so that for a moment it was like staring at the sun sparkling on lake waters.

"I'm kind of busy."

He squinted to clear the brightness from his vision. "What are you doing?"

She raised her eyebrows at his gruff tone. "Well, I'm dropping off these napkins here, and then I'm going to change the specials board."

No big deal, he told himself. But irritation flicked him. "You can't change things around here every time you feel like it."

She frowned. "It has nothing to do with how I feel. We're out of artichoke hearts, and the sign—"

"I'm not talking about the sign."

"Then what are you—oh." Blue eyes widened in understanding. "You're talking about the deer head. You're upset."

He inhaled. "I am talking about the trophy, and I am not upset."

"Good. Because I took it down."

"Then you can put it back up again."

"I don't want to. I don't like dead animals hanging up in my dining room."

"This is not your dining room. This is a bar." He saw Deanna glance their way and lowered his voice. "A bar that caters to hunters and fishermen."

Nicole looked taken aback for a moment. But she said, stubbornly, "Then we'll put up something else. An old wicker tackle box or—"

"We don't need something else. That stag was up there for twenty years."

He remembered—God, how old had he been? Four? Five?—sitting scrunched in the corner by the pool table, listening to his mother laugh at the bar. Waiting for his sister to find them and bring him home. And the deer watching out calmly over the noisy room, with its sharp horns and wise glass eyes.

"And it looked it," Nicole was saying. "It was filthy."

Yeah, it was. So what?

"It belonged," he insisted. "You make too many changes, you're going to kill the character of this place. Turn it into some chi-chi yuppie meat market and lose the regulars who keep us in business."

He watched her struggle to hold on to her temper. "I don't think taking down one dusty dead deer is going to cost us a lot of customers."

"You don't know that. You can't say."

"Maybe I don't know, but I can say. I am the owner."

There it was. She was the owner. She was the boss. He was...nothing.

Frustrated, he turned from her to wipe down the bar. "Fine. Do what you want. But don't say I didn't warn you."

She followed him. "Mark, please. Don't be like this."

"Like what?"

She bit her lip. But she wouldn't let it go. "It's possible you're being hostile because you perceive change as a threat."

"Where do you get this crap? Out of some book?"

He watched the blood sweep up her face, but it brought him little satisfaction.

"Try this one," he said. "It's possible I'm hostile because this change is a mistake."

She raised her chin in challenge. "Name one change you wouldn't consider a mistake."

He had to say something. He wasn't feeling threatened, damn it.

"New TV."

"Excuse me?"

"You want to make a change around here, make it one

the patrons can get behind. The TV over the bar is twelve years old. We could use a new one.''

''That's not change,'' she said dismissively. ''That's... maintenance.''

Sometimes maintaining was good. Sometimes holding the line was the best a man could ask of himself.

''What it is is a good idea,'' Mark said. ''Which, if you weren't trying to turn this place into something it was never meant to be, you would see.''

Nicole stared at him with those big blue eyes. She saw things, all right. She looked right inside him and saw...more than he wanted her to see. More than was there.

''I'll think about it,'' she said, like she already hated the idea. Well, he figured she would.

''You do that,'' he said.

''But the deer has to go.''

He didn't say another word about it, then or for the rest of the evening.

''I think maybe he's over it,'' Nicole said hopefully to her roommate on Monday morning.

Kathy stopped outlining her lips long enough to ask, ''What's to get over? You're redecorating the bar. It's not his problem.''

Nicole, inexplicably, was moved to Mark's defense. ''It is a problem if I alienate my regulars. Mark thinks—''

''You don't pay him to think.'' Kathy dropped her lip liner in her purse. ''You pay him to mix drinks, break up fights and count your money.''

Exactly. She had thought the same thing. And acted on it. *I am the owner.*

So why did it sound so awful coming out of someone else's mouth?

''He does more than that,'' she protested.

''Right. He's good for business.'' Kathy puckered her

lips at her reflection. "Like the naked lady over the bar in a saloon."

She hadn't seen him naked.

She'd like to.

Oh, God. No. She was his boss.

No, she was his friend.

Except he didn't kiss like a friend. He didn't act like a friend. He was sulking about his damn deer head.

It wasn't his deer head, she reminded herself. It wasn't his bar.

"Hello? Earth to Nicole."

She flushed. "Sorry."

In the mirror, Kathy's eyes sharpened. "You really went off on the naked bit, didn't you? Is something going on with you and Delicious DeLucca that you're not telling me?"

Her cheeks burned hotter. What should she, what could she, say? *I kissed him, but he thinks we should be friends?*

Any confession felt like a betrayal, of Mark…and of her own confused heart.

"I just don't want to ignore his feelings, that's all," she mumbled.

"My God, listen to yourself, Nicole. *His* feelings are not your problem. You want to be careful, or you're going to wind up in another user-loser relationship."

"I am being careful."

"But you're not being smart. Remember Charles."

Charles, her self-absorbed, graduate-student lover. "That was eight years ago."

"And Yuri."

The vodka-prone, out-of-work cellist. "We only dated a short time."

"Ted?"

Married Ted the insurance salesman. "He lied to me," Nicole said.

"They all lie to you. I remember when you called to tell

me about Zack. I warned you the man was a player, and you went on and on about trust and open relationships.''

Nicole closed her eyes. After her disastrous foray into pseudodomesticity with Ted, Nicole had formed a brief relationship with a long haired indie filmmaker named Zack. For a while she'd found his professed disdain for social convention up-front and fearless. Until she discovered he was using her apartment to shoot porn flicks and have sex with other women.

''Zack was a mistake,'' she admitted. ''But we learn from our mistakes.'' She had to believe that. ''Kevin was reliable.''

Kathy grinned. ''Oh, sure. Except that he broke up with you and fired you. Face it, Nicole. You're a lousy judge of men.''

Nicole burned with shame. It was true.

She had filled in the Guy Assessment Guide—GAG—at the end of Chapter Three, ''Are You a Relationship Addict?'' She knew she was a chronic relationship junkie with a desperate desire for approval and a humiliating history of recidivism. Her longing for nurturing was achieved vicariously by giving to men who displayed a ''need'' for her affection but were themselves unavailable, uncaring or unable to love her back.

Where do you get this crap? Out of some book?
I don't have friends. I don't need friends.
This is the only comfort I want.

How did she reconcile what her heart felt with what her mind told her?

''You did say Mark did a good job for the previous owner,'' she said weakly.

Kathy gave her a pitying look in the mirror. ''I recommended him as an employee. Not a boyfriend. Try to keep the two separate.''

It was good advice.

If she were smart, she would take it.

The trouble was, she didn't know how smart she could be where Mark DeLucca was involved.

Chapter 8

She wasn't giving up her plans for the Blue Moon because of Mark DeLucca.

Nicole hauled two cans of primer out of the back of her SUV, set them on the gravel and slammed the door. It simply made sense, now that the drywall was patched and the plumbing connected, to divert some of her energy to the upstairs apartment. She couldn't live with Kathy forever.

She picked up the gallons of paint, wincing as the wire handles dug into her palms. Actually, after this morning's mortifying rehash of the life and loves of Nicole Reed, she didn't want to live with Kathy at all. Things could have been worse, she comforted herself. At least Kathy hadn't known about the kiss. That mind-numbing, heart-stopping, shattering kiss she'd shared with Mark.

She staggered along the walk to the entrance. Swinging one can under her arm, she used the opposite hand to tug on the door. Her heart beat faster as she glanced through the glass. Was he in yet? He wasn't supposed to be. It was only two o'clock. But she noticed—how could she help noticing?—that he frequently came in early and stayed late, anticipated problems, outlined solutions. It was her bar, but in many ways he was still running it.

I recommended him as an employee. Not a boyfriend. Try to keep the two separate.

The door banged her hip. Gritting her teeth, Nicole maneuvered her cans through the narrow opening. It widened suddenly, and she almost fell through.

"Let me get that for you."

She glared up at the beaming square face of—she didn't remember his name, but he was one of her regulars.

"Thanks," she said.

"Not a problem." The big blond man didn't add "little lady," but he might as well have. "Give you a hand?"

This, she reminded herself, was why she had moved to a small town. This friendliness. This neighborliness. This willingness to help. Well, that and she had wanted to move a million miles away from her mother.

She certainly couldn't snap at this guy for adhering to some classic pattern of small-town social behavior...or an outdated code of male courtesy. The author of *Losing the Losers in Your Life*—Chapter Five, "A Few Good Men"—stressed a woman's need to be nurtured.

Maybe this was one of those men, nurturing and kind.

He was waiting patiently, still bracing the door, one large hand extended.

She passed him the primer. "Thank you," she said.

She deliberately avoided looking toward the bar as they threaded their way through the tables.

"Where do you want this?" her escort asked.

Nicole stopped. What should she say? Her new pal might talk like an Eagle Scout, but he looked like a Viking god. Did she really want to invite him up the stairs to her bedroom, however unfinished?

"Um," she said.

"Got it," Mark said smoothly.

He lifted the flap and slid from behind the bar. Nicole's heart did a little tap dance in her chest as the two men faced off: one big, blond and open-faced, the other lean, dark and watchful. Thor and Loki, she thought.

"Hey, Mark," Thor said.

Mark nodded. "Lars. I thought you were out of here."

"You two know each other?" Nicole asked. Stupid question. Mark knew everyone.

"Sure," said the giant. "Mark and I are both Wofers— Wilderness First Responders—for the county."

"Lars Jensen," Mark introduced him. "And he was just leaving."

Jensen raised one thick blond eyebrow. "That way, is it?"

Nicole frowned in bewilderment. "What are you talking about?"

"Thanks for the help," Mark said and took the can of primer.

"Anytime," Jensen said good-humoredly. "See you around," he told Nicole.

He was leaving, she realized. What had just happened here?

"I really appreciate—"

"What is this?" Mark interrupted her, lifting the gallon can.

"It's primer."

"I can see that. What is it for?"

He was threatened by change, she reminded herself. And probably worried she was going to paint the men's room pink.

"The upstairs. I thought it was time to start painting my apartment."

"I paint," Lars Jensen offered. He hadn't left. Mark gave him a hard look.

Nicole eyed him speculatively. He wouldn't need a ladder, either. "That's very—"

"You can't afford him," Mark said.

Jensen grinned. "No charge. For friends."

"You're not friends. You don't even know her."

"That could change," Jensen suggested.

Mark smiled. Not a very nice smile. "I wouldn't count on it."

Nicole blinked. Were they actually…? They were sparring over her. Like a mastiff and a Doberman over a bone. It was thrilling. Embarrassing. *Unacceptable*.

In the animal kingdom, the power of choice belonged to the female. That's what her books all said. Unfortunately the two bristling males in front of her hadn't read the same experts.

"That's one of the things I like about living in a small town," she said chattily. "Everyone helps everyone else."

Both men looked at her.

"You don't know much about small towns," Mark told her.

She stuck her chin out. "Enough to want to live in one."

"Yeah, well, that was your first mistake."

Not her first. But she wasn't going to remind him of that or ask what others she'd committed since.

Lars Jensen beamed blondly. "Don't listen to him. Most folks are glad you're here."

"Everyone's been very nice," Nicole assured him. She glared pointedly at Mark. "Almost everyone."

"Human nature is the same all over," Mark said. "If you're looking for different, you're out of luck."

He was cynical. That was sad. Or it would be, if Nicole believed him.

"So you don't think people in Eden are warmer? More open? More connected?"

"Nope."

She smiled triumphantly. "Then why do you stay?"

He met her gaze, and the bleakness in his eyes faded her smile. "I don't have anywhere else to go."

Lars Jensen tutted like an old man. "Listen to him. The world traveler. The war hero. Sure, no place else would have him."

"I was no hero. I disobeyed orders."

"You led your squad out of friendly fire in Kabul," Jensen said. "Your sister wrote about it in the paper. You got a medal."

"I got busted."

Nicole's head was whirling. Kabul? Mark had served in Afghanistan?

"You're a soldier?" she asked.

His face closed. His shoulders squared. "I was a marine."

She was stunned. Lost. Impressed. As if Tom Cruise from *Cocktail* had turned into Mel Gibson from *We Were Soldiers* in the middle of the movie. "How long?" she asked.

"Two tours," he said.

"Six years," Jensen translated.

She still couldn't believe it. "And you left because—"
I got busted. She flushed and shut up.

"I left because I took a swing at my division officer. Call it a bad career move."

Her eyes widened in sympathy. "You were discharged."

"No," he said. "I was provoked. There were enough witnesses willing to testify that I didn't get a Bad Conduct Discharge. I got demoted for insubordination and canned to the galley."

No more explanation than that. No excuses. But she could tell, from his absolute flat tone and stony face, how much the incident still bothered him.

Nicole drew in a shaky breath. He was being honest with her. He was taking responsibility for his actions. Both qualities were rare, too rare, in her experience.

Didn't she owe him equal honesty in return?

She twisted the rings on her fingers. "I wish you'd told me this before."

"Why? So you could fire me?"

Lars Jensen—with a tact that made Nicole suspect he wasn't as dumb as he looked—turned his back and studied the neon beer signs on the walls.

Nicole lowered her voice. "So I could understand you."

"Babe, I don't expect you to understand."

"But I do," she said earnestly, forgetting Lars. "If someone put people I worked with, people I cared about, in danger, I'd be tempted to throw a punch at him myself." She risked a slight smile. "Even if it meant I did kitchen duty for it."

Mark shook his head. "You still don't get it. Striking a superior officer is no joke. I was reprimanded for insubordination. It's in my record."

He was right about one thing. Nicole didn't know enough about the military to understand all the consequences of an official reprimand. But she could see the cost in the tight set of his mouth, the pain and anger in his eyes. Whatever had led to the disciplinary action taken against him, it had hurt his pride, touched his honor and ended his career. Her heart was a lump in her throat.

She swallowed it. Unlike every other man in her life, Mark wouldn't welcome her pity. And he didn't need it.

"I hardly need your record to tell me you have trouble accepting authority," she said lightly.

"No," he agreed. "You wouldn't."

"It can be a useful thing," she said. "Sometimes."

"Only sometimes."

"Well…" She couldn't possibly confess how much she relied on his opinion. How much she depended on his help. Bravely she met his flat, black gaze. "You were right about the ham-and-cheese."

And Mark—thank you, God—Mark grinned. The expression transformed his dark, closed face and almost robbed her of breath.

"Damn straight," he said.

Hugely relieved, she beamed back. The moment stretched between them, sparkling like a strand of web beaded with dew.

Lars Jensen coughed. "I guess you don't need my help anymore."

Nicole jerked back to the present, "Oh, I, um—"

"Nope," Mark said.

She glared at him, and the snake still looked amused. Relaxed. Her heart skipped. *Happy.*

But her mother hadn't raised her to ignore her social obligations. And she wasn't turning away a customer, either.

She smiled at Lars the Viking god. "Can I get you something to drink before you go?"

He looked surprised. "Thanks. A beer would be good."

They sat at the bar.

Mark slid a mug in front of Lars and then looked at Nicole. "What'll you have?"

Her pulse pounded. "Surprise me."

He narrowed his eyes and went away to fix her drink. He set it in front of her, a tall clear glass of something that fizzed faintly.

She sipped—club soda—and sighed in disappointment. At least it made a change from diet cola.

"Do you come here often?" she asked Lars and then cringed.

But he didn't seem to notice the pickup line. Either he was a little thick or he had excellent manners.

"Couple times a week." He reached for his mug. "It's a nice place you've got here."

Nicole watched as Mark—without asking, of course, where she wanted him to put them—retrieved her cans of primer and carried them in the direction of the storeroom.

"What? Oh, thank you," she said.

"So, you're fixing the upstairs into an apartment?"

She nodded.

"You live alone?"

Mark's warning rang in her brain. *If you don't see any problem with a young, single, attractive woman living alone over a bar, it's not my job to educate you.*

But she didn't see anything in Lars's broad, mild face to alarm her. Maybe it was a trick of size, but he looked dependable. Kind and safe and dependable. Exactly the sort of man all her books said she should be looking for.

Where was Mark?

"Or is that about to change?" Lars asked wryly.

She blinked. "I'm sorry. What did you say?"

He sighed and set down his mug, a nice man with broad shoulders and big square hands. When she met his gaze, she felt nothing: no zings, no tingles, no shivers or surges of lust.

"Never mind," he said. "What do I owe you for the beer?"

"Oh." She pulled herself together. "No charge for friends."

He was too polite to look disgusted, but he pulled out his wallet.

What was the matter with her?

Mark reappeared at the register and her heart zinged plenty. Wouldn't you just know it, she thought glumly. But it was hard to stay glum while her nerve ends tingled, her body shivered and her blood surged with lust.

She slipped off her stool and sidled along the bar, responding to the lure of Mark's presence like a paper clip sliding helplessly toward a magnet.

Beside the register, in place of the regular tip jar, was a hand-lettered can that read, Save Petey. Next to it was a clipboard with almost a page of signatures. Nicole regarded both with approval. This was the kind of community outreach she had been talking about, evidence justifying her decision to move to Eden.

She stuffed five dollars in the can and signed her name with a flourish.

Behind the bar, Mark went very still.

Lars was eyeing her with a mixture of confusion and admiration. ''You're a good sport.''

She flushed with pleasure. She'd never played team sports as a child, never been described that way before. But she didn't want to make a big deal out of it. She didn't want to seem an outsider.

So she shrugged. ''All for a good cause, right?''

Lars laughed.

Mark just stood there, his gaze fixed on her face.

Discomfort crawled under her skin. ''It is a good cause, isn't it?''

She looked again at the signatures on the clipboard, recognizing the names of many of her regulars, small-town residents rallying to save one of their own, a child, maybe, or a brother. It gave her a good feeling.

''Who's Petey?'' she asked.

Blond Lars looked away, embarrassed.

Mark was silent.

''Come on, guys. Who is Petey?''

Lars shuffled his feet. ''He, ah, it—''

''The pike.'' Mark's tone was abrupt, his eyes dark and oddly regretful. ''Petey is a fish—the stuffed pike hanging over the bar.''

''Boy, did you screw up,'' Lars said as both men watched Nicole stalk off.

Big-time, Mark thought.

''It was a joke,'' he said, not excusing it.

''Did it look like she was laughing to you? Because it didn't look like she was laughing to me.''

''Shut up,'' Mark said.

He felt like a heel. He'd been so wrapped up in his own fears, his own feelings, his sense of control slipping away, that he hadn't fully considered how his stupid joke might make Nicole feel.

Hell, he hadn't thought, period.

Until she looked at him with her stricken face and her eyes bright with tears or temper, and he realized that in publicly undercutting her he hadn't protected himself at all. He'd only hurt her. Nicole, whose cool manner hid her warm heart, who continued to donate to the local food shuttle, who—without pausing and without thinking—dug in her purse to contribute to a cause.

"Kind of too bad for you," Lars said, leaning against the bar. "Because I think you could have had her."

He had nothing. Sometimes he thought Tess was right, and he pulled dumb stunts to make sure he got nothing.

"Not a chance," he said.

"Kind of good for me, then," Lars said. "Maybe now she'll let me paint her apartment."

Maybe she would.

Mark glared at him. When he wasn't tromping through the woods in shorts rescuing campers, Lars owned and operated Cover With Care Painting and Construction. He was steady, thoughtful, reliable. He would do a good job for Nicole.

Or he could do a number on her.

"Stay away from her."

"Why?"

"She's—" vulnerable, Mark thought "—not your type," he said.

Lars shrugged. "Not your type, either."

She was exactly his type. He was a sucker for fragile-seeming blondes who turned out not to need him and totally wrecked his life.

"Just stay away," he repeated.

Maybe he should go after her. If he had a chance to

explain… Explain what? That he was a jerk? She knew that already.

He gave Jensen his beer on the house and mixed a pitcher of margaritas—gold, on the rocks—for the birthday party in booth four. The phone rang and cut off before he could get to it. A minute later Nicole appeared from the back.

"It's for you," she said, her voice as frosty as the pitcher.

He was *so* in the doghouse. The fact that he'd earned his place there didn't make him like it any better.

"Thanks." He picked up the phone behind the bar, wishing she carried the cordless phone from the kitchen so he had an excuse to brush her fingers, to touch her somehow.

Pathetic.

"DeLucca here."

"Mark, this is Jane Gilbert."

Nicole turned away. She wouldn't even meet his eyes.

"Well, that makes this day just about perfect."

The lawyer chuckled, which didn't improve his mood any. "I have news for you."

He watched Nicole's straight, stiff back as she headed back to the kitchen. "Good news or bad news?"

"Both, actually."

He waited.

"I received a copy of the results of your paternity test this morning."

His heart pounded. His grip tightened on the receiver. "Yeah, okay."

"You and Daniel are definitely a match."

The bar whirled like a skiff in a squall. They were a match.

He had a son.

Daniel was his son.

And even though he'd told himself he was prepared for this, for a moment he couldn't find his voice or his balance.

He took a deep breath; released it carefully. "Is that the good news or the bad news?"

''That rather depends on you, doesn't it?''

Right. All right. He drew in another breath, trying to force oxygen to his starving brain. ''What's the bad news?''

''The bad news is that Robert Wainscott is refusing to accept the test results.''

''That figures. If I wasn't good enough to marry his daughter, I'm sure as hell not good enough to raise his grandson. What does he want, besides for me to go away?''

''Will you go away?'' the lawyer asked.

''No.'' The word was out before he had a chance to consider.

''Good,'' Jane Gilbert said. ''Then we have to get Daniel retested.''

''Why the kid? Why not me?''

''You had a buccal swab taken with an appropriate chain of custody established.''

''So?''

''So even Robert Wainscott is going to have trouble disputing the accuracy of your DNA test in court.''

''Wait a minute. Are you telling me the kid's test isn't accurate?''

''On the contrary. Once the lab is successful in extracting DNA from a special sample, the test is guaranteed 99 percent accurate.''

''Then what's the problem?''

''Daniel's test was administered in my office. There's no proof the sample actually came from him.''

He was trying hard to understand. Was he Daniel's father or not? ''But you administered the test. Gave him the gum.''

''Yes. Unfortunately, Robert is no longer inclined to accept my actions on Daniel's behalf.''

''Why not?''

''Because I do not support his case against you.''

You could have fooled me, Mark almost said. ''Since when?''

"Since you turned your back on twenty thousand dollars and walked away."

Damn. Okay. He shifted his sweaty grip on the receiver. "Maybe you should wait for him to up the offer."

"Do you want to see him?" Jane asked unexpectedly.

"Wainscott?"

"Your son."

His pulse quickened. "Wainscott would never agree."

"He already has. In return for my agreeing to have Daniel submit a second DNA sample, he has accepted limited visitation. I felt it was in Daniel's best interest if you two had an opportunity to get to know each other."

The room—his whole world—tilted. "When?"

"This weekend? Friday?"

"So soon?"

"If your case goes before a judge, the court will certainly look for evidence that once you learned of Daniel's existence you acted promptly to secure your parental rights."

Mark thought about the dark-eyed kid in the photograph. "And if I don't?"

"Then the court will take that into consideration as well." Her tone suggested this would be a bad thing.

Mark stared at the bottles ranked behind the bar. For the first time in a long time, he was tempted to pour himself a drink—and another and another—to sear away his memories, to help him forget. Forget Betsy and her disapproving bastard of a father. Forget the lawyer and her talk of his rights. Forget the possibility he even had a son.

Yep, all he had to do was pour himself a drink, and he could be just like his old man.

"Friday," he said. "What time?"

Chapter 9

As a kid you could get used to almost anything.

Mark remembered sitting in parked cars and bars, outside the principal's office and inside the Eden jail, waiting for his mother, and later for Tess, to come and get him. He remembered the cold and the cigarette smoke, the ringing of the office phones and the shaky hollow in the pit of his stomach.

The law offices of Johnson, Neil and Younger were clean and quiet and smoke-free. But the kid sitting waiting in one of the big leather chairs, his sneakers dangling over the wall-to-wall carpet, looked up at the opening door with the same scared, hopeful expression Mark figured he'd worn twenty years ago.

Too bad the kid's mother would never come again to pick him up.

Mark nodded to the receptionist, who said, "Ms. Gilbert will be with you shortly."

He nodded at the kid, who was staring at him like he bayonetted babies for fun, and sat down. Not close enough to freak the kid out, but near enough to see him. Daniel Wainscott. Betsy's boy.

His son.

His chest felt tight. He drew in a breath and reached blindly for the periodicals aligned neatly with the edges of the table.

"The magazines here are boring," the kid volunteered.

So it wasn't "Hi, Dad." It was a start.

Mark made an effort to respond. "That right?"

The kid's head bobbed. "The first time I came they had a *National Geographic,* but they don't have it anymore. I looked."

Maybe now that he'd started talking, he wouldn't shut up.

Mark nodded again. Any more of this and they'd resemble a couple of floaters on the surface of the lake, bobbing and nodding at every conversational nibble.

"I brought a book this time," the boy offered. "About a dog. Do you like dogs?"

Where was the lawyer?

"Yeah, I guess," Mark said.

"It's a good book."

"Maybe you should read it."

The kid fixed him with large, dark eyes. "I can't read."

"Right," said Mark. Was it all right? The kid was what, six? When was he supposed to learn to read?

Panic struck. Mark didn't know. He didn't know anything.

The boy, Daniel, was still watching him.

The panic ballooned in Mark's throat. He coughed to clear it. "You want me to read it to you?"

The boy shook his head, adding with devastating simplicity, "I'm not supposed to talk to strangers."

Strangers.

Hell.

Well, they were, weren't they? Strangers who just might happen to be related.

"Then you shouldn't be talking to me, should you?" he asked, more harshly than he intended.

The boy shrank.

"Sorry to keep you waiting." Jane Gilbert's power heels sank into the deep, gray carpet. "I see you two have met. Shall we go back to my office?"

Mark rose slowly.

The kid scrambled off his chair. "Is that him?" he asked the lawyer.

"Yes," Jane said, smiling. "That's him."

Who? Mark wanted to ask. Who did she tell you I am?

"I thought it might be," Daniel said and slid another wide-eyed look in Mark's direction.

He skipped ahead of them down the hall.

Mark released his breath. This was so not going to work. He was *so* not father material. Let the kid go to the Wainscotts, where he belonged.

"Coming?" Jane Gilbert asked, no longer smiling.

He shoved his hands into his pockets and sauntered after her.

Friday night and the moon was out, along with most of the crazies.

The jukebox throbbed with vintage Stones and pounded out John Mellencamp. Nicole's head throbbed and pounded, too. She pressed the tips of her fingers to her temples. Apparently not all of her carefully thought-out selections were popular with the bar's patrons.

Like her decision to buy the place?

But she couldn't afford to think about that now.

She moved from table to table, refilling the little wooden bowls with snack mix, a compromise choice she had reached with Mark. Not as messy as the popcorn the bar used to serve, not as expensive as the mixed nuts that had been her preference.

Boisterous laughter erupted from one of the booths. She leaned forward to rescue an empty bottle and clear the empty bowl. A bearded customer patted her absently on her rear.

She was too depressed to object. It was acceptance, of a sort.

"Everything okay here?" a deep, male voice inquired.

It was Mark, lean and brooding and looking good enough to make an adjoining tableful of vacationing coeds nudge each other and finger their hair. He'd come on at seven, wearing attitude like a black leather jacket and his usual blank expression.

She refused to look at him. "Fine."

A blast of profanity rocked the bar. Heart thumping, Nicole turned. Two bristling, burly, middle-aged men in nearly identical faded jeans and plaid shirts faced off beside the line of bar stools.

"—anywhere near her," growled the one in the John Deere cap.

"—rip your head off!" yelled the other.

Nicole watched, horrified, as big-and-burly number one took a swing at big-and-burly number two. One of the college girls screamed. The first man staggered. A stool crashed.

"Ah, hell," Mark said wearily.

Nicole started. "I'll call the police."

"No." His strong, lean hand wrapped around her wrist. "I've got it."

Together, the two men must outweigh him by 250 pounds. They were built like stevedores or lumberjacks or something.

"But—" she protested.

He slipped through the tables. There was a shove. A

shout. A patron snatched his mug out of harm's way, splashing beer on the planked floor.

"Son of a bitch!"

The man in the ball cap lunged. Nicole stood, petrified, as stools scraped and a bottle shattered.

"Tom, Jerry, knock it off." Mark raised his voice. "I said, knock it off!"

They turned, blinking and growling, one nose bloody, one eyebrow cut.

"He said—"

"I won't—"

Mark cut them off. "That's enough. Take it outside, or I'll tell Marge on both of you."

Tom—or was it Jerry?—shuffled and cursed. Jerry—or possibly Tom—lumbered to his feet.

"Show's over," Mark announced. Nicole could only watch as he strolled forward, confident as an animal trainer in a cage full of bears. The guys around the pool table groaned, and one girl in a tight pink top clapped. Nicole had never felt so unnecessary. So inadequate.

"Tom, you owe me for that beer. Jerry, get a broom. We've got to sweep up this mess before somebody slips and gets hurt."

Amazed, Nicole watched as, grumbling, they complied. Mark paused by the jukebox as he passed, and Dusty Springfield's sexy croon took over the room.

"The only boy who could ever reach me…"

Shaking with reaction, Nicole carried the dirty glasses and empty bowls into the kitchen.

And then she locked herself into a stall in the ladies' room and cried.

Mark frowned in the direction of the hall. Where the hell was Nicole? He hadn't seen her in more than an hour. Not since Tom and Jerry put on their regular Friday-night cartoon show.

Was she upset because Bowden grabbed her ass?

He frowned and punched open the register drawer. He should have said something. But Bowden was harmless. And the temptation presented by Nicole's neat little, tight little, round little rear... Well, those curves just begged for the tribute of a man's hand.

Of course, if Nicole was upset about it, next time he'd have to break Bowden's arm.

"Good night, George. Roger, you good to go?"

He rang up his last tab and called a cab for Jimmy Greene. Jimmy tried to convince him he was walking home, but after nineteen years of living with Dizzy DeLucca, Mark knew all the signs and excuses of a road risk. Sulking, Jimmy gave in.

From the jukebox, a breathless female voice instructed her unseen lover in what a girl wants. Mark shook his head. Nicole and her changes. He didn't have a clue what she wanted. But if her new music chased the crowd from the joint before 1:00 a.m., well, he'd take it and be grateful.

"Yeah, good night," he said again, following the last lingering customers to the door. "Good night."

He flipped the dead bolt. Turned.

Nicole stood in the glow of the neon beer signs, bars of orange and blue sliding over her breasts and hair. She wore a button-down blouse of some silky material that left a long vee of her throat bare. Mark wanted to slip his arms around her and bite her neck.

He swung a chair up on one of the tables instead. According to Joe, she'd already put in a long day. She looked tired. She ought to be home in bed.

Yeah. And he'd like to be in there with her.

His muscles tensed. He lifted another chair. "What are you still doing here?"

She stood her ground. "I wanted to make sure you were all right."

"I'm fine," he said. "Go home. I can close by myself. I've been doing it for months."

She twisted her rings around on her pretty fingers. "I didn't mean to suggest... I'm sorry about what happened earlier."

"Yeah, so am I," Mark said gruffly. "It won't happen again."

She smiled faintly. "I don't suppose you can control that kind of thing."

"I can try."

She looked at him with those big, earnest blue eyes and he almost fumbled a chair. "I was afraid you were going to get hurt."

He frowned, insulted. "Not a chance."

"There were two of them," Nicole said. "And I was no help to you at all."

She wasn't talking about Bowden's hand on her butt, Mark realized. She was talking about the scene at the bar with Tom and Jerry. But he couldn't take any credit for that. Or let her take any blame.

"Those two have been mixing it up for years," he said. "Ever since Marge ditched Tom for Jerry back in high school. It doesn't mean anything."

"When I heard that bottle break—" Nicole shuddered. "I thought you would have to get between them."

"No, you never do that," he said. If she owned a bar, she ought to know. If she stuck it out, she had to learn. "You always keep your distance. Once you get close, once you get involved, then you're not in control anymore. That's when you get hurt."

She smiled suddenly. The impact shivered through him.

"What's so funny?" he asked, his voice rasping.

"You sound like one of my books."

He narrowed his eyes. "Do not."

"Yes. You do. 'Don't get close and you won't lose control'? 'Don't get involved and you won't get hurt'?'' She shrugged. "It's classic self-protection."

When she put it that way…

"I thought you believed in all that stuff."

"I do. Well, I did." She hesitated. "Now I'm beginning to think I don't know anything."

He upended another chair. "What are you talking about?"

"I thought I was doing such a great job giving orders, taking charge, being in control of my own business. But look at me." She met his gaze with disarming honesty. "I had no idea what to do when those two men started fighting tonight. I had no business buying a bar I can't run."

He agreed with her. Sort of.

Except she had ideas. Good ideas, some of them. She had hope. And being around her was beginning to make him feel that hope was rare enough and important enough not to be crushed.

"What about your strong work ethic and your business degree and all those other things you were telling me about?"

"What about them? What good are they without experience?"

Hadn't he said the very same thing the day they met? So why did it bother him to hear those words from her now?

"You can gain experience," he argued. "But you'll never know what you could have had if you don't try."

Nicole blinked. "That's very wise."

He thrust his hands in his pockets. Her regard made him uncomfortable. *She* made him uncomfortable, all fine-boned and blue-eyed and delicate, with that amazing rear end and her uncanny ability to get under his skin and into his head.

Maybe it was all those books she read.

"Not wise," he said. "I barely scraped through high school."

She moved closer. Her perfume, light and expensive, affected him like a finger drawn very slowly down the center of his chest. His stomach clenched and his nostrils dilated.

"I think you're very smart," she insisted. "And very sweet."

She took another step forward.

He balled his hands in his pockets. "What are you doing?"

She tipped her head sideways, like she was giving his question serious consideration. "I think…I'm gaining experience."

She put her hands on his shoulders. Her fingers touched the back of his neck. He sucked in a breath, but that only made things worse because her breasts were almost touching his chest and her perfume went straight to his head. And his groin. His jeans were too tight. He could feel them straining across his knuckles. Across everything.

"Not with me you're not," he said through his teeth. "I am not the kind of guy you want to get experience with."

She stood on tiptoe, stretching a little to make a better fit. "How will we know if we don't even try?"

She was going to kiss him. And, God forgive him, he was going to let her.

She kissed like a teenager with her first big crush: gentle, absorbed kisses. Curious, tender kisses. Kisses for the pleasure of kissing and the joy of sharing.

Sweet enough to make him ache.

Promising enough to make him hard.

He stood like a dummy, like a stone, with his heart doing 140 in his chest and his fists clenched in his pockets while Nicole kissed him. Her soft mouth caressed his upper lip and tugged gently at his lower one. Her tongue glided, touched, played with his.

As long as he kept his hands in his pockets…

He angled his head and kissed her back, sucked on her soft plump lips and explored her mouth. She tasted like seltzer and lime, tart and sweet and exciting.

She separated from him by a breath and smiled into his eyes.

"Well," she said. "That was nice. Different."

Different. He almost groaned. He didn't need different. He didn't want nice. Wham-bam, same-old sex was all he'd ever asked for. All he expected. All he could do.

"Yeah," he said hoarsely. "The first time I kissed you I was trying to scare you off."

She blinked. "And now?"

You always keep your distance. Once you get close, once you get involved, then you're not in control any more. That's when you get hurt.

"Now you're scaring me," he said.

"You're scaring me," Tess DeLucca said to her brother the following morning. "What is that?"

Mark dropped an empty pizza box into a black plastic garbage bag, barely sparing a glance for the great northern pike propped against the back of the couch.

"It's the fish," he said. "From the bar."

"Petey? What's he doing here?"

"I'm redecorating."

"I can see that. What I can't figure out is why."

Mark threw out some paper napkins, a handful of receipts, and an advertising flyer from the local gym. "You and me both, babe."

Tess grabbed an empty soda can from under the coffee table and held it in front of her mouth like a microphone. "Could it be maturity is coming at last to Mark DeLucca?"

She offered him the soda can for his commentary. He glared at her. It was like preparing for inspection, only worse. In the marines he hadn't had his big sister critiquing his every move.

Tess flopped on the couch, almost bumping heads with the pike. "Okay, not maturity. Hot date?"

"Something like that."

"Must be someone special. I can't remember you cleaning your apartment for a woman before."

He drew a deep breath. Hell. This was it. He had to tell her now.

"It's not a woman," he said.

Tess laughed. "Well, don't tell me you're gay, because I won't believe it."

He didn't say anything. He didn't know what to say. At least if he were gay, he wouldn't be dealing with the sudden intrusion of a six-year-old son in his life.

Tess sat up. "Mark?"

"There's something I've got to tell you."

Her eyes widened. "I'm listening."

He would have laughed if he hadn't loved her so much. Or if his news weren't so spectacularly unfunny.

"I've got a son," he said. "His name is Daniel, he's six years old, and he's coming for his first visit tonight."

Tess gaped. "When—how—"

Mark shrugged. "The usual way."

"His mother?"

Trust a reporter to get the important questions right. Mark cleared another pile from the coffee table, glad to have a reason not to look her in the eye.

"I heard from his lawyer two weeks ago. His mother is dead. Do you remember Betsy Wainscott?"

Tess shifted on the couch. "The little blonde who broke your— No, not really. Should I?"

"We both should. Daniel is hers."

"And there's no one else to take him?"

"The grandparents want him." And were prepared to pay to keep him. "But Betsy named me in her will."

He would tell his sister about the DNA testing later, he decided. How long until they got the second set of results from the kid? And what had they told him?

"I can't believe it," Tess said.

"I'm having some trouble with it myself. The lawyer called this morning. She wants to try the home visit thing."

"And the grandparents agreed to it?"

He shrugged. He would have to find out why.

"Tonight," Tess said, like she was testing the idea.

"Yeah. I'm scheduled to work. Joe can cover for me till nine, but I've got to close."

Tess narrowed her eyes at him. "You didn't tell me about this just to get a free baby-sitter, did you?"

He didn't deny it. "Look, it's bad enough I have to go in at all. I'm not leaving the kid with a stranger."

Tess tapped her red nails on her knee. "Why don't you ask Mom? She loves to sit."

Mark dragged his bulging bag of garbage to the door. When he trusted himself to speak, he said, "I don't think her maternal instincts are that highly developed."

"Oh, Mark. Give her a chance. I bet she was thrilled when you told her."

He walked to the kitchen and opened the refrigerator. The tiny bulb blinked on above the empty shelves. He had to buy food. Milk. Bread. Eggs.

"Mark." Tess followed him. "You did tell her, didn't you?"

He closed the refrigerator door and turned to face her. "What did I like to eat when I was six?"

"Peanut butter," she answered promptly. "Chicken noodle soup. Spaghetti."

"Spaghetti. Right." He unearthed an envelope from the counter and scribbled it down.

"Why?" Tess asked.

"Grocery list."

"No, I meant why won't you talk to Mom?"

He eyed her with a mixture of exasperation and affection. She wasn't going to let it go. She never let things go.

"How come you know all my favorite foods, Tess?"

She frowned. "Well, because I cooked them for you."

"Exactly. You got me fed, you kept my clothes clean, you made sure I did my homework—" he smiled thinly "—most of the time. Face it, babe. Our parents sucked. It's a little late for me to be turning to Mom for parental advice."

"She's changed," Tess said. "She hasn't had a drink since you went away."

"Good for her," Mark said, and he meant it. "But I have enough trouble right now dealing with something that went down seven years ago. Don't ask me to fix things that go back even further."

"As long as I don't have to fix things when Mom finds out she's a grandma," Tess muttered.

"Look, I've got to worry about getting the kid's hopes up. I don't even want to think about Ma's."

"Don't get mad at me."

"I'm not mad," he said automatically.

Tess snorted. "Yes, you are. You look exactly the way you used to when Billy Hotchkiss and Tom Dewey ganged up on you after school. Sort of broody and black-eyed and dangerous."

He was disgusted. "I am not mad. I do not brood. And the only danger is that if you don't shut up, I'm going to wring your neck."

He slammed another empty cupboard closed. He was so not ready for a kid.

Tess bit her lip. "So, have you met him yet?"

Mark had a sudden vision of the kid in his striped shirt and painfully clean sneakers staring at him with wide, dark eyes from the depths of the lawyer's chair.

He had to clear his throat. "Yesterday," he said. "In the lawyer's office."

Tess touched his arm. The DeLuccas were not a physically demonstrative family—well, Paul DeLucca liked to smack them around, but that wasn't the same thing. Anyway, Mark appreciated the gesture.

"How'd it go?" she asked.

"He didn't scream when he saw me."

She squeezed reassuringly. "Not screaming is good."

"And he wants to see me again." The words spilled out before he could catch them. He'd been keeping them close to his chest like dogtags, like a holy medal, ever since Jane Gilbert had called that morning. Who would have guessed? Not Mark. "The lawyer said he couldn't stop talking about me."

Tess's wide smile lit her face. "Mark, that's wonderful."

"Yeah, I bet the Wainscotts are thrilled." His hands clenched on the countertop. He loosened them deliberately. "Tess, I don't know if I'm going to get custody."

Hell, he wasn't sure he wanted custody.

"Take it one step at a time," his sister advised. "At least he likes you."

Mark shrugged. "Maybe. It's not like he has a lot of choice. Kids don't get to reject their parents."

"Tell that to Mom," Tess said.

His head snapped back as if she'd slapped him. "Hey," he said. "I asked you for a favor, not a lecture."

She patted his cheek. "And you got both."

"Does that mean you'll sit for me?"

"Absolutely. DeLuccas forever, remember?"

Mark remembered. It was their childhood pledge, their playground battle cry, their pact against the world.

But as he cleaned his bachelor apartment and stocked his empty kitchen with child-friendly foods, the question played in his head and churned in his gut.

Was his son a DeLucca? Or a Wainscott?

Chapter 10

"**I** understand our friendly neighborhood painter put the moves on you the other day," Kathy said as she poured herself coffee.

Nicole hit the wrong key and watched her figures scramble. She was doing her books on the dinette table because she couldn't concentrate at the bar and her roommate was supposed to be out all day showing commercial properties to clients. Nicole had been careful not to use Kathy's desk. But wherever she set up, Kathy had a knack for making her feel in the way.

She clicked on the screen to restore her work.

Kathy raised her voice and her eyebrows. "I said, I heard Lars Jensen bought you a drink."

Nicole sighed. "He didn't buy me a drink. I own the bar. But he was there."

"And interested?"

Nicole pretended to check her totals. There was no denying that upstanding, good-looking Lars Jensen had been interested. Or that his mild flirtation had restored some of her confidence.

"Maybe a little interested," she said.

"Well, he's thick as a plank, but he's built like a god," Kathy pronounced. "You should go for it."

Nicole shrank inside. Maybe she was looking for love in all the wrong places, but at least she believed it was out there. Somewhere. Kathy had given up hope.

"Oh, I don't— He's not— I'm not interested in him that way," she said.

Kathy set down her mug, depositing a coffee ring on a stack of invoices. "Why not? You could do worse. In fact, you have."

Ouch.

"He's not my type," Nicole said lightly.

"That's exactly my point. The last thing you need is to fall for another tall, dark and emotionally inaccessible male."

Nicole felt the betraying heat sweep up her face.

"Oh, my God," Kathy said. "That's it, isn't it? You've fallen for the bartender."

"Mark," Nicole said. "I think I may have misjudged him."

Anyway, she hoped so.

"No, you didn't. Unless maybe you mistook him for some nice, responsible, ready-to-settle-down boy next door. Which he is not."

"He's been nice," Nicole said fairly. Stubbornly. Sometimes he was nice. "And he's responsible."

"Which doesn't mean he's about to settle down."

"No. But—"

"What makes you think he would even be interested in you, anyway?"

It was a good question. A hard question. Mark hadn't exactly come after her with roses and a box of chocolates. But—

"He said I scared him," she offered.

It gave her hope that he was vulnerable. She liked believing she threatened his badass bad-boy routine.

Kathy rolled her eyes. "Oh, puh-leeze. Honestly, Nicole, that is the biggest kiss-off line. It's right up there with 'You deserve better' and 'I want to be your friend.'"

Mark had said that, too, Nicole remembered. At least, he hadn't objected too strongly when she claimed she wanted to be friends with him. But—

"He's different," she insisted.

"How do you know?"

She didn't really. Her books had rules and warnings, check lists and assessment tables. She had only the promptings of her heart.

"Maybe I should have said I'm different. I'm better at knowing what I want now. I'm better at asking for it."

"Whatever." Kathy lifted her hip from a pile of daily register receipts and strolled across the kitchen to dump her cup in the sink. "Ask for it tonight, why don't you. Because there are a few things I've been wanting, and I can't get them with a roommate around."

Nicole blinked. Tonight?

The prospect made her shiver with nerves and desire. She knew what she wanted. But what if what she wanted was bad for her like champagne cocktails or chocolate? Maybe Mark was only good for her taken in moderation. Did she trust her own judgment and restraint that much? Did she trust him?

She thought of the way he'd kissed her last night, keeping his need leashed and his hands clenched in his pockets.

I am not the kind of guy you want to get experience with.

But he was.

Tonight she would ask him... Tell him... Show him what she wanted. She'd seduce him. If she could.

How would she? How could she?

There had to be a book somewhere.

Oh, no. She wasn't looking this up. Not with Kathy looking on, mocking her, offering her advice. Sometime since their college days, Kathy had let experience blind her to the way things could be, *should* be, between a man and a woman. To things like respect and tenderness and possibility.

Nicole's heart beat faster. So… No books, she decided. No advice.

She would do this on her own.

She would do this from the heart. She would throw herself at his head and into his arms. Whatever it took.

Tonight.

Tonight was a real winner.

Usually Mark enjoyed the action on a Saturday night. But this one had chafed his nerves and strained his patience.

He didn't like being in a bar while his kid was home. Never mind that he wasn't a drunk like his parents, or that he'd made sure the boy had plenty to eat and clean sheets on his bed before he took off. He ought to be home. He knew it. Tess knew it. And from the abandoned look in the kid's eyes when Mark went into his room to say good-night, Daniel knew it, too.

No way could Mark close early, either. Nicole had her hands full tonight. The room had an edgy, end-of-week fever. A party of sailors had found their way in from the Great Lakes Naval Base. Some college yahoo turning twenty-one had decided to celebrate his new manhood by sneaking drinks to all his underage buddies and mouthing off to the surrounding tables.

Mark cut the kid off, but it was too late. The damage was already done. The four swabbies Mr. College had chosen to get smart with were flush with liberty and spoiling for a fight.

When they swaggered over to the college boys' table, Mark pulled Nicole behind the bar.

Her eyes were worried. But her voice was perfectly steady as she asked, "This time can I call the police?"

He appreciated her calm. And her trust.

A visit from his future brother-in-law the police chief wouldn't do anything to save his evening. But it might save Nicole's bar.

"Yeah," he said. "Now would be good."

She swallowed and picked up the phone. Good girl, he thought, but at that moment the biggest, youngest swabbie—new recruit, Mark judged, with the shortest haircut and the most to prove—grabbed a fistful of shirt and pulled the college yahoo from his seat. The kid yelled. Chairs scraped back all over the room.

"I wouldn't do that," Mark called.

The recruit turned his head. "Why the hell not?"

Mark strolled bare-handed from behind the bar. The previous owner used to keep a baseball bat handy, but Mark figured any threat only stirred things up.

"Your pal there is two sheets to the wind," he said. "No challenge at all."

The recruit's fist wavered. "There are eight of them."

Mark continued to move forward, keeping his tone light and his eyes steady. "There are four of you. And they're civvies. They may have to appear before a judge for creating a public disturbance, but you'll end up in jail for drunk and disorderly." He addressed the group. "Is it really worth it?"

Another sailor—a little older and slightly less drunk, a petty officer, maybe—stepped forward. His gaze slid over Mark before it found the tattoo riding just below his sleeve on his right arm.

"You Navy?" he asked.

Hell. Four of them, Mark thought with a sigh. But he said, "Marines."

The petty officer grinned. "No challenge at all."

All the frustration of the past two weeks seethed and

surged through his bloodstream like lava, seeking a crack in his calm, an outlet. But Nicole was here, wide-eyed and silent. The whole bar was watching.

And he had a kid at home.

Mark didn't have a model to go by, but he was pretty sure daddies weren't supposed to show up at the breakfast table sporting split lips and black eyes. He had a responsibility here to keep the peace. To hold his tongue. To control his temper.

He balled his fists. "Guess not," he said. "You guys want to move this party someplace else? It would be a shame to end your night early in the brig."

The petty officer thought it over, his brain cells well lubricated but still working.

The shaved recruit—he looked the same age as the college boy and just as incapable of holding his liquor— sneered. "Are we too much for you, jarhead?"

"No," Mark said clearly. "Too drunk."

Wrong answer. Seaman Stupid threw a jab to his stomach. Mark had to end this. Fast. And without breaking up the bar.

He stepped to one side, grabbed the sailor's wrist and elbow, and twisted his arm behind his back. His buddies lurched forward, but Mark was holding the cursing recruit in front of him like a tackle dummy.

He made eye contact with the petty officer, giving him his best dead-eye glare and his easiest tone. "Do you guys really want to go up on charges because some townie was a jackass and your pal here is a little quick on the draw?"

The older man's bleary gaze sized up the situation. Mark decided to help. Alcohol did not promote clear thinking.

"You could take me, no question," Mark said. "But I've got a barful of witnesses and the police on the way. You got to ask yourselves if it's worth it." In case the other guy still didn't get it, he added, "I'm betting you'll say no."

He might have lost his bet.

But before the befuddled sailors could make up their minds to take him and his bar apart, red lights flashed on the glass outside. Mark released his breath in relief. The cavalry was here. Or at least, an Eden police department squad car.

Police Chief Jarek Denko was a lean man of medium height who should never have been able to command a room simply by walking in. But he did, Mark thought, both admiring and resentful. Maybe it was his fourteen years' experience as a homicide cop in Chicago's notorious Area 3. Maybe it was his freezing-as-the-lake-in-March-gray eyes. Maybe it was his gun.

Whatever it was, he depressed the atmosphere in the bar like a cold front blowing down from Canada.

"Mark. Ms. Reed." He nodded in Nicole's direction. "Having some trouble this evening?"

Nicole frowned. "That's why I—"

Oops. Hell. For a smart woman, she could be really dumb sometimes.

"No trouble," Mark said, shifting his grip on the sweating recruit. "In fact, it's been a little too quiet. Which is why some of these guys were leaving."

"That right?" Jarek asked mildly. He angled toward the sailors, keeping his shoulder back and his gun arm free. "Were you about to leave?"

The petty officer had enough working brain cells left to recognize the hint and the opportunity. "Yes, sir. On our way."

"Well then, you have a pleasant evening," Jarek said, and stepped aside.

Mark turned away from the locked door, already running through the evening routines in his mind, the register, the tables, the floor, trying to figure the shortcuts that would get him out of here—get both of them out of here—before two in the morning.

Nicole was standing by the open cash drawer, but she wasn't counting bills or punching numbers. She looked over at him with an open, warm regard that made his lower body clench and the hair on the back of his neck rise in warning.

"You were wonderful tonight," she said.

He rejected her praise instinctively. He was never wonderful. Nobody ever told him he was wonderful. He did his job, and sometimes he didn't screw up.

"Thanks," he said. "You, too."

She shook her head. "I didn't do anything."

He smiled to himself. So he wasn't the only one who had difficulty accepting compliments. "You kept your cool. You called the police."

"You kept a fight from breaking out in my bar."

"No. Jarek did that."

"You took down the Save Petey petition."

He felt the heat move in his cheeks. "That was a mistake."

"And the fish."

He was gratified. Embarrassed. "You noticed that?"

"I noticed." She came around the end of the bar. Her breasts shimmered distractingly under her shiny blouse. "I kind of miss it, though."

It? His mind blanked as her scent reached him. She was talking about the pike. Petey. "I hung him up in my apartment. Over the couch."

She moved closer. Her tongue touched her bottom lip. "If you're not going to bring him back, maybe I could visit sometime."

Mark's body, already revved with adrenaline and tensed with frustration, tightened even further. If he didn't know better, he'd swear she was coming on to him. Which of course she wasn't.

Unless... What had she said the other night? She wanted to gain experience? His brain exploded with images. He almost groaned. If he wasn't careful, if she didn't stop him, he could give her some experiences neither one of them would recover from anytime soon.

Right. Like that was going to happen with a six-year-old sleeping in his other bedroom. With his sister waiting up for him to come home, like he was sixteen again.

Maybe he'd misunderstood her. "You want to visit my fish?" he repeated.

Nicole smiled ruefully. "I didn't want to sound clichéd. You think maybe I should ask to see your etchings instead?"

Okay. He hadn't misunderstood. He still didn't have time for this. He didn't have the space for this.

But he sure as hell had the inclination.

He looked her right in the eye. "You don't have to ask, babe. For anything."

She raised her chin. "I think maybe I do. You're sure not doing the asking."

"It's…complicated," he said.

"So explain it to me."

Explain Betsy, the lawyer, Daniel? He really didn't have the time. Or the words.

"I can't right now. I've got to go."

Or Tess would kill him. Jarek would kill him. It was after one in the morning.

"I could go with you," Nicole offered. "We could get coffee somewhere."

They could get coffee here. That wasn't the point. He appreciated what she was trying to do—*Friends talk to each other,* she'd said—but no way was he launching into an explanation of his life right now. Especially when he didn't understand it himself.

As far as launching into anything else…

He looked at Nicole, at her dark pupils and her distracting breasts and her pink cheeks. She wanted him. She was no different from any of his other women, really, he could have her or not, no big deal.

Only her blue eyes were anxious. Her shoulders were stiff. This was Nicole, his hopeful, hardworking, infuriating boss. Nicole, who had lousy luck with men and a big, soft heart.

And he couldn't do it to her, couldn't take what she was so clearly offering.

Yeah, he was tempted. But it wouldn't be right. She deserved more than a fifteen-minute standing bang, with him on his way out the door.

It wouldn't be fair. Not when she had no idea that he had become a package deal.

He shook his head. "I've got to go home."

She took a deep breath, making the fabric over her breasts shimmer some more.

"I could go with you," she repeated. Hopeful. Stubborn.

"It wouldn't work," he said.

Her chin quivered, but she tried to make a joke of it. "What's the matter? Got someone waiting for you?"

"Yeah." Regret roughened his voice. "Yeah, I do."

Rejected.

Parked at the curb outside Kathy's town house, Nicole leaned her forehead on the steering wheel and cried.

Oh, God. She should be used to rejection. It shouldn't hurt this much. He wasn't Charles or Zack or Kevin, she hadn't even slept with him...

And the thought of what she'd missed, of what she was still missing, made her cry harder.

Pathetic. That's what she was.

Nicole knuckled her eyes and wiped her nose on the back of her hand. Maybe she'd had a lucky escape. Maybe she should be counting her blessings. Maybe she should be grateful Mark hadn't accused her of sexual harassment.

She winced. Oh, God. How was she going to face him at work tomorrow?

She didn't have to. Tomorrow was a Sunday. The bar was closed.

The realization made her feel slightly better. Drawing a shuddering breath, she climbed out of her SUV on shaky knees and tottered up the walk to Kathy's porch. The front light was on. She fumbled in her purse for her keys and— quietly, so as not to wake her roommate—unlocked the door.

The end-table lamp was turned down low. But even in the dim light, Nicole could see the flash of Kathy's red hair, her long pale legs…and a man's bare buttocks, moving busily up and down among the cushions of the couch.

There are a few things I've been wanting, and I can't get them with a roommate around.

Nicole's mouth dropped open, but no sound, no breath escaped. Her chest ached. Obviously, not everyone got turned down tonight.

She shut her jaw. She closed the door and stole quietly back to her car.

Chapter 11

"I hung up the towel," Daniel announced, appearing around the end of the counter. The top of his head barely cleared the cutting surface. It was like living with Yoda.

The gas flared as Mark adjusted the heat under the frying pan. "What towel?"

"For my hands. I washed my hands." He sounded anxious.

"Well, that's good," Mark said. Wasn't that good? His sister used to make him wash his hands. "How many eggs do you want for breakfast?"

Daniel hovered just beyond arm's reach. "How many are you having?"

"Two."

"I'll have two, please."

The kid had good manners. He wanted to fit in. Was that enough to make this father-son thing work?

"You'll have to get out another one, then," Mark said.

Daniel stared at him, wide-eyed.

Mark jerked his head toward the fridge. Thank God he went shopping yesterday. "Another egg. In there."

The butter sizzled. Mark swirled it in the pan as the boy scooted into the kitchen behind him. He heard the refrigerator door open and close and then a wet smack, crack, as something—an egg—hit the floor.

Mark said a word you weren't supposed to use around six-year-olds and turned.

Daniel stood beside the fridge with empty hands and a horrified expression. "I dropped it," he said unnecessarily.

Mark grinned. "I noticed."

"You said a bad word."

"Yeah. I shouldn't." The kid still looked upset, so he added, "Sometimes I forget I'm not onboard ship anymore."

"Mommy said—" The boy stopped.

Mark reached for the roll of paper towels. "What did your mom say?"

Daniel stepped back from the spreading egg. "She told me you were a sailor. In the war."

"Marine," Mark corrected and squatted to wipe the floor. He felt cold. Warm. Nervous. Betsy had talked about him. To their son. To make the kid feel better, presumably, about his lack of a father.

Mark could sympathize. He'd sat alone at too many "Dads and Doughnuts Days" himself. But he couldn't let the kid think he was some kind of hero.

"And we aren't at war, exactly."

"She said that was why you didn't come to see me."

Hell.

Mark folded the paper towels with the runny egg inside and wiped his palms on his jeans. Crouched like this, he was almost eye-to-eye with the boy. "That was kind of why. When Betsy—your mom—found out she was expecting you, I was probably—" *Gone*. Doing his thirteen weeks of basic on Paris Island instead of two-to-five years in jail.

"—really hard to get hold of," Mark said.

Had she even tried?

What could he say that wouldn't sound like a criticism of the child's dead mother?

He cleared his throat. "So we haven't had, you know, much chance to—"

The kid was staring at him with those big eyes that belonged on some cartoon character. Pinocchio, maybe, or Bambi. Mark stopped himself from saying another bad word.

"—get to know each other. Before this, I mean," he finished lamely.

The boy blinked once. "Are you mad?"

"You mean, like, crazy?"

The kid looked confused. "I mean about the mess."

"Oh. No. No big deal."

"Okay." Daniel smiled. And then he padded barefoot to the refrigerator and carefully took out another egg.

Okay.

Mark released his breath. And smelled butter burning. He snatched at the frying pan with one hand, made a grab for the control knob with the other.

The doorbell rang.

"I'll get it," Daniel, unnaturally helpful or maybe just curious, volunteered.

"You're not supposed to—"

The egg the child had set on the counter rolled. *Splat,* on the floor.

Bad word, bad word, bad word, bad word.

Nicole stood on the weathered landing outside Mark's apartment, light-headed with nerves and lack of sleep, her stomach churning and her pulse racing. The platform was dark and slick from last night's storms. Over the lake a fresh wind scoured the clouds away and ruffled the surface to sunlit peaks.

She should not be here.

She had humiliated herself enough already. Mark had rejected her for another woman, a woman who was probably still inside with him. It was only ten o'clock. They could be having brunch. Couples did that on lazy Sunday mornings. They could be having sex.

Nicole hunched her shoulders, shivering in the breeze from the lake. She should have called.

Except she didn't know what she was going to say. She'd spent the night in her unfinished apartment among the unpacked boxes, tearing them apart in search of answers. She was bleary-eyed from reading the advice of a dozen different gurus, from poring over a dozen different self-help guides.

When Loving Yourself Means Hating Him
Getting the Love You Deserve
I'm Okay and You Have Problems
When Your Lover Leaves You

Except her lover hadn't left her. Her bartender had.

Sometime during the long and sleepless night, it occurred to Nicole that she'd not only acted completely out of character, she'd been completely out of line. She had confused work and sex, repeating the mistake she had made with Kevin. Only this time she was the one with the power to make things right. The power and the obligation.

And until she did, she would be existing in this sleepless, anxious limbo. Unless she acted, she would not see Mark until Monday night. Their first meeting was bound to be awkward. Awful. Much better to get it over with quickly, with no one to witness her humiliation.

At least, that's what she told herself, driving her hands deeper into her pockets, praying for him to answer the door. She had to put their relationship back on a business footing.

She would tell Mark that her only focus right now was

the Blue Moon. He could go back to tending bar and having hassle-free sex with women who didn't want to be his friend, and she could go back to minding her business and being miserable and alone.

She sniffed. She was getting gradually better at the first part. She had the second down pat.

Where was he, anyway? It shouldn't take this long to come to the door. What if she had interrupted him? Interrupted them. Her heart pumped faster with shame and rage. She would kill him. She would die.

The door opened six inches.

Nicole jumped back, prepared to bolt.

But there was no one there.

"Hi," said a voice from the vicinity of her waist.

Mark was dating a midget? Bewildered, she looked down. A little face, a little boy, hovered in the crack of the door. A beautiful little boy, with soft dark curls and big dark eyes.

Helplessly enchanted, Nicole smiled.

The boy smiled back.

"Daniel?" She recognized Mark's voice, deep and impatient. "Who is it?"

The boy turned his head. He had a cherub's profile, round cheeked with long lashes. "I don't know."

"Then you shouldn't have answered the door," Mark instructed roughly.

His voice came closer. The boy shrank back.

Nicole wanted to shrink, too.

She was not here as Mark's rejected lover, she reminded herself. She was here as his employer. She would be professional and conciliatory.

And brief. She wanted to be very brief.

Mark yanked the door wide. His eyes widened in surprise and then narrowed. He looked hot and rumpled and distracted, as if he'd just rolled out of bed.

Nicole's heart bumped.

She moistened her lips with her tongue and gave him her most conciliatory professional smile. "I realize this is probably an inconvenient time. But—"

"Yeah, it is." He turned from her and addressed the child. "She's okay. But don't do that again."

Nicole cleared her throat. "I, um—"

Mark walked away, saying over his shoulder. "You might as well come in. You want coffee?"

"No, I, um—"

"You look like you need some. God knows I do," he muttered and stalked across the main room of the apartment.

It looked like a den, like a lair, decorated all in browns and greens. The walls were planked. The furniture was rough. Petey the Pike leered at her from above the sofa as Nicole edged over the threshold.

The angel child watched her with wide, interested eyes. "I'm Daniel. I'm six."

"Hi, Daniel. I'm Nicole."

"I learned three new words today."

"Don't say them," Mark warned from the kitchen. "Cream and sugar?" he asked Nicole.

"Just milk, please." She smiled again tentatively at the little boy. Professional, she reminded herself. Conciliatory. And then she blew it. "Do you live here?"

The boy shook his head. "I'm visiting."

She almost sagged with relief. Mark wasn't keeping things from her. He wasn't lying to her. He wasn't— "Is Mark your—" Uncle? Cousin?

Mark returned bearing a coffee mug and wearing a hard, closed expression. "Daniel is my son," he said flatly.

Nicole looked like he'd just splashed ice water in her face instead of handing her a cup of coffee. Not the reaction he'd hoped for. Pretty much what he expected.

Single dad and chick magnet were not the same thing at

all. He'd already screwed up last night by not being straight with her. Finding out this morning that she'd been dumped for a six-year-old obviously wasn't scoring points either.

She hid it pretty quick, though. At least from the kid. Mark appreciated that.

"That's nice," she said. "Do you live with your, um—"

Mark crossed his arms, watching her with grim amusement. "Grandparents," he supplied.

"My mom died," Daniel said. "A car hit her."

Oh, now, that was good, Mark thought, grabbing for his customary cynicism. If they didn't scare her off completely, maybe he could work the pity angle. For some women a cute kid with a dead mom played better than a chocolate Lab.

"I'm sorry," Nicole said. She looked at Mark, her blue eyes warm and sincere. "For both of you."

He felt like a jerk. He was a jerk, looking for ways to use her soft heart against her.

But he didn't want to let her go.

"It's not like you're thinking," he said.

She tilted her head. "So explain it to me."

"It's a long story."

Her gaze cooled. "Of course. Some other time."

He was losing her. "No, I meant—"

"It's really none of my business. We don't have the kind of relationship where you have to feel compelled to share the details of your personal life with me."

He wanted to agree with her. But he didn't like the way she was withdrawing behind that bright, blank barrier she erected against hurt.

"So what should we talk about? The bar? The weather? Did you know our average rainfall this year is eleven inches above average and seven of those inches fell in the last month alone?"

Her cheeks turned pink. "Very funny. Actually, I came to discuss—"

"After breakfast," he interrupted.

"Excuse me?"

"We can talk about whatever you want after breakfast. You look like you need some, anyway."

Her free hand went self-consciously to her hair. She looked—not less perfect, she was still and always a knock-out—but less pulled together than usual. Her face was pale, her eyes were tired, and her clothes looked slept in.

"Well, I—"

"We're making eggs," Daniel announced unexpectedly. "You can have two."

Her whole face softened when she turned her attention to the child. Mark doubted she was even aware of it. "Two eggs?"

"Unless we break any more," Mark said dryly.

Daniel's eyes widened. His lower lip quivered. "You said it was no big deal."

Ah, hell.

"It's not," Mark said.

Nicole smiled with sympathetic understanding. She must be used to kids. Married Ted, the insurance salesman, had had three boys.

"Problems?" she asked.

Mark curled his hand around his son's bony shoulder, willing it to relax under his palm. "Nothing we can't handle," he said.

But it was nice, he discovered, to have some adult backup. Nicole helped Daniel set the counter with silverware, praised the eggs and dealt competently with toast crumbs and spilled milk. And Danny seemed more relaxed in her company, chattering about starting first grade and sliding from his stool to show off his collection of plastic lizards that traveled with him in a special shoe box.

"I like dogs," he announced. "I want a dog. But Grandpa says they're dirty, so I have lizards."

A boy ought to have a dog, Mark thought with sudden, fierce conviction.

A dog would be somebody to play with. To take care of. To look up to you with unconditional, unquestioning love.

Yeah, Daniel needed a dog.

And Mark needed…

Well, he sure as hell had never had a pet. Any dog dumb enough to sniff around the DeLucca household would have run away from his dad's abuse or starved from neglect.

He watched his son arrange the lizards among the crumpled napkins and dirty glasses. Nicole was talking to him, getting him to explain the difference between lizards and salamanders—man, the kid was smart. Who would have guessed he'd know something like that? And Mark thought, This is okay.

It felt right to have the kid here.

It felt good to have Nicole around, asking all the right questions.

He could get used to this.

The thought rippled like a storm flag on a cloudy day. Danger. Alert.

He shouldn't want to get used to this. What if he decided having them around was a good thing and then it blew apart? What if he came to need them and they didn't need him back? Mark set the dirty dishes in the sink. Wouldn't that be a kick in the teeth.

Robert Wainscott had made it clear he would fight to keep Daniel.

Danny himself might not want to leave the grandparents he knew for a father he'd only just met.

Nicole was recovering from a series of hit-and-run lovers. Despite last night's offer, probably the last thing she needed was drive-by sex with someone she had to work with day in and day out.

Mark ran cold water over the egg-crusted plates. Face it. He didn't have what it took to make things work for the

long haul. Tess was the one with the caring gene. He was
the screwup with the short attention span.

He'd never met a relationship he couldn't louse up or a
responsibility he couldn't walk away from. By now he
knew better than to set himself up for disappointment.

Didn't he?

Every book and article Nicole read stressed the impor-
tance of communication. That was why she had barged in
on Mark and his little boy: to communicate to him her
determination to reestablish their relationship on a busi-
nesslike footing.

Well, that, and because she couldn't keep away from
him.

She cradled her mug in her hands, feeling the warmth of
the coffee seep through the thick china, letting the warmth
of Daniel's chatter seep into her bones.

Okay, maybe she had allowed herself to be diverted from
her original purpose. But Mark had promised to tell her
about Daniel's mother—*it's a long story*—and that was still
communication. Wasn't it?

So her objectives were good. Basically. Her motivations
were pure. Mostly.

It wasn't her fault that none of her books offered any
guidance on how to launch into a complicated discussion
of involvements and intentions when your lover—*employee,* she corrected herself hastily—was distracted by
breakfast dishes, and his six-year-old son was marching lizards up your leg.

She stirred reluctantly. "I should probably go. Thank you
for breakfast."

"More coffee?" Mark asked.

She was tempted. And by more than the coffee. Mark's
eyes were warm and dark, his jaw attractively stubbled. He
looked as if he'd just rolled out of bed and with very little
encouragement would roll back in.

Her pulse quickened. She tightened her grip on her cup. "No, I—you obviously have plans for the day."

"You could come with us." Daniel, standing by her knees, turned his head toward his father. "Couldn't she come with us?"

Mark frowned slightly. "Is that what you want?"

Nicole cringed. He might as well have spray painted a huge No Girls Allowed across the front of the clubhouse.

She stood, making a grab for one of the plastic lizards as it tumbled to the floor. "Really, I—"

"Please?" Daniel asked, still looking at Mark.

Mark hesitated. "Sure," he said. "That would be fine." And then, before Nicole could tell him she wouldn't dream of intruding on the DeLucca-male, Sunday-morning bonding ritual, he smiled at her crookedly. "In fact, it would be great."

Her insides turned to warm mush. Nicole Reed, Human Oatmeal. She sighed. "Where are you going?"

"In a boat. A big boat. On the lake." Daniel's eyes were wide with excitement…or nerves? He clutched a big blue lizard. "You'll have fun. Please?"

A big boat on the lake. Nicole looked at Mark. "Will you make me walk the plank?"

"No. We have other uses for our female prisoners."

Her heart beat faster. "Oh, now, *that's* reassuring."

"Relax. You have a chaperone."

"But no clothes." She was still in the khaki pants and silk blouse she had worn the night before.

"You can stop at home."

Her stomach clenched. The thought of facing Kathy and her overnight guest was more than she could bear. "No."

Mark shrugged. "Then we'll find you something."

"Please?" Daniel repeated, like little Oliver Twist requesting another bowl of gruel.

She had always been a sucker for male persuasion. The combined coaxing of father and son was too much to resist.

She needed to be wanted, and she wanted to be with them. Maybe it wasn't smart, but it was true. And Nicole was sick of lying to herself.

"If I'm really not intruding—"

"Daniel wants you," Mark said.

She searched his gaze, black, challenging. "Does he?"

"We both do," he said.

She took a deep breath. "Then…yes."

"Cool," said Daniel.

"Good," Mark said. "Let me get you something to wear."

The "somethings" turned out to be a large white T-shirt, a zippered black sweatshirt and a snug blue bikini.

Nicole held the pile up and raised her eyebrows. "Yours?"

Mark paused stuffing a duffel. "The T-shirt is."

"And the bathing suit?"

He shoved a child-size sweatshirt and a pair of shorts into his bag. "Somebody must have left that behind."

Somebody female. Somebody temporary.

But it did fit very well, Nicole thought, craning to look at her reflection in the bathroom when she went to try the suit on under her clothes. She wasn't falling out the top, and the blue flattered her coloring. Should she take it as a sign her luck was turning?

Or as a warning?

It was hard to cling to gloomy thoughts when the lake sparkled and the sky gleamed and the wind whipped her hair from her eyes and her doubts from her head.

They walked down the dock. Or rather, Nicole walked, Daniel skipped and Mark strode after him. Boats tugged gently at their moorings on either side, their ports of origin ranging from Batchawana Bay to the Florida Keys, their names ranging from the sentimental to the silly: *Sea Dreams, Annie's Yacht, Kawabunga.* Flags and beach towels bleached in the bright sun. A dog launched itself from the side of a boat, splashing and barking.

Danny stopped. "Is he okay?"

Nicole looked to make sure. The dog's head was a sleek wet arrow in the water. Its legs churned beneath the surface. "I think so. He's chasing that ball. See?"

"He's swimming." The boy's voice quivered.

Mark stopped beside a long white boat with deep red sails bundled to the—whatever that part was that stuck out from the mast. *Under Way* ran in red letters down the side.

"Technically, that's a dog paddle," he said.

Nicole raised her eyebrows. "Which you, of course, can identify because of your advanced marine training."

His mouth quirked. "Well, yeah. And because he's a dog. That was a big clue. So, can you swim?" he asked Daniel casually.

The boy shook his head.

"Don't go jumping in after any ball, then, okay?" Mark said.

"What if I—" The boy snapped his mouth shut.

"Fall in?" Mark finished easily. "Not going to happen. But I've got a vest for you to wear that would keep you afloat."

"Where is it?" Daniel asked.

"Right onboard." Mark stepped over the low side and onto the deck of the big white sailboat. It rocked under his weight.

Nicole gaped. "This is yours?"

"Every inch," Mark said.

"It's—" Gorgeous. Expensive. "—big," she said.

"Twenty feet." He caught Daniel under the arms and swung him aboard. The boy clutched at his shoulders. "Easy, sailor."

"But how could you—" Crass, Nicole scolded herself. She might as well come right out and ask how much he made.

Except she knew how much he made. She paid him.

"I had a lot of pay saved up and waiting for me when I got out," he said. "Not that I could have afforded her if some forty-six-foot ketch hadn't dragged anchor in a storm off Mackinaw and plowed right into her. I've spent the past year doing repairs."

He fit an orange life jacket onto Daniel and guided him to a padded bench before extending a hand to Nicole. She grasped it tightly, trying to ignore the foot or more of dark water separating them, and lurched toward him.

He caught her, chest to chest. His was lean and strong.

Her heart hammered. "Thank you."

He smiled. "Welcome aboard."

He handed her to the seat beside Daniel and tossed her a matching vest.

"What can I do?"

His grin flashed. "Enjoy the ride."

Oh, my.

She watched him untie from the dock, long arms reaching, strong back flexing. He moved with speed but without apparent haste, pushing, adjusting. The breeze flipped back his hair. The engine thrummed under her feet, and she looked at him in surprise.

"I want to get clear of the marina before I put her under sail," he explained. "Someday I'll take you out on Lake Michigan and show you what she can really do. But today—" the boat shuddered gently as he urged her away from the tie-up and into open water "—we'll just take a little tour of Paradise."

The lake, he meant. He wasn't really offering to show her heaven. Although... Nicole lifted her face to the wind, the sun warm across her shoulders, the cold night only a memory. Danny leaned against her side, shivering with excitement, like a puppy.

Maybe heaven was like this after all.

"Now you'll see something," Mark promised.

He moved nimbly, working the lines. The main sail rattled as he raised it. It billowed, snapped and filled, lifting above their heads, deep red and glorious as a flag. The boat leaped. Mark scrambled out on the pointy front part of the boat, only a gleaming silver rail separating him from the rushing water.

"Is that safe?" Daniel whispered, pressing closer for reassurance.

She put her arm around his shoulders. "I'm sure your father knows what he's doing."

She hoped so, anyway.

And he certainly seemed competent, fearless, as he set the second sail against the wind. He dropped back into the cockpit and took the wheel. The breeze flattened his shirt against his hard chest. His feet were braced against the deck. His strong hands were easy on the wheel.

He looked like every romantic picture to come out of Hollywood or from between the covers of those books she bought and devoured in secret. Of course, she knew better than to fall for the fantasy completely. Pirates were thieves and marauders. Sailors had a girl in every port. Even Odysseus took ten years to train his wandering heart toward home.

But there was no denying that something in her leaped and filled at the sight of him as the sails leaped and filled with the wind.

The bank slid by to their left—trees tinged with autumn, and the shops, all gray shingles and red brick, and the spire of the Catholic church rising in the distance.

"There's the Blue Moon," Mark called, lifting a hand from the wheel to point.

She had never seen him like this before. Cocky, yes. But not this happy. This relaxed. This young.

He grinned. "Want to give her a try?" He eased the wheel suggestively toward her, and the boat angled in response. Thrilling. Scary.

She shook her head vigorously. "No, thank you."

He straightened them out with a slight adjustment. The boat surged forward. The shore rolled past, sandy beach and dark pine and the broad white steps of the Algonquin hotel.

"Daniel?" Mark invited.

The boy stared yearningly at the wheel. But he didn't move from his seat.

Mark held out his hand, palm up. "Come on," he coaxed. "We'll do it together."

Very slowly the boy stood. He took one hesitant step forward. And stopped, his fingers curled around the edge of his seat.

"Way to go," Mark said. "Almost there."

Nicole wasn't sure she would choose to walk across the moving deck herself. The boat wasn't heaving or pitching. But the water was moving by awfully fast, and the floor, that is, the deck, tilted.

Mark released the wheel—Nicole's heart rocketed to her throat—and extended both hands to his son. But he didn't close the space between them.

"It's okay. I've got you."

White-faced with terror and determination, Daniel flung himself forward.

Mark wrapped both arms around him and hoisted him up. He turned so that Daniel could grasp the wheel and put his own hands alongside his son's. "There you go. Now you can see everything."

Daniel's smile lit his face and brought tears to Nicole's eyes.

She looked away, willing the wind to dry them. She was falling for him. She was falling for both of them: head over heels, overboard, fathoms deep falling.

And she wasn't at all sure she trusted herself to swim.

Chapter 12

They had lunch in a quiet inlet far from the vacationers' cottage, where trees ringed a strip of rocks and sand and the water was deep and the current flowed slow. It was one of "his" places, private and solitary. He only brought the kid there because of the beach and because the water's depth accommodated the boat. Even with the recent high lake levels, the *Under Way*'s draft wouldn't allow him to pull in just anywhere.

He brought Nicole there because… He didn't want to think too much about why he brought Nicole.

Mark dropped anchor and carried the kid through the hip-deep water to shore. Daniel clutched his neck, but once they hit the beach he was okay with letting go. Mark set him on the sand and turned to fetch Nicole.

But she surprised him. She had already stripped to her bikini and slipped into the clear, dark water. It came up to just under her pretty breasts.

"Oh!" she exclaimed.

Despite his appreciation for the picture she made, Mark grinned at the comic outrage in her voice.

"It's cold!"

"It's September," he said.

He watched her find her footing and slog cautiously for the shore, holding his sweatshirt over her head to keep it dry.

"Want a hand?" he called.

He certainly wouldn't mind getting his hands on her sleek, wet curves. The cold did interesting things to her nipples under the blue nylon bikini.

"I'm fine, thanks." She sounded breathless.

When she reached the sand, she shook out his sweatshirt and pulled it on, which was too damn bad. But the glimpses he caught of her smooth chest and pale belly framed by the open zipper almost made up for it. And the sight of those long legs disappearing into the short, black cover-up made his groin tighten.

Maybe it was a good thing the water was so cold. He sure as hell wasn't ready to give his six-year-old son a demonstration in sex education.

Not that Daniel was paying particular attention to the two grown-ups. He was running around acting like a little boy instead of a polite, nervous old man. He threw rocks and buried his lizards in the sand and dug them up again.

"He likes it here," Nicole observed, leaving her investigation of Daniel's fossil dig to stand beside Mark.

Something in his chest eased. "Maybe he just likes being on solid ground," he said.

But when it was time for lunch and he ordered the boy back to the boat, Daniel came along happily.

They took turns changing out of their wet clothes in the boat's cabin. Nicole exclaimed over the galley—the previous owner's tastes had run to brass and teak—and Daniel liked the food, box lunches from the Rose Farms Café.

Nicole inspected her turkey sub, the throwaway container

of pasta salad, her slightly bruised apple and chocolate chip cookie as if she were already calculating costs in her head. "We could do these at the Blue Moon," she announced. "We have a better menu, and we're closer to the marina than they are."

Mark had had the same thought when he went shopping yesterday. But he only grinned. "Eat your cookie, babe. It's your day off."

He figured she needed one. When she showed up on his doorstep this morning, her eyes had been bruised and puffy and her mouth tight with strain. Now her eyes were bright, her cheeks were pink, and she was smiling.

She narrowed her eyes at him. "That doesn't mean you can order me around."

But she bit obediently into her cookie. Her pink tongue chased a smear of chocolate at the corner of her mouth, and his lower body tightened. He shifted uncomfortably, glad that he was at least out of the wet, revealing denim.

Daniel yawned.

"Tired?" Mark asked, grateful for the distraction.

The boy nodded. And then, in a surprise move, he slid off the padded bench, crossed the deck and crawled up on the seat beside Mark, leaning his head on his father's arm.

Holy hell.

Mark took a shallow breath. He felt like a grenade had landed in his lap and any sudden movement would set it off. His heart hammered.

And yet nobody else seemed to feel anything was wrong. Nicole nibbled at her cookie. Daniel yawned again and burrowed deeper into Mark's side.

Very cautiously he put his arm around the boy's bony shoulders. Just so he wouldn't fall off the bench.

"Maybe you should take a nap or something."

"I'm too old for naps," Daniel informed him sleepily.

Right. Okay. What did he know?

"Mom used to sing to me." The words were muffled

against Mark's chest, but they hit his heart with the force of shrapnel. "When she wanted me to sleep? She would lie on my bed and sing to me."

Mark was silent for a long time. Nicole put down her cookie.

"I don't know any songs," he said at last.

The boy raised his head. "Not any?"

"Not many." Lullabies had never been Isadora De-Lucca's strong suit. Some Joplin, maybe, a little Judy Garland, the anthems of doomed and self-destructive women. "Unless you count 'Barnacle Bill the Sailor.'"

He knew lots of verses to that. All of them obscene.

"That sounds funny," Daniel said hopefully. "Sing that."

"Uh." What the hell. He could edit as he went along. The beginning wasn't too bad, as he recalled. He cleared his throat and warbled, "'Who's that knocking at my door? said the fair young maiden.'" So far, so good. He lowered his voice to pirate gruffness to sing the part of the sailor. "'It's only me from over the sea, says Barnacle Bill the sailor. I—'oops—uh, 'dumpty-dum and a bottle of rum, says Barnacle Bill the sailor.'"

Jeez. Okay, so editing was going to be tougher than he thought.

But Daniel giggled. Nicole was biting her lip, as if she was trying to keep from laughing, too.

"Is that really how it goes?" Daniel asked.

Not even close.

"Something like that," Mark said. "It's not really a kids' song."

"Too many bad words," the boy said wisely.

"Way too many," Mark agreed.

They sat awhile in silence, as the child's breathing deepened and slowed. The boat rocked gently.

"You really don't know any other songs?" the boy asked at last, wistfully.

Mark drew a deep breath. "Maybe. One. Yeah." He closed his eyes, trying to remember all the words. Don't blow this, DeLucca. Get this one thing right.

And with his eyes still closed, he opened his mouth and sang every drunken Irishman's favorite bar tune.

"'Oh, Danny boy, the pipes, the pipes are calling…'"

It was a long song. Four verses, and he sweated every one of them.

"'…then I will sleep in peace until you come to me.'"

When he finished, the boat was very quiet. Even the breeze had died. Danny was sleeping, finally, against his side, and Nicole was staring at him with wide blue eyes that saw—what did she see when she stared at him like that?

"That was beautiful," she whispered.

He lifted one shoulder, uncomfortable with her warm, open regard. "It's no big deal. Every bartender who's worked one St. Patrick's Day knows 'Danny Boy.' Especially in Chicago."

"It was still very special," she insisted.

He hoped so. He hoped he could give the kid one good memory of him, even if— But his mind slid away from the thought. It was his day off. Maybe he was entitled to a cookie, too. Maybe today he could pretend he was the kind of father a kid like Danny deserved.

He carried the boy below to lay him on one of the berths. Man, he was small. Mark could remember being six—the start of first grade, a long time ago, and he didn't have the kind of childhood you wanted to dwell on, anyway—but he couldn't remember ever being that small. He took time to cover the kid with a blanket and make sure he was still asleep.

A tactical error, that was.

Because when he came up on deck, Nicole had had time to think. She was curled up on the port bench like a little

girl on a window seat, staring absently over the water, her
eyes thoughtful and her mouth sad.

He eyed her warily. He was used to women who went
overboard on drama: sex partners who wanted the excitement of fighting and making up, lovers who made wild
demands. His mother, when she was drunk, was given to
fits of laughter and weeping. Even his sister, the one emotional anchor in his life, had a temper.

Nicole was different. She didn't put her emotions on dis-
play. And if she occasionally sounded as if she was reading
from a script—or quoting from one of those books of
hers—at least he never got the feeling that she'd already
written his part. Or that she'd prefer some other actor in
the role.

He crossed his arms and waited.

"Tell me about Danny's mother," she invited.

So he gave her the same basic spiel he had given the
lawyer: they were young, they were dumb, they weren't
married, her parents hadn't approved.

"Did you love her?" Nicole asked quietly, which was
the one question the lawyer had never asked.

He answered her honestly, surprising them both. "I think
I did. As much as I could love anybody at nineteen. I sure
as hell would have wanted to know if she was pregnant."

"So you didn't learn about Danny until…?" She paused
expectantly.

"Two weeks ago." He grinned at her stunned face, but
there was no humor in him. "Yeah, it was a shock to me,
too."

"I don't want to pry, but—"

He looked at her.

She turned pink. "All right. I am prying. But what will
you do now?"

He turned his head to starboard, staring out at the bound-
less blue sky and the lake stretching wide and open. An
illusion, Mark knew. Just out of sight the water was

hemmed in by trees and the beginnings of development. To really feel the freedom of open water, a sailor had to leave Paradise for the Great Lakes and beyond.

Nicole was still waiting for an answer.

"I don't know." He looked back at her. "I don't know if I can take care of him."

"You're doing fine. You'll find a way."

He was tempted to believe her. And that scared him.

He jerked one shoulder. "Maybe. Or maybe I'll just find someone else to do it."

The light in her eyes dimmed. "Is that why you invited me along? To take care of Danny?"

"No. Maybe." When she didn't say anything, only looked at him with those serious blue eyes, he admitted, "Well, he wanted you to come. And he likes you. You look—you're blond, like Betsy. Maybe I thought it would be a good idea to have someone else along while we got used to each other."

She nodded. "I can accept that."

So he'd dodged that bullet. His muscles relaxed a fraction.

"I've had a lovely time," she continued. "He's a wonderful child."

But? he thought.

She straightened on her bench seat. "But that's all the more reason for us to examine our expectations before beginning a relationship."

The jargon was a bad sign. He raised both eyebrows. "There's no beginning about it, babe. We're already together ten, twelve hours a day."

"In a *professional* capacity," she said earnestly. "This is personal."

"Personal, fine. It still doesn't have anything to do with Danny."

"Until you need the night off or a week away to be with him."

"You got a problem with time off?"

"No! No, of course not. I just can't help wondering… How much do you want me? And how much do you simply want a buffer with your son? Or a baby-sitter."

"Is this about that Ted guy?" Because he could sympathize with that. Once burned…

But she shook her head. "No. Well, it could be. This is about me. About us." Her tongue touched her lower lip. Her eyes sought his. "Do you want me?"

Hell, yes.

"Yeah, I want you," he said. "I told you I want you."

"Why?"

His laughter cracked like a rifle shot. "I thought I made that obvious."

"Sex." Her voice was flat. Not mad, he thought, as much as…disappointed?

He ground his teeth. He was no good at talking about this relationship stuff. He was no good at relationship stuff, period.

"If you want," he said.

"We're not talking about what I want."

"Well, maybe we should." Maybe she needed to. And maybe it would get him off the hook. "What do you want, Nicole?"

Her gaze slid away. "I guess I made that clear, too."

Last night, she meant. When she came on to him in the bar.

His heart beat faster. He sat beside her on the bench. The sailboat leaned at their uneven distribution of weight, but Nicole did not protest. That was a good sign, wasn't it?

He took her hand, the back faintly sunburned, the fingers sparkling with rings. "Okay," he said. "So, I want you. You want me, too. That's simple."

Her fingers twined with his. "But it's not. You know it's not."

He knew.

He just didn't care. Her hand was warm and smooth in his. Her scent teased at his senses, lake water and mud overlaying her perfume in a weird combination that made him want to lay her back against the seat and lick her skin.

He inhaled sharply. "Let's see what we can do to simplify it, then."

"With your six-year-old sleeping downstairs?"

Maybe not. But—

"He has to go back," Mark said. A circumstance that didn't exactly fill him with joy, but he had to admit that in this case it was convenient. "To his grandparents. This afternoon."

Nicole wasn't convinced. "Workplace relationships are rarely successful and frequently awkward."

She sounded like she was reading from a book again. But there was real hurt in her eyes and real apprehension in her voice. She'd worked with her other lover, Mark remembered. The dot-com boss. The son of a bitch.

"What are you afraid of? It's not like I'm in a position to fire you."

She flushed. "No. But—"

"You planning to fire me?"

"Of course not. But we still have to work together."

"Tomorrow. We have to work together tomorrow. Today is our day off, remember?"

She bit her lip. "What are you suggesting?"

"Come with me to Chicago. We'll drop off Danny, and I'll take you out someplace."

"You mean, like a date?"

Jeez, he was smooth. "Yeah, a date. Dinner. Just you, just me. No roommate, no sister, no bar, no responsibilities. What do you say?"

She pulled her hand back to fiddle with her rings. "And after dinner?"

After dinner he wanted to drive her to a nice hotel and

take her standing against the wall the minute he locked the door behind them.

He cleared his throat. "Let's keep it simple, okay? Let's take it one step at a time."

She nodded, her eyes wide.

Ah, hell. Did she have any idea at all what he was getting at? What she was getting into? For a woman with a string of loser boyfriends in her past, she was remarkably trusting.

"You might want to pack a toothbrush," he said, just so she got the idea.

Again she nodded. "I'll pick up a few things when I go home to change. What time do you want me to come over?"

She was going to do it.

She was going to come with him.

Even if it turned out it was only for dinner.

He was stunned.

"Five o'clock," he said. "We'll pick you up."

That would make it seem more like a date, he reasoned.

"That way you won't have to worry about your car sitting outside my place," he said.

She smiled, that wonderful smile that lit her eyes and warmed his insides. "Five o'clock," she agreed. "I'll be ready."

Hot damn.

Her legs were shaved, her eyebrows were plucked, her underwear was color coordinated and her toothbrush was in her purse along with a condom she'd stolen from Kathy. Heart beating and hopes high, Nicole had prepared herself for a night on the town with a man who turned her bones to water.

But for the past twenty minutes, she'd felt frustratingly as if she had somehow hopscotched horribly past courtship, love and marriage and landed smack in the middle of the family vacation from hell. The Jeep's wiper blades shuddered and squeaked. Danny whined in the back seat. And beside her, Mark drove, white-knuckled and tight-lipped.

Nicole sighed. She needed to get herself a new fantasy.

She dug in her purse for a roll of Lifesavers and turned in her seat to offer one to Danny. He accepted it and subsided, sucking. Mark threw her a grateful glance.

On the other hand she wasn't sure she would trade her present reality for a dozen romantic fantasy scenarios. Maybe it was enough to be here with him, with them. Included. Wanted. Necessary.

Mark took the exit for Kenilworth, an exclusive suburb of old oaks, putting-green lawns and granite-slab houses. The rain let up. The gray light gleamed off the high stone walls and marble beasts that guarded Chicago's old money. Keep out, they growled. Go away.

Nicole understood their silent warning. She'd grown up behind those walls.

Mark turned the Jeep under the blank stone stare of two lions and onto a curving brick drive. The three-story house overlooking the lawn had more steps than a museum. The front door opened as soon as they pulled up, as if someone inside couldn't wait to welcome Daniel back.

Or didn't want Mark to come into the house.

Nicole shivered.

"This will only take a minute," Mark said. His voice was without expression. So was his face.

Not good, she thought. He could hardly miss the contrast between his modest, masculine digs and this imposing residence. Did he resent it? Or was he simply sad to be saying goodbye to his son?

I don't know if I can take care of him.

Nicole vaguely recognized the man who came down the steps: Robert Wainscott, another mover and shaker in her father's legal circles. He was golf-course tanned with a naturally spare frame and unnaturally dark hair. His wife, waiting at the top of the stairs, had equally improbable coloring, but her champagne-blond hair was much softer and more flattering. She smiled when she saw Danny.

He waved.

"Thanks for the visit," Mark said. Nicole wasn't sure if he was addressing the Wainscotts or Danny.

"Thank you for having me," the boy said politely. "I had a nice time."

Nicole believed him. She hoped Mark did.

They didn't hug, she noticed. Mark touched the boy's shoulder in brief farewell, and then both men watched as Danny trudged up the steps. He had almost reached the woman at the top when Nicole heard him humming. Two more steps, and the words of his song drifted down.

"'...dumpty-dum and a bottle of rum, says Barnacle Bill the Sailor.'"

Mark laughed.

Robert Wainscott turned on him in fury. "I only agreed to this visit because your lawyer insisted. I hoped a taste of responsibility would make you run. But if this is what I can expect—"

Mark's face wiped clean of amusement. "You can expect me to deal with my son in my own way. And you agreed because you didn't have any choice. Daniel is my son."

"So you say."

"It's what the test said."

"That test is not admissible in court."

Nicole bit her lip. She shouldn't listen. She couldn't resist.

"Danny's lawyer submitted the sample. Where do you think she got it?"

"How should I know? From any one of your other bastards, I suppose."

Mark shook his head. "You are so full of crap."

"The agreement was for you to take the boy for one night," Wainscott insisted. "I should have known that even that brief a time would subject him to corrupting influences.''

"'Corrupting influences'? What are you, nuts? It was a song.''

Wainscott threw a venomous glance into the car. "I'm not talking about the song.''

"What the hell are you talking about?''

"The woman. Did she spend the night with you?''

Nicole shrank.

"That's none of your damn business,'' Mark said.

"It's my business if you're screwing her in front of my grandson.''

Nicole sucked in her breath.

Mark went as still as a coiled snake. "Given that your wife and my kid are watching from the top of those stairs, I won't knock your teeth down your throat for that remark,'' he said softly. "We'll let the testing center settle this.''

Wainscott puffed his narrow chest. "We'll let the court settle this.''

Mark shrugged. "The courts in Illinois favor the rights of the natural parents. I read enough to know that much.''

"I have friends on the bench in Cook County. And no judge in the world would consider you a fit guardian for a child.''

"Your daughter did.''

"Elizabeth had no idea what she was doing.''

"Yeah, that's what you said seven years ago.'' Mark's eyes were flat and cold. Nicole felt a chill chase up her spine. "The difference is this time I won't go away without a fight.''

Chapter 13

"This was a bad idea." Mark roused himself to stare across the table at Nicole, her perfect hair, her perfect face, every freaking thing about her perfect and out of place. "You want to leave?"

She straightened on her high-backed wooden chair. Behind her, the rollicking Greek music—bouzouki and drums—kicked up a notch. A roasting lamb rotated in the window. A waiter added a shot of ouzo to a sizzling plate, and cries of "Opa!" went up from the surrounding tables as blue flames shot toward the ceiling.

"No." She smiled, and something in his chest unclenched. "I like it here. It's very lively."

"Which is more than you can say for the company," he said dryly.

"You have a lot on your mind," she said.

Now there was an understatement. But he didn't need her to excuse his bad mood. Or his bad manners.

"I promised you a good time."

"You promised me dinner. Which you provided. I liked the moo—the moos—the lamb dish."

"Moussaka." He appreciated the way she'd plowed into her food. And the fact that she hadn't ordered the most expensive item on the menu.

He leaned forward to refill her glass with *roditys,* the raw red wine he'd ordered to go with their meal. Under the table their knees brushed.

She touched her fingers to the lip of her glass. "You'll make me dizzy."

"Maybe I want you dizzy."

She arched her brows, but took a sip of her wine. Setting down her glass, she observed, "You're not drinking."

He shrugged. "I don't, much."

"Isn't that unusual? A bartender who doesn't drink?"

"Not really. A bartender who depletes the stock or loses control with the customers is going to find himself out of a job pretty damn quick. Besides—" He shut his mouth.

"Besides…?" she prompted gently.

After the scene with Wainscott this afternoon, he owed it to her to let her know the worst.

Maybe he owed it to himself.

"My father was a drunk. My mom was a lush. I don't want to end up like that."

"You haven't. You won't."

He played with his knife, watching the candlelight gleam off the silver handle so he wouldn't have to see the look in her eyes. "It runs in families, you know. Alcoholism."

"Are you warning me? Or playing on my sympathies?"

She surprised him. Her tone was almost tart. And the expression in her eyes wasn't disgust or pity.

It was almost…acceptance.

His heart thumped. But he made one more effort to be straight with her.

"I'm telling you I'm no prize. Old man Wainscott's probably right about me."

"I'm not interested in Robert Wainscott's opinions," she said in that snooty, blondes-know-best voice that amused him and turned him on.

"That's good. Seeing as he's full of—" bad word, he thought, practicing for Danny "—hot air."

"I'm sorry if my being in the car this afternoon created difficulties for you." The words were stiff, but her eyes were genuinely concerned.

"Don't be," he said roughly. "Wainscott's the one making things difficult. You just got caught in the crossfire." He was sorry for that. "You okay?"

She swallowed. Nodded. "Did he really think that you would—that we would—"

"He'll think whatever he wants. Whatever makes him right and me scum, so he can keep telling himself that what's his should never be mine."

"You sound…bitter."

He smiled thinly. "Damn straight."

She tilted her head. "Is that why you want Danny? To show him you can take something that belongs to him?"

"No." *Maybe.* He glared at her. "That's stupid."

But she didn't drop it. "Is that why you want me? So that he'd see you with another blond, Gold Coast lawyer's daughter and know there was nothing he could do about it?"

He expelled his breath in frustration. "You read too much, you know that?"

"It's not what I read. It's what I observe."

She saw a lot. But this time she was wrong.

"Well, you're blind on this one, babe. I don't need an excuse to want you. I just do."

She sat back, crossing her arms and raising her brows. "Really."

If he had been a drinking man, he would have reached for the bottle. He wanted her until he ached with it. Wanted her nervous conversation and quiet understanding and can-do earnestness in his life. Wanted her soft mouth and blond hair and pale limbs in his bed. His hunger for her was a heaviness in his groin, a hollowness in his chest.

And he didn't have the words or the guts to tell her.

"Yeah, really," he mocked.

Her cheeks were pink. "Then why are we still sitting here?"

Mark couldn't believe it. But he wasn't about to question his luck. Once the objective was in sight, a marine never retreated.

He signaled the waiter and stood. "Let's go."

Nicole stood under the opulent arched ceiling of the Palmer House Hotel, rain spotting her blouse and dampening her hair. Mark leaned over the high counter to speak to the reservations clerk. She shivered from a combination of air-conditioning and nerves.

The Palmer House didn't cater to guests without luggage. They didn't rent rooms by the hour, either. How on earth was Mark going to afford this?

And what in heaven's name was she doing here?

He strode across the blue-and-gold lobby in his black jeans and dark shirt, lean and hot and dark as the devil. A white-haired matron in a pastel pantsuit nudged her companion. A sleek brunette in Armani turned around frankly to gawk.

Nicole nibbled her lip. Women would always look at Mark DeLucca. Women would always respond. Could she compete with that? Could she live with it?

One step at a time, she chastised herself.

He stopped in front of her, the light of the lobby making his black eyes appear even darker than usual. His expression was all male and so satisfied her breath stuck in her throat. "We're in luck. They had a cancellation."

Her heart thudded. She moistened her lips. Attempted a smile. "So, do we—did you—"

"I've got the key. Did you pack a toothbrush?"

It was in her purse, along with the condom.

Her face burned. Her body burned with embarrassment and heat. She could be making a mistake. She could be repeating her mistakes, which was worse.

But it was hard to think of that with Mark's black gaze focused on her face, with his body close and taut and almost steaming with heat in the cool lobby air. It was hard to think at all.

Toothbrush. Did she have one?

"Yes," she said.

Satisfaction flashed across his face. "Outstanding." He took her elbow. "Let's go."

She let him steer her past the low, plush couches, the interested women and the carefully incurious bellman, feeling as obvious as Julia Roberts in *Pretty Woman*. Mark didn't put his arm around her, didn't twine his fingers with hers or fondle her bottom.

Maybe she would have felt more reassured if he had.

In the elevator he stood behind her and slightly to one side, his shoulder warm against her back. She met his eyes in the mirrored doors. His gaze sharpened, became almost predatory. Her stomach fluttered with…

It wasn't fear, she told herself. She wasn't afraid of him. She wasn't afraid of anybody.

But he was looking at her as if he was the Big Bad Wolf and she was Red Riding Hood and he could eat her up in a single bite.

She shuddered with excitement and dread.

"Cold?" he murmured close to her ear.

"I— Not really."

"Second thoughts?"

"No."

To convince him, to convince herself, she turned, flattening her breasts against the hard planes of his chest, enjoying the instant response of his body. She put her hands on his shoulders, surprised when his arms didn't wrap around her in return.

"It's not like I'm a virgin," she said.

"A woman of experience." His voice was bland.

If he was laughing at her, she would die. No, she would kill him.

She stuck out her chin. "Yes."

A crease deepened in his cheek. "I'm going to have to work harder to impress you, then."

She panicked. "No. Mark, I—"

He stopped her with his kiss, his mouth hard and sure as he took hers with devastating skill. Her mind blanked. Her knees melted.

He sucked in his breath and raised his head. "It's okay," he said against her lips. "It'll be good. Better than good. I promise."

He'd made promises before. Promises that mostly hadn't been wanted and a few that hadn't been kept.

I'll never hurt you, to Betsy.

I'll never leave you, to Hayley.

I'll call you, to the beautiful women who sometimes occupied his evenings or his bed.

They used him for excitement. He used them for release. He figured it was a fair exchange. They got their stories or their memories of "How I Spent My Summer Vacation," and he got off. Everybody was satisfied.

Except he wanted more from Nicole than recreation or physical release. Wanted to give her more than a brief thrill or a bout of hot, sweaty sex.

It was a jarring thought. An alien thought. He'd played out this scenario too many times with too many women to welcome a change in the script.

But Nicole was special. Or maybe it was just the situation that was different. After all, they worked together. Unlike his summer women, he would see her again. Tomorrow he had to be able to look her in the eyes, had to face himself in the mirror.

Which meant that when the door to their hotel room finally closed behind him, he couldn't fall on her like a starving dog on a piece of meat.

He bolted the door, dragged in his breath, and turned. And practically salivated at the sight of her, slim and pale and pretty at the foot of the bed. Her face was shadowed. Her hair gleamed in the dim glow of the distant street below. Against the rain-streaked, gauze-covered window, he could make out the shape of one breast and the curve of her hip.

His libido grew fangs and bit deep.

Easy, ace. He reached under the silk shade to turn on a lamp. "Nice room."

She winced at the sudden brightness, or maybe the stupidity of his observation. "Do we really need a light to see it?"

Hell, no.

All he needed was the bed.

He didn't even need the bed as long as she was in the room.

But he wanted her to see that he hadn't brought her to some cheap dive with stains on the sheets and lipstick on the bathroom glass. He wanted to see her, wanted to watch the rise and fall of her body and the shifting expressions of her face, like the changing moods of the sea.

"You want to do it in the dark?" he asked, half-joking.

Her shoulders squared like she faced a firing squad. "I would be more comfortable with the lights off, yes."

"Comfortable is good." He switched off the light. "Even relaxed would be an improvement."

"I am relaxed," she insisted.

Her voice was strained. She was rigid as a board and nervous as a nine-year-old embarking on her first solo sail.

He stalked her carefully. "Good. That will definitely make it easier to seduce you."

She sputtered. He hoped with amusement, but it could have been outrage. "You don't have to seduce me."

"Sure I do." He reached her, damp silk and subtle curves in the dark. His lips skimmed her forehead. He pressed a kiss to her hair. "You're shaking."

"So are you," she announced with bravado.

"Mmm." He slid his hands up her back, pulled her close and tight against him. His senses swam with her. She smelled so good. The urge to touch, to taste, to take, gnawed on his bones. "It's because I'm nervous," he said, hoping she would think he was joking.

"You?" she scoffed. "Nervous? Of what?"

He trailed his mouth down the side of her face. What the hell. Maybe she was right about the dark. Maybe he could tell her in the dark the stuff he never would admit in the light of day. "Of this. Of you. I don't have a lot of experience at this sort of thing."

A snort of disbelief escaped her. He felt some of the tension leave her shoulders. "Oh, please. No experience seducing women?"

"Nope."

It was true, he realized. The marine groupies, the bar bunnies…they kind of threw themselves at him. He mostly just picked them up and moved on. "Anyway, I don't have to work for it."

"You don't have to work for me, either," she pointed out. Her voice was stiff, her body fluid against him.

He nuzzled the curve of her jaw. "There's a difference."

She drew back her head until they were face-to-face, nose to nose. "What difference?"

"I like working for you," he whispered against her mouth and then bit into her lower lip so that she clutched at him.

But she didn't surrender, not right away, not all the way.

Her nipples were tight little points against his chest, her fingers curled into his shoulders, but he could feel the hesitancy in her mouth, the resistance in her mind. She was holding out on him. She was holding back.

So he kissed her again, long and wet and deep, pushing for her response. She cooperated, winding her arms around his neck, welcoming his tongue. Oh, baby. His blood surged. But he eased back to study her face in the dim light that filtered through the window: her soft, slick mouth and her warm, smooth cheeks and the tiny pleat between her eyebrows.

His lust developed claws that raked his gut. He could have her. He could take her right now, standing, pressing her back against the wall with his pants down around his ankles, and she would not object. He beat the thought back into its cage.

"Stay or go?" he asked harshly.

Her eyes fluttered open. Narrowed. "What do you mean? I'm here, aren't I?"

"Your body is. Your head isn't."

She smiled at him uncertainly. "Well, it's my body you want."

Oh, yeah. He definitely wanted that. He was so hot for her, so ready, he'd probably carry the imprint of his zipper around on his body for days. The problem was, he wanted more.

"I want all of you," he said, and took her mouth again to prove it.

Nicole's heart pounded because of the things he was doing. Because of the risks she was taking. And mostly because of what he'd said. *I want all of you,* just like that, his voice rough with frustration, his hands rough as they dug down inside her slacks—her waistband cut briefly into her stomach—and then up the bare skin of her back to her bra.

She should break their kiss. She should explain, apologetically, that her bra had a front closure, chosen in anticipation of being with him tonight. But before she could get the words out, his lean, long fingers slid along her ribs, grazing the underside of her breast. Obviously, he didn't need instructions from her. He knew what he was doing. Her nipples tingled. Ached. She gasped, and his tongue filled her mouth, hot, seeking, sleek, as he flicked open her bra, pushed the satiny cups aside and rubbed his whole hand over her breast.

Boy, did he know what he was doing.

There was something vaguely disquieting about that fleeting thought, like a shadow under the surface of the water, but before she could dive after it, he swept her up and dragged her under. She felt herself softening, melting, as he squeezed her breast, as he brushed her nipple with his thumb, as he rolled it between his fingers.

Her thighs loosened. Her head dropped back. And he took exquisite advantage, pressing his hard body between her legs, setting his lips and teeth against her throat.

Her hands gripped his shoulders. Her mind flailed. She ought to... He would expect... But her half-formed resolves sank under the onslaught of his urgent mouth, under wave after wave of response.

He yanked her blouse off her shoulders, tangling her arms in the sleeves. With her hands trapped behind her back, he bent her over his arm and trapped her breast in his mouth. The damp heat, the suction, made her quiver. She squirmed. He feasted, releasing her only long enough to pop the button of her slacks and drag down her zipper. She tried to tug her hands free—to help him? To cover herself?—but his hot mouth glided down her torso, nipping, sucking. She trembled as his breath gusted against her lower belly and between her thighs.

She sucked in her stomach. It was too soft. Too pale, despite her hours in the blue bikini. Zack used to tell her she didn't do enough crunches. If she'd gone to a tanning parlor—

But Mark didn't seem to notice. He grasped her hips. Her heart jerked in her chest. She was wet. In a moment he would see... He would know... She was too open to him. Open and vulnerable.

She struggled for balance, but he held tight to her buttocks, nuzzling between her legs, his hair brushing the swell of her belly. His breath was hot. A choked cry escaped her throat. Eagerness. Doubt.

She felt his tongue stroke and plunge, and her blood roared in her ears. Her knees gave way, as if she stood in a sucking tide, but he held her, supported her, as he licked and flicked and swirled his way inside her.

Oh, he knew exactly what he was doing.

She was drenched. Drowning. She tried to hold her mind above, separate—*this is only sex, you've had sex before, what an interesting technique*—but she could not resist his pull on her senses and her heart. He lifted her—he was strong, his arms corded with muscle—and laid her on the bed. Stood over her while he ripped his shirt off over his head, while he yanked on his buckle and shoved down his jeans.

Do something.

She couldn't just lie here and let herself be taken. The thought shivered through her. Yes, she could. But she had a responsibility to her partner.

She wrestled with her blouse to free her hands. By the time she rolled free and sat up, he was already naked, sinewy, lean and naked, lit only by the thin gray light that sparkled through the rain on the glass.

Her breath abandoned her. *Oh.*

"I—" *Say something.* "I have a condom."

And instead of sneering, he smiled. "So do I."

He wasn't objecting. Gratitude made her blink. "It's in my purse."

He raised his hand, revealed the packet in his palm. "Mine's closer."

She opened her arms to him.

He came down on her, his lovely hard bone and muscle pressing her into the mattress, the silky weight of his arousal thrusting against her hip. His hands went everywhere.

She was overwhelmed. Overcome. Battered by sensation, swamped by need.

I want all of you.

Turning her head, she opened her mouth on his shoulder, tasting salt and skin as his hands, urgent and sure, spread her legs and opened her. She arched against the bed, her hands gripping and slipping on his smooth, damp back. She locked her legs around his hips.

Any second now. Any second. Now.

He hesitated.

"What can I do?" she cried, frantic.

He raised his head and smiled into her eyes.

"Enjoy the ride," he said, the way he had on the boat that afternoon, and plunged into her.

The shock quivered through them both. And then he began to move, over her and inside her, thick and hot, swelling inside her, thrusting inside her, making her stretch and throb. Making her pulse and surge. Making her gasp. Making her—

"Come on, baby," he said hoarsely, working her body, working her, until sensation built, until it flooded and filled her.

She gave a sharp, surprised cry and let herself be swept away. He shuddered like a swimmer at the limits of his strength and went with the tide.

Chapter 14

"You have a tattoo."

A finger traced the curve of Mark's biceps, tickling him from sleep. He was wrecked, sprawled facedown on a bed—not his bed, his few working brain cells noted—with his arm resting heavily on a warm, naked woman.

Nicole.

He smiled and turned his head on the pillow.

God, she was pretty. At some point she must have switched on the bedside lamp, and her blond hair, spilling over her face and his arm, glowed in the yellow light. Her cheeks were pink. Her lips looked thoroughly kissed, licked, sucked.

Her eyebrows lifted. She was waiting for him to say something. Right. Like she wanted to hear any of the things he had to say.

I want you. Well, that had worked.

I need you. Too wussy.

Let's do it again. Too soon.

Although maybe… His mind was struggling, but his body was definitely waking up.

"What?" he said.

"A tattoo," she said patiently. "You've got words on your arm."

This was a hell of a time to remind him of that.

"Beats having an anchor on my butt," he joked.

But she wasn't distracted. Her fingers stroked his arm. "What does it say?"

"Semper fi." His voice was muffled by the pillow.

"Semper—"

"—fi." *Semper fidelis.* Always faithful.

"That's nice." Her voice was dreamy. Wistful. Her touch was light and loving on his skin. Her interest jabbed him like an inking needle. "Did you get it to remind you of the U.S. Marine Corps?"

"No."

She frowned, either at his answer or his tone. "But isn't that their motto?"

"Yeah."

"Then, why—"

"Look, could we drop this?"

Her fingers stilled. Her body stiffened. "Of course," she said politely.

Mark said a bunch of bad words all strung together in his head. Now he'd hurt her. Which meant he owed it to her to explain.

He rolled away from her to sit on the side of the mattress. "I got it because of a woman, all right? Like some guys get 'Suzy' or 'Rosie' on their chests. It was a woman I—" Damn it, he was not going to say the *L* word "—I thought I was going to be with. Marry, even."

He risked a glance over his shoulder.

Nicole's eyes were very wide and blue. "Then why not get her name?" she asked quietly.

"Because she was already married," Mark said. The

memory was bitter in his mouth. "To a superior officer in my platoon. I figured this way I could show her I was serious about us and still, you know, protect her."

"That was considerate."

"It was stupid. Hayley never had any intention of leaving a captain's pay grade and the officers' wives club for me. Which her husband was happy to let me know after she decided a tearful confession could leverage her a move off base and a bigger kitchen."

"Bitch," Nicole said clearly.

He couldn't believe he'd heard her correctly. "What?"

She blushed, sitting up in bed, tugging the sheet to cover her pretty breasts. But her tone was firm and fierce as she repeated, "She was a bitch. I can't stand people who use other people for money."

Well, that kind of figured. She had enough experience being used herself to make her sympathetic to the chump he had been. Only he didn't want her pity. He wanted… His gaze slipped to the outline of her nipples through the sheet before he looked away.

"It could have been worse."

"Yes. You could have tattooed her name on your arm and need laser surgery."

Her unexpected tartness surprised a laugh from him. "Maybe I'd leave it," he suggested, just to see what she'd say.

"Why?"

"As a reminder."

"Of what? That women aren't deserving of faithfulness?"

Well, yeah.

"She wasn't," he said.

"Just because your parents didn't model a good relationship, just because you may have recreated a dynamic of rejection, doesn't mean you can't move past it." Her voice rang with sincerity. "We can learn from our mistakes."

A dynamic of rejection? Like hell.

"That sounds like something out of one of your books," he said.

She raised her chin. "What if it is?"

She was so sweet. So earnest. So damn determined to help.

"Then I'd say—" Too late he saw the land mines ahead. "I'd say maybe there's something in them after all."

Her lips parted. "Do you mean that?"

He shrugged. "Sure."

"And you reached this startling new conclusion because…?"

The best thing to do in an interrogation, he'd discovered with his sister and the one or two reasonable COs he'd known in his career, was to go with the truth. Or part of the truth, anyway.

"You've made some mistakes, right?"

She winced. "Yes."

He nodded. "Right. So if I want to be the new guy in your life, I'd be stupid to tell you our relationship is just another mistake."

She sat there, naked except for the sheet, her brain chugging away like that little laptop computer of hers digesting data. And then—thank you, God!—she smiled.

"Is that what we have?" she asked softly. "A relationship?"

Panic time. *Let's keep it simple,* he'd told her. *Let's take it one step at a time.*

But now that he'd had her, *simple* didn't cut it. Dragging his feet wasn't what he wanted anymore. And it was way less than she deserved.

He pretended to consider. "Kind of soon to call this a relationship. We've only been to bed one time."

She went from bed warm to ice cold in five seconds. "I see."

"I don't think you do." It was too easy to tease her. He

stopped her retreat across the mattress by the simple method of grabbing the sheet. "Now, if we do it again, *that's* a relationship."

She resisted his pull on the covers. "What makes you assume I would want to do it again?"

He leaned over her, kind of digging the fact that he was bigger than her and stronger than her. Okay, so it made him a pig, but it turned him on. He trapped her beneath the sheet, beneath his weight, enjoying the way the color surged into her cheeks and her eyes darkened.

"I don't assume anything," he assured her.

He bent his head to her throat, finding the tiny beat of her pulse with his lips. The light, expensive perfume she wore mixed with the heavy narcotic scent of sex. Her pulse raced under his kiss.

"I like to work for it," he said.

She laughed then, and let him.

"You're home late," Kathy observed, bending to fish a shoe from under the coffee table. "Or do I mean early?"

Nicole tried hard not to feel like a high school junior sneaking home after curfew. It had been six years since she'd last roomed with Kathy. And while the redhead knew where the bodies—where *all* the bodies—were buried in Nicole's romantic past, Nicole didn't want to conduct a postmortem on her weekend while the memories were still fresh and warm.

"Oh, I, um—"

Kathy held on to the arm of the couch while she wriggled her free foot into her shoe. "Got lucky?" she suggested.

Nicole's face was hot. But there was a glow in her chest that had nothing to do with embarrassment. *Get lucky?*

Maybe she had.

Maybe her luck had changed at last.

She set her purse on a chair. "How do you know I wasn't visiting my parents this weekend?" she countered.

Kathy straightened, stamping her foot to get it all the way into the heel. "Honey, nobody goes out the door plucked and polished like you were yesterday to spend the night at their parents' house. And you didn't get that hickey playing Scrabble with Mommy, either."

Nicole's hand flew to her throat. "I didn't know it showed."

"Girlfriend, you've got dinner, drinks and a sex chaser written all over you."

"It wasn't like that," Nicole protested instinctively.

"It's always like that." But instead of sounding jokey and confiding, Kathy's tone was flat and bitter.

Was she right? It had been like that before. Nicole couldn't prove this time was any different.

If I want to be the new guy in your life, I'd be stupid to tell you our relationship is just another mistake.

No, she couldn't prove it. But she felt it.

She believed it.

"You look nice," she said, changing the subject. She was, amazingly, happy. She could afford to be kind. "Anything special?"

Kathy shrugged. "Monday morning. Back to the real world." She rummaged on the end table. "Now, where did I put my earrings?"

Nicole roused herself to be helpful. "When did you have them last?"

"Saturday night. I wore them when I went out. Gary didn't spring for dinner, the cheapskate, but he gave me what I wanted afterward." Kathy slid Nicole a look bright with humor or malice. "Right here on this couch."

Nicole had a sudden image of the couch and a man's bare backside, moving.

"Oh," she said faintly.

"Here they are." Kathy swooped. The earrings sparkled in her hand. She tilted her head to insert one. "So, how was he?"

Nicole blinked. "Excuse me?"

"Delicious DeLucca. How was he?"

Nicole opened her mouth, but no words came out. It was as if she and her college roommate spoke different languages. Kathy was talking about sex. About getting it and taking it from faceless men whose hearts were not involved. There were no words for what Nicole had shared with Mark, for what Nicole had felt with Mark, in Kathy's vocabulary.

Maybe, Nicole acknowledged, Mark didn't feel all the things she felt. Maybe his heart was not involved.

But hers was. She knew that now.

"He was, um—"

She was suddenly impatient with herself, with Kathy, with her own reluctance to trust her feelings and speak her mind. Language barrier or not, she did not graduate from the University of Chicago so she could go around saying "um" all the time.

She took a deep breath. "I had a wonderful weekend, thank you."

Kathy looked at her cockeyed, but maybe that was simply the effect of inserting the other earring. "That's it?"

Nicole considered. Nodded. She was not exposing what ought to remain private and precious to Kathy's corrosive cynicism. "That's it."

For one second, something lost and ugly peered out of Kathy's eyes. And then she smiled. "Well, good for you," she said. "And goodie for him. I can't guess how he is in the sack, but he certainly knows what he's doing otherwise."

Nicole felt cold. "What are you talking about?"

"Oh, didn't I tell you? I guess not." Kathy swung her purse onto her shoulder and fluffed her hair with her fingers. "Mark DeLucca was the other interested buyer for the bar."

* * *

"So, it's definite now, right?" Mark repeated into the phone. Despite the previous test results, and his own gut-level response, he could hardly believe it. "Wainscott can't contest my paternity in court."

"I can't tell you what Robert Wainscott will decide to do," Jane Gilbert said in her precise lawyer's voice. "No test can prove with 100 percent certainty that an individual is the biological parent of a child. However, this second test is court admissible and establishes your paternity with a 99.8 percent certainty, which is in excess of the 99 percent required by the court."

Mark released his breath slowly. "You're joking, right?"

Jane chuckled. "Not necessarily. Have you hired a lawyer yet?"

He turned his back on the empty bar room. He wouldn't open for another hour. "Do I need one?"

"Well, you're not fighting for custody because you did anything wrong. You didn't neglect Daniel or beat him. But if the Wainscotts argue that you are unfit in some other way—if you knew of Daniel's existence, for example, and chose to abandon him and his mother—then things could get sticky. A lawyer would help."

Anger swelled in him like the wind filling a sail. "Hold on. They can't say he's not my kid and then turn around and claim I abandoned him."

Jane Gilbert was silent.

A little of Mark's anger spilled out as fear. "Can they?" he appealed.

"You should really get a lawyer," Jane said.

When he hung up the phone, his hand was shaking. Damn it. He turned just as Nicole walked into the bar. His heart gave a great leap, which annoyed him even more, because it reminded him how vulnerable you were when you let yourself get close to somebody, when you let yourself care, and where did that ever get you except alone and needing a lawyer?

Although maybe that wasn't going to be a problem, because the way Nicole was looking at him right now, he doubted they were ever going to reach a stage where lawyers were necessary. Unless, say, she murdered him and had to hire one to get her off.

He leaned against the bar, crossed his legs at the ankle and his arms against his chest, and waited for her attack.

But she stopped before she reached him, twisting her rings around on her fingers, her mouth a tight, miserable line. "I talked to Kathy."

The roommate. The real estate agent.

"So?"

"So." Nicole dragged in a slow, painful-sounding breath. "Why didn't you tell me you were a prospective buyer for the bar?"

Boom. He wasn't expecting an assault on this front. True to his training, he scrambled for cover and launched a counteroffensive.

"Why should I?"

"Well, because I—because you— Don't you think it might have a bearing on our relationship?"

Quick fear cramped his gut. That's why he hadn't told her. She was so damn afraid of being used, so quick to believe no man could want her for herself.

"No," he said.

Her jaw stuck out. "You still could have mentioned it."

"Why? Did you want to hear more about my 'inadequate business plan'? Or my 'inability to obtain the necessary bank funding'?"

She flushed, recognizing her own words from their first meeting. But she said stubbornly, "I don't like secrets. I especially don't like secrets about money."

"You're just looking for some kind of proof that I can't be trusted."

"No. I'm asking you for proof that I'm wrong."

"There is no proof, babe. I don't come with a guarantee."

Her chin quivered. "Fine. As long as you understand I don't come with the bar."

She might as well have hit him over the head with one of his own liquor bottles. How could she say that? How could she think it? Did she honestly have that low an opinion of herself? Or was it him? Fear and fury spilled together inside him, and he came back at her like the fighter he had been.

"You think I'm screwing you for the bar?" He laughed without amusement. "Babe, for that I'd have to marry you."

She flinched. "And of course you would never commit yourself to that extent."

"And aren't you glad?" he taunted, as if she'd even think of contradicting him.

Right. As if.

"At least now we both know where we stand." Was it his imagination or did her voice quaver slightly?

"I guess we do."

"So." She twisted the thin gold rings on her hand. "Where do we go from here?"

Directly to jail, he thought bitterly. *Do not pass Go. Do not collect two hundred dollars.*

"That's up to you, isn't it?" he said. "Where do you want this to go?"

"I don't know." She looked at him then, and the hurt in her eyes echoed the ache in his own chest. "I honestly don't know."

Chapter 15

"Lady here to see you."

Mark shoved the lunch ticket at Louis and turned to Joe, his heart thudding with dumb hope.

"Who is it?"

"Never saw her before." Joe shifted his toothpick to the other corner of his mouth. "Older lady. Nice looking, though."

"Right. Be there in a minute."

But Joe stuck in the kitchen doorway, his chubby face concerned. "You expecting someone?"

Nicole.

He kept expecting to see her walk through that door to ask him something, to tell him something, her eyes shiny with some bright new idea, her voice rising in enthusiasm.

It was stupid. Really stupid, because she was never coming after him again for anything. He hadn't even seen her this afternoon.

Anyway, Joe wouldn't be calling her a lady.

"No," Mark said. "I'm not expecting anybody."

And he went to the front of the house.

He spotted the blonde right away, upright and awkward at the end of the bar, her white wine untouched in front of her. He put her age around fifty, her hair color, her figure, her way of life all carefully maintained.

It took him a second more to place her. Helen Wainscott.

His gut clenched hard. Just what this day needed to make it absolutely perfect. A close encounter with the Queen of Cold.

"Hi-ya, Helen."

He had to give her credit. She stiffened at his use of her given name, but she managed a small, polite smile. "Mark."

He waited. But that was all she could give him, just his name, and that slight, nervous smile. He nodded at her glass. "You don't like the wine?"

"No, I— The wine is fine. I drove up here myself."

Nice. So his kid didn't have two alcoholic grannies. But Mark wasn't about to swap family stories with Helen Wainscott. She disliked him enough already.

"Why?" he asked bluntly.

She played with her cocktail napkin, Nicole's jaunty moon rocking over a stylized wave. "Is there someplace we could talk?"

He glanced around the nearly empty bar. It was still early. He bet she'd timed her visit so she could be home before rush hour started in Chicago.

"What's wrong with here?"

"Nothing," she said a little too quickly. "Here is...fine."

"Right. So now we've established the wine is fine, the place is fine. How are you, Helen?"

"I'm f—very well, thank you."

A new thought struck him. A new fear. "Danny?"

She pleated the edge of her napkin. "That's what I came to talk to you about. Danny."

"Is he all right?" Mark demanded.

She looked at him directly for the first time, and something in her face relaxed. "Danny is fine. He's in school today."

"So, when does he get home?"

"Maria is there when he gets home," Helen said quietly, answering his unspoken accusation. "Won't you sit down?"

He came around the bar and sat.

She took the first sip of her wine. "As you might imagine, this has been a somewhat…difficult year for Bob and me."

"Yeah," Mark said. Joe came out of the kitchen. He warned him away with a look. "Sorry for your loss," he added.

"Thank you. Elizabeth was— We had no other children. She meant everything to Bob. To me. I wonder sometimes if we were too protective of her, if we took too active a role in her life, but—"

"I know you loved her very much," Mark said.

Enough to separate us, he thought. Enough to keep Betsy from telling me about our baby.

But he didn't say those things. The woman had lost her daughter. Putting her down as a mother at this point was pretty much useless. Not to mention cruel.

"Yes," Helen said gratefully. "And we love Daniel."

Hell. He *so* did not want to go there. Not now. Not with her. He could deal with this as long as he concentrated on what was right, on where his duty lay. He was not getting into a pissing match with Helen Wainscott over who loved Danny longer or who loved Danny more.

Because she might win. And then where would he be? And what would happen to his son?

"He's a good kid," Mark said.

"He's a very confused kid right now," Helen countered.

"To lose his mother, to be in danger of losing the only home he's ever known, is enormously difficult for him."

Mark crossed his arms. "He seemed okay when he was up here."

"You don't know him like I do."

"And whose fault is that?"

Helen winced. "I suppose we deserve that. Elizabeth often asked... That is—"

His heart beat faster. "Asked what?"

"She wanted to see you again," Helen admitted. "To tell you about the baby."

"Then why the hell didn't she?"

"You were gone," Helen said simply. "I told her it was reasonable to assume you weren't ready for a relationship. Certainly not for fatherhood."

"How would you know? I never got the chance to prove myself."

"You sound like Elizabeth. But Robert said—" Helen's gaze dropped to her wineglass.

"What? What did he say?"

"He said if she contacted you we wouldn't help her with the baby's expenses. She had to choose, he said. We would help her with Daniel. We would help her with college. We would help her find child care and a place to live, but she had to decide then and forever who her family would be."

Oh, God. Mark thought what that ultimatum must have meant to a scared, sheltered, pregnant seventeen-year-old forced to choose between the well-being of the child she carried and loyalty to a boyfriend who'd already skipped town.

"Poor kid," he said. "So you won."

Helen smiled sadly. "No. We lost. Because once she finished college, we didn't see Elizabeth very often. She kept her promise. She never contacted you. I think she was happy with her work, her life, her son. But in the end she chose you anyway."

He was shaken. "Too bad for you," he said flippantly.

Helen Wainscott's nostrils narrowed. "I'm not here for myself. I'm here for Daniel, to ask you to consider what he needs. A child his age deserves a stable home and a two-parent family."

"It's a little late for that," Mark said. "Seeing as his mother and I never got the chance to work things out."

"It's not really too late. Bob and I are his family."

"And Maria. We can't forget Maria. Who is she, anyway? The nanny?"

"Maria is our housekeeper," Helen said stiffly. "She's been with us since Daniel was two years old. And she adores him."

"Which explains why she's taking care of him after school today."

"I hardly think you're in a position to criticize my child care arrangements. Or do you imagine that as a single, working father you will have so much more time to give Daniel than we do?"

The problem was, he didn't think that at all. He couldn't imagine the impact that keeping Danny full-time would have on his life. That didn't mean he didn't have the responsibility to try.

"We'll figure that out when we get there."

"When you get there, it may be too late to figure something out."

He looked at her levelly. "What do you want, Helen?"

"Mark." She put a well-manicured hand on his arm. "Have you ever asked yourself if it's really in Daniel's best interest to be with you?"

Hell, yes. He asked himself all the time. He just hadn't answered himself yet.

"That's what the lawyer's for, isn't it? The guardian ad litem. To decide what's in Danny's best interest."

"Lawyers can be wrong."

"That's really interesting coming from a lawyer's wife."

"You, more than anyone, should understand that we might have made mistakes. That we might have regrets. That doesn't change the fact that we love our grandson. And we are in the position to offer Daniel the things he needs."

"You mean money," Mark said flatly.

"Is that so bad, to want our grandson to grow up with certain material advantages? Can you honestly say your childhood wouldn't have been easier if your parents had been able to provide better for you and your sister? That you wouldn't have benefited from the opportunity to go to college? Even now, wouldn't more money make it possible for you to live a better life?"

Unexpectedly Nicole's voice came back to him: *I can't stand people who use other people for money.*

Mark shook his head. "You almost had me till the last one. I can't be bought off, Helen. Your husband already tried."

"I'm not offering you money."

"What, then?"

"A chance for Daniel. Please, think about it." She collected her purse and folded her raincoat over her arm. Mark watched her select a five-dollar bill from her wallet and leave it beside her full glass of wine.

He picked it up and handed it to her. "My treat," he said.

"My tip," she replied. "Give it to the bartender, if you want."

A chance for Daniel. Think about it.

Mark scowled at the empty bottles of Pabst Blue Ribbon lined in front of him. Right. Like he'd been able to do anything else but think. And drink. And wish he could go back to last night, to the time before Helen made her big emotional power play and Nicole was all that occupied his heart and his brain.

He couldn't do a damn thing about Helen. At least, not tonight. He didn't even know what he should do.

So he tipped his chair back on two legs and closed his eyes, letting himself sink from deep funk into fantasy, seduced by longing and the memory of Nicole arching under him, smooth and soft and slick.

With the bar shut out and a nice buzz from the beer going, he could almost imagine he had it all back, had her back, the glow in her eyes and the scent of her skin and the sound of her voice saying—

"You said you didn't drink much."

Okay. Definitely not part of the fantasy. Which meant…

He dropped the front legs of the chair and opened his eyes.

Nicole wavered before him.

"I thought you went home early," he said.

"I did." When he continued to squint at her, she explained, "I moved in upstairs today."

Without his help. Without even telling him. Even through the beer, her rejection stung. "I didn't see furniture."

"It's still in storage."

"So you're camping out?"

Despite the way she'd taken to his boat, he didn't see her as the sleeping bag type.

"Well…" She met his gaze, and the rueful humor in her eyes snagged in his chest. "I have plumbing. And paper supplies. I've been raiding the kitchen down here until I get my boxes unpacked."

"Why the rush?"

"I had a—call it a difference of opinion with my roommate this morning."

She was doing that thing with her rings again, twisting them around on her fingers.

Concern slid through his pleasant fog and nicked him. "What about?"

She stopped fussing with the rings and jerked up her chin. "I don't want to talk about it."

"What happened to 'friends talk to each other'?"

"We're not friends."

Ouch.

"No?" He slid out of his chair, noting smugly that her eyes widened and her breath quickened as he got close. "You better hope we're friends, babe, or I'm going to start thinking of things I'd rather do with you than talk. What's up with you and the vampire real estate agent?"

Nicole snickered. A release of tension, she told herself. "You shouldn't call her that."

"Are you telling me she didn't try to suck the life out of you this morning?"

She was gratified by his quick defense. She was too used to parents who found fault, to bosses who blamed her, to boyfriends who were quick to point out the ways she'd failed or fallen short. "How did you know?"

"Because I've met her." His gaze was direct. Unapologetic. "I was the other prospective buyer for the bar, remember?"

Remember? She couldn't forget.

Except it was really hard to care when he was standing so close with his hot, dark eyes and his lean, hard body promising her everything she'd ever wanted. Respect. Understanding. Sex.

"So, are you okay?" he asked.

"I— Yes," she said, surprised because it was true. "She only…she tried to make me feel small. I think maybe she always has, and I just never noticed it."

He nodded, not interrupting.

Nicole swallowed. "You don't do that."

He reached up with one hand, barely toying with the ends of her hair where it touched her shoulder. Her scalp prickled in reaction. "That's because I like that light you carry around inside you. Somebody like Kathy only sees that you outshine her.''

It was so unexpected a thing for him to say that her mouth dropped open.

''A light?'' she repeated.

He looked embarrassed. ''Forget it.''

''No, I like it. What do you mean, a light?''

''You're just…you know.'' He shrugged. ''You've got all these ideas and all this hope. Even when things go wrong for you, you don't give up.''

She wanted to bask a little in the glow of his compliment. But there was an edge to his voice and a shadow in his eyes that tamped her own pleasure.

''Did things go wrong for you today? Is that why you're drinking?''

''Three beers,'' he said. ''I'm not turning into my old man yet.''

''You're still sitting here alone after closing in the dark.''

''I wouldn't be here alone if you hadn't dropped me like a wet glass this morning.''

Her heart beat faster. ''I didn't drop you.''

''No?''

She shook her head. ''No.'' She'd had the strength to walk away. Did she have the confidence to come back? She smiled ruefully. ''I just put you back on the shelf for a while.''

A corner of his mouth quirked. ''Does that mean you plan to take me down and use me again sometime?''

Her knees wobbled. *Oh, yes.*

''Don't try to distract me,'' she said. ''Tell me what happened.''

He sat at the table and pushed out the chair opposite him with his foot. She obeyed his silent invitation, pressing her weak knees together.

But instead of answering her, he asked, ''Did your parents ever read to you when you were a kid?''

Nicole blinked. "I guess. I think it was supposed to prepare me for reading or something. My mother used to take me to the library."

"We didn't do the library. But Tess used to read to me out of this book of Bible stories my mother had around. Anyway—" he dragged in a painful breath "—she used to read me the story of Solomon."

Oh, my. Half-remembered images and phrases teased Nicole's memory: "Let him kiss me with the kisses of his mouth; for thy love is better than wine... A bundle of myrrh is my well-beloved unto me; he shall lie all night betwixt my breasts."

Mark stared at the row of bottles. "There was a really cool picture in the book, these two women kneeling at the feet of the old king with this baby, both claiming to be the kid's mother, right? And this big slave standing there with a sword, which is probably why I liked it."

Not the "Song of Solomon," Nicole realized. The story of the king's judgment. Sadness clogged her throat.

"So neither one of the women will give the baby up, and the king says, 'Cut the baby in two!', which, when I was like five or something, I thought was great."

"Mark—"

"Almost done. It's a short story. What I remember, anyway. When the king says that, one of the women says fine, that's fair. And the other says no, give him to the first woman, it's okay, just don't kill the baby. And the king gives the child to the woman who was willing to give him up for his own good, because that proved she was his mother." Mark picked up the last half-empty bottle and tilted it in salute. "'The Wisdom of Solomon.'"

Her heart wrenched. There was more to this story than an ancient king in a picture book.

"What happened today? Did the lawyer call?"

"You know, she did. The second set of DNA results came in. There's a 99.8 percent chance that Danny's mine."

Relief loosened the knot in Nicole's chest. "Then you have your proof. You don't need a king's judgment."

Mark set the bottle precisely next to its fellows. "I also got a little visit today from Danny's grandmother."

Oh, dear. Oh, Mark.

"Are they going to fight you for custody?" Nicole asked.

"Only if I fight them first. And why should I? They love the kid. He's known them all his life. They can give him everything he needs."

"Except a father. They can't give him that."

Mark met her gaze, an arrested expression in his eyes. And then he picked up the bottle again and drank.

"Maybe he doesn't need one," he said.

Nicole straightened. "Cut it out. You know better than that. For heaven's sake, I've been trying to win my father's approval my entire life, and I know better than that."

Mark stopped looking dark and brooding and started to look annoyed. A definite improvement, in Nicole's eyes.

"Fine. Maybe he needs a father. And maybe he needs somebody better than me."

"What's wrong with you?"

"For starters, my pop did not exactly stick around long enough to pass on his parenting skills."

She waved that away. "Then you didn't learn bad habits."

"I work as a bartender."

"As a valued associate in a successful service business," she corrected.

He sat back and crossed his arms. "My hours suck."

She arched her brows. "I am sure your employer could be persuaded to adjust your work schedule to accommodate a change in your lifestyle."

"Look, I appreciate what you're trying to do here. But what if I'm just not father material? I'm not Jarek, okay?"

"And what does Jarek have that you don't have?"

"A house. A career. A fiancée."

Oops. There was no way she was going to touch on his lack of fiancée. And the career thing was problematic, too, since she'd like nothing more than for him to stay on as manager of the Blue Moon. But—

"You have a Jeep," she said. "And a boat."

"Great. So I can hit the road or sail off into the sunset. Think the kid will want to come along?"

"I think he'll want to stay in Eden. I think you do, too, or you would never have come back here. Your roots are here. Your family."

"Some family. I never talk to my mother."

"Then maybe you should try."

"We don't have anything to say to each other."

Nicole wondered if Isadora DeLucca would agree. "How about, 'I love you'?" she suggested.

Mark shook his head. "I'm no good at that stuff."

He certainly hadn't said it to her. On the other hand…

"You're close to your sister."

"My sister is the warm and caring type. My sister could form a close personal relationship with the Grinch."

"You're good with Danny."

"Short-term, yeah. One night and one day. That doesn't mean I have what it takes for the long haul."

She didn't know enough to contradict him. And if he was right, what did that mean for Danny's future? Or theirs?

But she said, stubbornly, "You'll never know unless you try."

"Trying and failing could really screw the kid up."

"Not trying could hurt him even more. He needs to know you want him."

I need to know you want me, she thought but did not say. This wasn't about her.

"I want him," Mark said.

"Then show him. Fight for him."

He watched her over his crossed arms, his black eyes inscrutable. "In court."

"If necessary."

"And that's your advice," he mocked gently. "The big expert on love."

She stuck out her chin. "I read a lot of books," she told him loftily.

He smiled for the first time that night, lazy and dangerous, and her pulse kicked into high gear.

"I can show you things that aren't in those books," he said.

"Oh, I don't know," she said, amazed when her voice remained steady. "You'd be surprised what gets published these days."

His eyes were hot on hers. "So, surprise me."

Her breath went. What was left came out in a squeak. "Here?"

He scraped his chair back from the table, still watching her. "Sure. Unless you think the owner would object."

He was asking permission to seduce her?

No, he was asking her to seduce him. Here, in her bar, with the front door locked and the beer signs flickering on the walls.

She shivered with doubt and with lust. "Have you ever done this before?"

"In the bar?" He moved his head once, slowly, side to side. No.

"Is it—" She hesitated. Clean? Private? Possible? "—safe?"

"How safe do you need it to be?"

She swallowed. "I still have a condom in my purse."

"You brought your purse downstairs with you?"

"It has my keys in it. And my mace."

His brows jerked together. "You carry mace?"

Maybe she had succeeded in surprising him after all. "You told me a woman living alone over a bar needed protection."

"So you bought mace."

She nodded. "And condoms. Well, I didn't buy those. I took one from Kathy, but—"

"Go get it." His voice reached the pit of her stomach.

"The mace?"

"The condom."

She frowned, uncomfortable with him ordering her. Uncomfortable, period. "And what are you going to do while I do that?"

"Watch you."

Oh.

He sounded so smug she wanted to hit him. So predatory she wanted to run. And then she looked in his eyes and saw the raw need there, and everything in her was moved and softened toward him.

She tossed her head, so her hair shimmied on her shoulders.

"Be my guest," she said.

She sucked in her breath, drawing his attention to her breasts. She turned slowly, and slowly sauntered to the table by the hall where she'd left her purse, feeling his gaze hot and heavy upon her.

When she walked back, her legs were shaking. But the condom was clutched in her hand, and her back was straight. She stopped in front of him, so close her knees brushed his thighs as he slouched in the chair.

She touched the tip of her tongue to her dry lips. "Now what?"

"Whatever you want," he said hoarsely.

She wanted to make him see himself as she saw him.

She wanted to feel she could comfort him, to explore the extent of her feminine power.

She wanted to love him.

"I want you," she told him, claiming him as he had once claimed her, and undid the top button of her blouse.

If she wanted him to, he would beg.

If she wanted him to, he would do, say, be anything for her.

As long as she didn't stop.

She undid all the buttons of her blouse and then the zipper of her slacks, letting them slide to her ankles. He watched her step out of them, trying to figure how he had reached this point with her but not much caring. He was too grateful.

And when she unclasped her bra and spilled her panties down her long, smooth legs, he was too stunned.

In the dim room, she burned like a candle, pure and straight and white. She stood so close he could smell her fragrance, could see the fine down on her thighs and the slope of her belly. His heart hammered.

She rested her arms on his shoulders. The curve of her breast brushed the side of his jaw. He turned his head to take her nipple, but she was already climbing, moving, straddling his lap, and his mouth found her throat instead.

She raised his face between her hands and kissed him long and sweetly. Balancing herself with one hand on his shoulder and one foot on the floor, she tugged and shoved his jeans from his hips.

It was awkward. Arousing. Incredible.

Before he could decide how he should play this, before he could pull his mind back to the place where he could please her and protect himself, she took him inside her. The shock stopped his breath. She wrapped him in her arms and rode him, and took all his troubles away.

Chapter 16

Nicole had been watching out the window all day, like a ten-year-old with an eye out for the boy down the street, like an elderly woman on the lookout for prowlers. When the Jeep finally pulled in front of the Blue Moon, she felt giddy with relief and apprehension.

Mark got out, still wearing the blazer and tie he'd put on that morning to go to court. His sister Tess climbed down from the passenger seat before he could go around to open her door.

Nicole couldn't read Mark's expression, but his sister was smiling.

Please, Nicole thought. *Oh, please.*

But no one else got out of the car.

Her heart contracted, but she pinned a smile to her face and hurried out the entrance to greet them. "How did it go?"

Brother and sister exchanged glances, not speaking, and then Tess said brightly, "It went well."

Nicole didn't believe her, but that didn't matter.

I want that, she thought. I want that connection, that closeness, want to look at him and know what he is thinking and what I should say.

Of course, Tess had an edge here. She'd known Mark longer. Twenty-seven years longer. But she was his sister and she was getting married soon.

"Did Jarek go with you?" Nicole asked.

"He drove down in his own car," Tess explained. "In case he had to leave early. But he hooked Mark up with a really good lawyer."

Nicole met Mark's eyes. "How good?"

He smiled finally, holding her gaze, and even though she suspected he was still holding out on her, she started to feel better.

"Good enough," he said. "Daniel's coming to live with me."

She beamed. "That's wonderful."

"Yeah." He tugged at his tie. "It is."

"So…where is he?"

"He went home with his grandparents. To say goodbye and pack a bag. Wainscott's bringing him up tonight, and I'll go down next week to get the rest of his stuff."

It all sounded right. So why did she get the sense that something was subtly wrong?

Tess fingered her purse strap. "I should get going. They're expecting me at the paper. Give me a lift?" she asked her brother.

"Sure. Get in the car."

Tess rolled her eyes. "You could at least pretend you weren't in a hurry to get rid of me." She seized Nicole's hand and pressed her warm cheek to Nicole's cool one. Surprised and touched by the embrace, Nicole squeezed back.

Tess released her and jerked open the Jeep's door. "Take care. I'll see you at the wedding."

"At the…"

"You did tell her," Tess said to her brother.

"I was going to."

"Mark, my wedding is in three days. She needs time to pick out a dress."

"She's not the one getting married."

"You are so clueless," Tess said. She turned back to Nicole. "Saturday at eleven o'clock. St. Raphael's. Jarek and I want you to come."

My sister is the warm and caring type. My sister could form a close personal relationship with the Grinch.

Nicole was powerless to resist. "I'd love to come."

"Good," Tess said, and got into the car.

Mark raised his eyebrows. "Pizza at seven. My place. Danny and I want you to come."

"Oh, I couldn't," Nicole said instinctively.

"Why not?"

"I can't intrude on your first night."

"You're not intruding."

Maybe it was a family thing. Maybe—

"Will your sister be there?"

"Nope. Just the three of us."

Us. The three of us. Her heart thudded with possibility.

"It's no big deal," Mark said, and her pulse steadied. "You don't even have to buy a dress. Come naked, if you want."

Nicole ignored the dark little thrill that ran through her at his words. "Now that would be really inappropriate."

"Forget appropriate. Will you come?"

He grinned at her, dark and charming as his sister and just as irresistible. More irresistible, if you were female and breathing.

"Seven o'clock," she promised weakly.

"What did she say?" Tess demanded.

Mark reversed out of his parking space. "About what?"

He watched in his rearview mirror as Nicole went into

the Blue Moon without looking back. He told himself that was okay. It was starting to rain. Why should she get wet?

"About dinner. Is she joining you?"

"Yes."

"Well, that's good." When he didn't say anything, Tess stole a look in his direction. "That is good, isn't it?"

"What is this, you're getting married, so now the rest of the world has to line up two by two, like the animals on Noah's ark?"

"I'm happy. I want my only brother to be happy, too."

"Fine. Don't push me."

Tess grinned. "How about a little nudge?"

"No pushing. No nudging. She's not ready."

"Ready for what?"

Mark regarded his sister with exasperated affection. "You don't give up, do you?"

"Nope. It's a large part of my charm. Ask Jarek."

"I'll pass, thanks." He didn't want to think too closely about what drew the cool, in-control police chief and his hot, volatile sister together.

"Ready for what?" Tess repeated.

He flipped on his wiper blades. Anybody else he would have kicked out of the car. With Tess he tried to explain. "Look, I'm still easing into this thing with Danny myself."

"You mean, fatherhood?"

"Yeah. I don't want Nicole thinking I just want her as some kind of surrogate mother."

Tess shook her head. "She can't think that. I've seen the way you look at her. Unless you spend all your time together talking about child development theories or something."

He'd spent all of the past week that hadn't been taken up with Jarek's fancy lawyer trying to figure ways to get Nicole alone and naked. But he wasn't telling his sister that.

"Mostly we talk about the bar," he said.

"There you go, then," Tess said with satisfaction. "Common interests. That's good."

"Not if she thinks I'm more interested in real estate than in her."

"Why would she think that?"

The memory of his own words haunted him, punctuated by the swish-click of the wiper blades. *You think I'm screwing you for the bar? Babe, for that I'd have to marry you.*

And so he couldn't ask her to marry him.

Not for a long time.

"I'm just saying I don't want to rush her, that's all."

"You don't ask, you don't get," Tess observed.

"You don't ask, you don't get stomped on, either."

"If she stomps on you, I'll pull her hair."

He slanted her a look. "Leave it alone, Tess. I'm a big boy now."

"Oh, sure. Couple of grown-ups, that's us." She shook her head. "Who'd have thought a year ago we'd both wind up married with kids?"

He winced. "Aren't you getting a little ahead of yourself?"

"You don't want to marry her?"

A month ago he would have said no. But after three weeks of Nicole Reed, with her big ideas and her big blue eyes and her heart as open as a target on a firing range, he wanted…all kinds of things he couldn't have.

"I haven't asked her. Anyway, you're not married yet, either."

"Three days," Tess said. She scowled through the windshield. "And it better not rain."

She sounded so tragic, he smiled. "Jarek's not going to call off the wedding because of a little rain."

"It's not a little rain. The lake level's two feet above average. There are flood alerts upriver. City crews in Fox Hole are filling sandbags."

"Don't sweat it," he said. "Haven't you heard the forecast?"

Her eyes narrowed in suspicion. "What forecast?"

"Clear skies, babe." He smiled at her crookedly. "Nothing but fair winds and smooth sailing from now on."

It was raining again. Nicole huddled on the landing outside Mark's apartment, trying to protect her load of packages as she stabbed at the bell with one finger.

The door jerked open. She looked down, for Danny, and then up at Mark. He looked so good—strong hands, lean body, hot, dark eyes—that for a moment she forgot the rain and why she had come and simply stood there, drinking in the sight of him.

He frowned. "You want to come in?"

Did she…? She swallowed. "Yes."

He was barefoot, in a short-sleeved shirt and jeans. She sidled past him, feeling overdressed and ridiculous in her silk blouse with her arms full of offerings. She was trying too hard, and it showed.

Mark studied her with hooded eyes, her damp hair and her damp blouse and the rain-spotted packages she carried. Nicole felt herself grow warm from embarrassment and because he was looking at her.

"Can I take something for you?" he asked like a polite host, when what she really wanted was for him to throw her over his shoulder and carry her to the bedroom.

"Thank you. I brought brownies." She thrust a foil-covered pan at him. "For dessert."

"I like brownies," he said solemnly.

If he was laughing at her, she was going to eat them all herself.

She held out a bag from the Silver Thimble, which carried everything from fine Irish linens and local art to puzzles and games for kids. "This is for Danny."

Mark didn't take it. "Why don't you give it to him yourself when he gets here?"

"He's not here?"

Mark's mouth tightened. "Not yet."

"Is anything wrong?"

"Not yet," Mark repeated. "I know the Wainscotts don't want to give him up, but short of kidnapping him, there's nothing they can do."

Despite his assurances, he looked so grim she wanted to put her arms around him. But she wasn't sure that would be wise or even welcome.

So instead she offered, "I brought you something, too."

"You brought me something," Mark said blankly.

"Nothing much," she said hastily. "I was just browsing—" searching, comparing, agonizing for over an hour "—and I thought…I found…"

He took the bag from her and tore it, exposing the thick hardcover inside. *All They Can Be,* the title proclaimed, *A Guide to Your Child's Growth and Development.*

He stood there a long time, staring at the book in his hand.

Oh, dear. What if he was amused? Or worse, offended?

"I kept the receipt," she said. "If you don't like it you can—"

"This is great." He turned the book over, studying the jacket. "This is—"

He met her eyes, and her heart beat faster, but not from nerves anymore, this was—

"Great," he said again, and kissed her.

Nicole sighed and let herself sink into the kiss, let his chest support her and his mouth drive her doubts away. She needed this. She wanted this. She loved—

A series of knocks rattled the door in its frame.

Mark broke their kiss. Nicole smoothed her hair and made a grab for her composure. He opened the door.

Robert Wainscott stood on the landing, his eyes narrowed

in his red face. "If you can keep your hands off each other for a minute, perhaps you could take Daniel's suitcase."

Nicole flushed.

Mark lifted an eyebrow. "Nice to see you, too, Bob." His gaze dropped. His face gentled. "How's it going, Danny?"

The six-year-old edged around the stiff, disapproving figure in the doorway. "Grandpa said you didn't have a lot of room. Do you have room for me?"

"Sure, I've got a room for you," Mark said easily, putting a deliberate spin on the words. "Same one as last time. Come on, and I'll show you." He stepped close to Robert to take the suitcase and said in a low voice, "I want to talk to you."

"I have nothing further to say."

"I have plenty." He plucked the case from the older man's grasp and walked with Danny down the hall.

Robert Wainscott watched them go, love and loss and fury in his eyes.

"He'll be fine," Nicole said gently, moved to compassion and well-trained in rescuing sticky social situations. "Mark will take good care of him."

"Mark DeLucca never looked out for anyone but himself." Robert ground the words out. "He only wants my grandson as a means to get his hands on my daughter's estate. Or didn't he tell you about Elizabeth's trust fund?"

He smiled thinly at Nicole's shocked face. "I can see he didn't. Be warned, young lady. DeLucca's always been motivated by money." His gaze flicked her up and down. "Although in your case, I suppose there might be other…compensations."

"That's enough." Mark's voice was cold and hard as hail. He strolled out of the shadows of the hall, his face dangerous. "I told the judge I was willing to agree to some kind of visitation schedule. But if you ever speak to Nicole or about Nicole again with anything less than respect, I will make it very difficult for you to see your grandson. Do we understand each other?''

"You can't stop me from visiting Daniel. I am the executor of his mother's estate.''

"And I'm his father.''

Nicole trembled at the tension between the two men.

And then Robert turned and left, slamming the door.

Mark looked suddenly weary. "Gee, that was fun.''

She thought, The heck with *wise,* and put her arms around him.

"You were wonderful," she said.

He shook his head against her shoulder. "Danny doesn't need us at each other's throats.''

Danny came down the hall. "Is Grandpa gone? I wanted him to see my room.''

"He will next time he comes to visit," Nicole said.

When I'm not here, she thought.

The doorbell rang. She tensed.

"Pizza delivery," Mark said, and she nodded, relieved and ashamed of her reaction.

They ate pizza in the kitchen. Danny was happy, Mark was indulgent, and Nicole relaxed.

"I never get enough pizza," the boy confided.

"Well, now you're going to get too much," Mark said. "At least until I learn to cook.''

"I could get you a cookbook," Nicole said, pulling the foil off the brownies.

He smiled at her, and she felt warm all over.

"That reminds me.'' She fumbled for the bag from the gift shop. "I brought Danny something.''

The boy wriggled on his seat. "Cool. What is it?''

"Open it and find out.''

He stuck his hand into the bag and drew out a reproduction from a museum collection of reptiles, six inches long and rusty black with white spots.

"It's a Mexican beaded lizard. One of only two poison-ous lizards in the world," Nicole offered anxiously.

Danny beamed. "Awesome."

"Pretty smart," Mark said.

Did he mean, because she knew the species of lizard? Or did he think she was trying to buy her way into Danny's affection?

But when she met his gaze, his eyes were alight with approval. Her heart stuttered and then was still. At peace. Secure in a way she could not remember being secure in all her life.

"Are you guys going to get mushy?" Danny asked.

Nicole goggled.

"Probably," Mark said. "Not until you're in bed, though."

"Okay." He helped himself to another brownie.

"You got a problem with any of that?" Mark asked, not challengingly, but as if he really wanted to know.

"No." Danny washed the brownie down with a gulp of milk. "Are you going to sing to me?"

Mark's face cracked like an iron mask, and the incan-descent tenderness, the vulnerability, the longing that shone through in that moment flooded Nicole's heart.

"You want me to sing to you?"

The boy nodded. "If I go to bed? Please?"

"Are you making me a deal?"

Danny nodded again, his expression uncertain.

Mark cleared his throat. "Yeah, sure. Whenever you say."

The boy scrambled from his seat, clutching his lizard. "We could go now."

"What's your hurry?" Mark asked.

"I like her," Danny announced, with a sideways glance at Nicole.

"That's good," Mark said. "I like her myself."

Nicole smiled.

Danny nodded, as if he'd just had something confirmed. "Well, if you get mushy a lot, then maybe you'd get married. And then I could stay, and we'd be a real family with a dog and everything."

Dogs again. Mark laughed.

But Nicole's smile faded and her eyes were troubled.

Mark came out of Danny's bedroom cautiously, like Nicole was a sniper waiting to blow his head off.

Maybe she was. Not a sniper, but the rest of it. Ever since Danny's not-so-innocent comment, Mark had been waiting for a replay of her declaration on the boat.

All the more reason for us to examine our expectations before beginning a relationship.

He had one anxious moment when he returned to the empty living room and figured she had gone. But he followed the sound of running water and found her in the kitchen, doing dishes.

"You don't have to do that."

She gave him a flickering smile over her shoulder. "A couple glasses. I don't mind."

And she really didn't. That was the amazing thing. He'd never met a woman before who didn't keep score.

Gratitude went to his head. He came up behind her and slid his hands around her waist. She was warm and smooth under his palms. Her hair tickled his jaw, and the scent of her perfume mingled with the detergent smell made him crazy. He nuzzled her neck, wondering how quick and how deep Danny slept.

Nicole sighed and tilted her head to give him better access.

And then she said the words that for most men ranked right up there with "My mother called" and "Turn your head and cough."

"We need to talk," she said.

He thought a few words he wouldn't use with Danny

around. But he remembered what his sister said—*You don't ask, you don't get*—and he figured that after Robert Wainscott he owed Nicole something.

Anyway, she was still here, which was encouraging.

So he kissed the side of her throat and said, "I'm listening."

Her throat moved as she swallowed. "Not here," she said. "Can we sit down?"

Not good, he thought.

"Yeah, sure," he said.

He watched as she dried her hands and walked into the living room. She barricaded herself on the far end of the couch, behind a couple of throw pillows. Pete the pike leered down at them from the wall.

Not good at all.

Nicole took a deep breath. "I…care about you," she said to the pillow in her lap.

Okay. That one was easy.

"I care about you, too," Mark said.

"And because I…care, it's important to me not to make a mistake in this relationship."

"A mistake," he repeated flatly.

"Yes. It's obvious it's not just my feelings that are at stake here. Danny's feelings have to be considered, too."

"And mine."

She bit her lip. "And yours, of course. But Danny's feelings are more…problematical."

Problematical. Big word. If she was getting this out of a book, he was screwed.

"Danny doesn't have a problem with us. With you."

"Danny barely knows me. It's a little soon in our relationship to ask him to accept me on faith."

Her words poked at Mark's own fears like fingers pressing a bruise. "Danny barely knows me, either, but he's accepted me." He hoped. "Anyway, it's not like he has a choice. I'm his father."

"But I'm not his mother," Nicole pointed out. "He ought to have a choice about how involved I become in his life."

Panic licked along Mark's nerves. Was Nicole truly worried they were moving too fast for Danny? Or was she using the kid to hide her own reluctance?

"Look, he likes you. What are you so upset about?"

"I'm not upset. I'm—" She pressed her lips together on the word; parted them to admit, "I'm scared."

Oh, hell.

"Is this about Wainscott?" he demanded.

She blinked. "What?"

"I knew you'd be like this when you found out about the trust fund. That's why I didn't tell you." He resented having to defend himself, resented having to explain. But he did it anyway. Only for her. Only because he…cared. "For your information, Wainscott set up that trust himself for Danny's education. I don't get a penny. I don't want a penny."

Her eyes shone. With tears? "This isn't about money!"

Fear and frustration churned inside him. "Then tell me, please, what the hell it is about. Because I'm damned if I know."

Her hands twisted in her lap. "It's not about you at all. It's about me. I'm afraid there's something wrong with me. With my judgment."

"There's nothing wrong with you." She was perfect. Why didn't she see that? "It was those guys you dated." He reached out and stilled her hands with his. "I'm not going to hurt you."

Her fingers tightened gratefully. But she said, "I know you don't want to. And I trust you, I do. I just don't trust myself yet."

"Why not? You're smart. You work hard. You read books. You believe in people. Why the hell won't you believe in yourself?"

"I've made mistakes."

"So you learn from them and move on."

But Nicole—hopeful, determined Nicole—shook her head.

"What if I haven't learned? Knowing why I made stupid choices doesn't guarantee I won't go on making them. Sometimes I think understanding simply allows me to excuse my own behavior." She raised her gaze to his. "I want love, Mark. I want a family. Maybe I even want a dog. What if I'm grabbing at what I want without stopping to consider if it's a mistake?"

He had an opening there. He recognized it later. But he blew it.

It was that damn word again. *Mistake.*

Sweet God, he was tired of being everybody's mistake.

Just once he'd like to be somebody's white knight. Somebody's Captain America. The best thing that ever happened to…somebody.

Right. Like that would ever happen.

"Is that what you think I am? Another mistake?"

Her mouth dropped open. "No! No. But I'm worried that *we* might be. And this time I'm not the only one who would get hurt."

His heart turned to stone in his chest.

He dropped her hands. "Well, isn't that just great. I can't make you promises because you won't believe them. I can't make you guarantees because I don't know what's going to happen tomorrow or six months from now or twenty years down the road. So what can I do? What do you want from me?"

She picked at the pillow in her lap. "I just want to know everything will be all right," she whispered.

He stood. He'd had too many disappointments in his own life to lie.

"That's something else I can't tell you," he said, and walked away.

Chapter 17

She had done everything by the book.

Nicole carried a load of paper napkins to the bar, where the napkin dispensers lined up waiting to be refilled. She had tried to communicate. She had used "I" language. She had expressed her own needs while considering the feelings of others.

I want love, she'd told him. *I want a family. I want a dog.*

And what had he said? *I can't make you promises.*

"Hey, Nicole." Louis wandered out of the kitchen, his dark face creased with concern. "You been watching the news?"

"No, I—"

He snapped on the set over the bar. The set Mark said needed to be replaced.

The local news anchor flickered above the liquor bottles, her hair stiff with spray and her voice heavy with self-importance. "...rising river submerged a stretch of railroad track this morning, forcing passengers between Fox Hole and Chicago to board buses to reach their destinations.''

Nicole looked out the window. The sky was overcast, the lake swollen and gray, but—

''It's not raining,'' she said.

Louis held up one hand as the anchorwoman continued. ''As rivers crest, residents in nearby towns are cautioned to be on the lookout for rising lake levels. Water is already seeping into basements and crawl spaces west of Paradise Lake. Police have closed several parks along the water's edge.''

Nicole felt as if her last bit of solid ground were being sucked from beneath her feet. ''We're not in any danger here, are we?''

Louis shrugged.

She wanted Mark. The instinct to turn to him came as naturally as the rain, automatic and unsettling, especially in light of what he'd said to her last night. *I can't make you guarantees. I don't know what's going to happen tomorrow or six months from now or twenty years down the road.*

Well, it was tomorrow. And the river was rising and she was alone and he was—oh, God, he was over a boathouse. Right by the water's edge.

She expelled her breath. ''I need to call Mark.''

''He already knows,'' Louis said.

''Knows what?''

''More than you and me. He's a Wofer—Wilderness First Responder for the county. Anything happens, anything bad happens, he'll be one of the first called.''

''Oh, that makes me feel better,'' Nicole muttered. So if the water didn't come and get him, he could still go drown himself.

''What do you want to do?'' Louis asked.

She looked again through her wide, clean windows at her beautiful view. The lake was still several feet below the deck, high, yes, but no cause for worry. Except she didn't know the first thing about rivers and lakes, didn't know whether to be worried or not.

What should she do? She couldn't afford to ignore the newscaster's warning. But how could she be sure she was acting with appropriate caution and not overreacting from fear?

The way she had with Mark?

She pushed the thought away, but it kept returning like a persistent error message on her computer screen. She had followed all the outlines and strictures in her books, and she was just as frustrated and even more alone.

Louis was still waiting for her answer. Think, Nicole. If the old plan wasn't working, she needed a new one. But where would she be without her manuals and experts? At the mercy of her own heart, with only the guidance of her own judgment.

She did not trust her judgment.

But she was ready—maybe—to listen to her heart.

"Where do you live, Louis?"

He met her gaze. "Green Road."

On the west side of town. By the flooding river.

"And your family…?"

"My wife's at home. She's moving things upstairs."

Her life might be rushing out of her control. But here, at least, she had the power to do something right.

"You go home and help her," Nicole said. "We're closed today."

She needed to call her employees, Nicole thought as she closed and locked the door behind her grateful cook. All her employees, to let them know they should not come in today. And she would start with Mark.

Her mouth dry and her palms clammy, she punched in his number, while the television over the bar returned to its regular morning happy news program. Pressing the receiver to her ear, she counted the rings on the other end of the line.

He didn't pick up.

Oh, well. That was okay, she assured herself. Maybe he was in the shower. Maybe he was taking Danny to school.

Maybe he had caller ID and he'd decided she was too much trouble and he was never going to speak to her again.

She sniffed and tried the next number on her list.

"Yes, thanks, Deanna. Yes, I will call and let you know. Thanks. Take care."

"...from the Channel Seven Weather Center," the television announced.

She hung up the phone.

"Students at Edenton High School are the only ones so far directly affected by the flooding, with two playing fields and a portion of the student parking lot now several inches underwater. An updated list of school closings—"

Someone tried the locked door. She hurried toward the entrance to tell whoever it was that she was sorry but the Blue Moon was closed.

"Nicole?" It was Mark's voice, rough, impatient.

Her heart beat faster. She yanked on the door. He was standing on the other side, dark and lean and safe.

"I was trying to call you," she blurted out.

His brows flicked up. "I tried calling you, but your line was busy. What are you doing here?"

"Well, I—" Not a lover's greeting. She struggled to respond. "I was letting people know not to come in to work today. Where's Danny?"

"In the Jeep. I got called in to the hospital. I'm taking him to my sister's."

"He could stay here," she suggested tentatively. "With me."

"No."

His immediate dismissal hurt. "It's no trouble," she said.

"He can't stay here. You can't stay here. You're too close to the water."

She looked out the window at the lake, still reassuringly within its bounds. "I'll be fine."

"You don't know that. You have no idea what the water is capable of."

He was right.

And yet the thought of leaving her bar—her business, her livelihood, her second chance—to the whims of the weather and the likelihood of looters sickened her. Everything she owned and everything she'd hoped to make of herself was on these two floors. Everything she wanted was right here.

Except for Mark and Danny, and they were driving away.

"I'll keep the TV on," she promised. "If it looks bad, I'll get out."

He scowled at her, thinking hard and not saying much at all. Typical DeLucca stuff.

"Fine. Make sure that you do. I'll be back," he said, making her feel like Linda Hamilton being stalked by Arnold Schwartzenegger in *The Terminator*.

He kissed her, a brief, hard kiss that for some stupid reason brought tears to her eyes.

And then he left her, standing in the doorway as the rain began to fall.

Tess wasn't at her apartment.

Mark hustled Danny back to the Jeep. Now what? He was supposed to be at the hospital. It wasn't his regular call day, but every dispatcher, dog handler, ranger, firefighter, EMT and paramedic in the county who wasn't already committed along the river had been mobilized for the emergency relief effort. It was what Mark was trained for. What he was good at.

But before he could go, he had to get Danny settled somewhere safe.

He punched in his sister's cell phone number, but with phone lines starting to fail, all circuits were busy.

"Why can't Aunt Tess come to our house?" Danny asked.

Because in a couple of hours, his place could be underwater.

"Because she can take better care of you at her house," Mark explained.

Or Jarek's. That was it. She had to be at Jarek's. Jarek lived well away from the flood area. Tess was probably watching Jarek's ten-year-old daughter, Allie, while he did the emergency management thing. Mark turned east on Old Bay Road, avoiding South Lake Street, where the puddles were turning into creeks.

"Nicole could take care of me," Danny said.

Mark glanced at his son, his short legs sticking over the edge of the seat, his Mexican beaded lizard—one of only two poisonous lizards in the world—clutched in his hand.

"We'll be fine," he told his son. "We can manage on our own."

"Then why do I have to stay with Aunt Tess?"

Mark set his jaw. "Because I'm going to be busy, and Aunt Tess is family."

He pulled in front of Jarek's house, looking for signs that somebody was home. His sister's car was missing from the driveway. But the living room light was on, and, running up the walk through the rain, Mark heard the sound of a television from inside.

Thank you, God, he thought, and leaned on the bell.

The door opened. His prayer dried up.

Isadora DeLucca, his mother, stood in the doorway, thin and dark and nervous as always. "Hello, Mark."

Danny clutched Mark's pants leg. "Who's she?"

There was no way Nicole could carry the pool table upstairs to her apartment. Or the jukebox, or the long, polished bar. She wouldn't even think about the condition of the refrigerator and the oven if water got back into the kitchen, although she supposed the sealed components might be protected.

But she could save her laptop and the cash register. She filled the bathtub and sink upstairs in case her water supply became contaminated. She spent anxious minutes in the rest rooms searching for the check valves on the sewer traps. She stacked the tables in the booths.

Gray light filtered through the windows. Was it her imagination, or was water beginning to creep up the pilings that supported the dock?

But no urgent weather bulletins interrupted the station's morning programming. Secure above the bar, a roundtable of women discussed whether the sexes would ever be equal in their ability to focus on and nurture relationships.

Nicole started to stack her chairs and lug them two by two up the narrow staircase to her apartment.

"You said a bad word," Danny observed.

"Yeah. Sorry. Don't repeat it, okay?" Mark ran a hand through his hair. "Hello, Ma. Tess in?"

Isadora DeLucca shook her head. "She's out covering the flood. Would you like to come in?"

"No, I—" Damn. "Jarek?" he asked without much hope.

"Down at the station. They've had to divert traffic around the flood. Did you have trouble getting here?"

"No, we took Old Bay Road," he said absently. "It wasn't too bad."

What the hell was he supposed to do with Danny now? A first responder's primary obligation was to get to the scene as quickly as possible. But he had new obligations now.

His mother turned her dark, anxious gaze to the boy. "You must be Danny," she said, a little tremor in her voice. "Allie and I are baking cookies in the kitchen. Would you like to join us?"

"You're kidding," Mark said.

Isadora straightened her thin shoulders. "I often stay with Allie when Tess and Jarek have to go out."

"Yeah, but you never baked a cookie in your life."

"Who's Allie?" Danny asked.

"Your aunt Tess's little girl," said Isadora.

Mark shifted impatiently on the step. "I told you about her, remember?"

Danny nodded. His gaze slid back to Isadora. "But who is she?"

Mark looked from his mother's anxious face to Danny's curious one. He took a deep breath. "This," he said tightly, "is your other grandmother."

Danny tightened his hold on Mark's pants leg. "Nice to meet you," he said politely.

"It's very nice to meet you." Isadora smiled at Mark. "He has beautiful manners."

"Which I can't take credit for."

She ignored him, speaking to Daniel. "The cookies are almost ready to go into the oven. Do you want to help?"

Danny looked at Mark for permission. Or rescue?

"We can't stay," Mark told his mother. "They're evacuating the hospital. I've got to go."

"Then go," Isadora said. "Danny can keep Allie and me company."

"I don't—"

"Mark, I know I wasn't there for you when you were growing up. Let me be here for you now."

What could he say?

Nicole's voice, warm and firm, spoke up in the back of his mind. *How about 'I love you'?*

He cleared his throat. "Yeah, all right. Thanks."

Isadora beamed as if he'd handed her a bouquet or one of those stupid handmade cards he used to bring her in kindergarten before he figured out she didn't save them like the other mothers.

"I don't want to stay here," Danny said.

Poor kid. He was probably tired of being passed around his new relatives like potato salad at a family reunion.

Mark hunkered down so he could look his son in the eye. "We don't have a choice," he said gently.

"I could go with you."

"No, you can't. Really. You'll be safer here."

Danny clutched his lizard. "What if something bad happens?"

Isadora stirred. "I won't let anything happen to you, I promise."

Danny looked doubtful. Mark knew how he felt. And yet…

He had a sudden, years-old memory of fear, of crouching in a corner while his father raged through the shabby living room. Where was Tess? He couldn't remember. Tess had always protected him. But he remembered his own helpless hate, his sick terror as his father's thick fingers curled into his shoulder and dragged him from his hiding place.

And Isadora, white-faced, shrieking, fastening herself to her husband's burly arm. "Don't you hit him! Don't you ever hit him!"

The fingers slackened.

He remembered dropping to the couch and scrambling away.

And he remembered his father's roar and his mother tumbling to the floor.

God. He shook his head.

Isadora's face fell. "I will," she protested, but quietly, as if she didn't expect him to believe her.

And affection for her eased his shoulders. Tess kept telling him their mother had changed. Maybe this was one more time his sister was right. "Yeah. I know you will. It'll be okay," he told Danny. "You bake cookies with Grandma. Everything's going to be okay."

It was a promise. The promise he'd denied Nicole. And it wasn't so hard to make after all.

Danny regarded him solemnly. "Can I save you a cookie?"

Love for the child swelled Mark's chest and tightened his throat. But he didn't want to foist his emotions on the kid, didn't want to embarrass either one of them with a scene.

"That'll be great. Thanks. I bet I'll be hungry."

From the window of the Jeep, he saw them framed in the doorway, watching him go. He'd never had anybody waving goodbye to him on the job before. Never had anybody waiting for his safe return.

He saw his mother stoop to whisper in Danny's ear. His son lifted his skinny arm, his high voice carrying clearly through the rain.

"Bye, Daddy!"

Nicole was on her fifth trip down the stairs when the lights in the bar flickered and went out.

Her heart pounded. Things could be worse, she told herself. You've just lost power. Some lines are down in the storm.

She made her way by feel down the narrow staircase, willing her eyes to adjust to the dark.

Rain lashed the windows. The TV was silent. She felt as if she'd lost a companion, her last connection with the world outside. Was it time to go?

The bar looked eerie. Empty. Dark. The tables stacked in the booths blocked the pewter light that filtered through the windows. Nicole held on to a table leg and peered at the lake outside.

She sucked in her breath. The water had risen to the level of the dock. Wait or go? There were still things she could do. Things she could save.

Echoes haunted the empty bar. Mark's warning: *You*

have no idea what the water is capable of. And her own promise: *If it looks bad, I'll get out.*

Go, she decided. *Go now.*

She ran upstairs to grab her purse, her pulse thudding, her mind racing, as she felt her way a second time down the steps. She should call Mark.

No, she shouldn't, she would be fine. She had her car, her lovely new Lexus with four-wheel drive for winter and all the other bells and whistles. And he had work to do. He couldn't be worrying about her.

She left the bar and locked it, trying not to think of all she was leaving undone. All she was leaving behind. She ran through the rain—there were puddles in the parking lot—and unlocked her car door. The engine caught on the first try. She gripped the wheel, shuddering with cold and relief.

Where should she go?

South and east, she decided. Away from the river. Away.

She pulled her cell phone from her purse and put it on the passenger seat beside her where it would be handy in an emergency. She was not going to become a flood statistic. She bounced through puddles and onto the street, turning left on Harbor, toward the center of town. Her wiper blades churned furiously to clear the windshield. Except for the parked cars and the water rushing in the gutters, the streets were deserted. The streetlights weren't working. The buildings were dark. Nicole crawled forward through the rain, her tires throwing up water.

At the intersection of Harbor and Main, the water stretched from curb to curb, brown and impassable. A truck, an oversize gray pickup, blocked the road, its windows rolled up and its cab empty.

Nicole slowed, stopped, sickened. If a truck couldn't make it…

She looked around for light, for signs of life, for help. But on this side there was nothing. Only the traffic lights swaying above the street and darkened windows and a brown-and-white dog pressed into a doorway.

Just half a block away the road rose solidly from the water. The lights from an emergency vehicle flashed strobelike on the street. A single figure in a yellow slicker disappeared around the corner. Should she call for help? Get out and ford the street? But she'd read somewhere a person could be swept off her feet in six inches of water, if the current was fast enough. Better to stay in the car. Safer to stay in the car.

Only the car wasn't going anywhere, and the water was rising.

She had to go back. She couldn't turn around. Empty cars lined the sides of the street. Water foamed along the gutters. Her pulse thrummed. She would have to back up.

Now.

Nicole undid her seat belt and twisted in her seat. With one hand on the steering wheel and the other gripping the upholstery, she eased the Lexus into reverse and started creeping through the water.

A patch of white caught her eye. The dog had left the shelter of the doorway. It ran to the curb and back, to the curb and back, trapped by the rising water.

It would be all right, she told herself. Dogs could swim.

Only this was sort of a little dog: a little, wet, ugly dog, its short brown-and-white coat plastered to its skinny body.

There was nothing she could do. She backed the car another two yards. The dog barked, its wide eyes dark and frantic. She could see some sort of collar, black, but no broken lead or dangling tags.

She couldn't possibly stop. Rain rattled on the roof. If the water surged— If the engine flooded—

The dog barked again, and Nicole stopped the car, pulling as close to the curb as she dared.

She opened the door. "Come on," she said.

Bark. Bark. The dog danced at the water's edge. Rain soaked her sleeve and pelted her face.

"Here, boy," she called, feeling foolish.

More barking, more dancing. Its tail wagged. Its whole body shook.

"You have to come now," she told it firmly. "Or we're both going to be stuck."

The dog whined and ventured a few inches into the current. The water swirled around its stubby legs.

Oh, dear. Oh, damn.

Leaving her keys in the ignition, Nicole swung one foot out and dipped it in the water. The shock of it almost took her breath away. It was cold and dirty and moving alarmingly fast. She blinked water from her eyes. Holding tight to the door, she took a few tentative steps away from the car.

"Come on, dog," she said. "Here, puppy."

And the dog quivered and jumped.

Twenty pounds of wet, frightened, frantic dog hit Nicole in the chest and knocked her back on her seat. Its nails scrabbled and scratched her thighs. Its sleek, wet head shoved at her shoulder. It pushed past her and scrambled to the passenger seat, leaving a nice long gouge in the leather.

Nicole glared at it. "Good dog," she said.

The dog barked and dripped on her upholstery.

Her windshield was clouding. She turned on the air-conditioning, shivering as a blast of cold air hit her wet clothes.

She backed the Lexus cautiously down the middle of the street, water whooshing away from her tires, until she reached the Blue Moon.

And her heart sank.

The parking lot now resembled a river delta, long fingers of gravel surrounded by brown, slow moving water.

Okay. Not good. But how bad could it get? The anchorwoman this morning had reported that most flooding in the area occurred with the snow melts in the spring. The recent heavy rains had saturated the ground and flooded the narrow river channels. But the lake was not expected to rise.

So she could ride out the storm. She could wait out the flood. She was going to be—she drew a deep breath—fine.

On the seat beside her, the little dog whined.

She looked at it, wet, cowering, miserable.

"It's okay," she said reassuringly. "Things can only get better."

She hoped.

She put her purse on her shoulder and pocketed her keys, opened her door in the driving rain.

"Come on," she chirped. "Let's go."

She jumped from the car and waited for the dog to follow. It didn't.

She reached back in and tugged on the blank, black nylon collar. "Dog. Come on. Come."

The dog lowered its head, its knobby paws scrabbling on the edge of the seat.

The hell with it. Nicole grabbed the dog and bolted across the flooded parking lot.

Chapter 18

"How come I always have to be the one on top?" Mark asked. His knuckles scraped the wall. Up front, the orderly's flashlight beam jumped in the darkened stairwell. The cement steps were slippery with humidity.

"I thought you liked being on top," Lars said. He raised his end of the backboard over his head. "Easy. Step." He started down the next flight of stairs. "At least you're not going down backward."

"No, just doubled over." Mark glanced at the monitor on the transport ventilator. This patient was lucky. On some floors, nurses were using hand pumps to aid in respiration as backup batteries failed. "Airway pressure is good," he reported. "How's pulse ox?"

"Holding. We'll make it down."

Downstairs in the E.R. staging area, a medical team, including a doctor, would take over the patient's care until an ambulance or chopper became available to escort him to a new facility. And Mark and Lars, as they had for the past six hours, would hump it up the stairs and grab another backboard. The elevators were down. So were the lights. Four hours ago, to conserve the drain on the emergency generators, the hospital had shut down everything but the most essential life support. And then water had flowed into the subbasement, shorting the switches that directed power to the generators.

McCormick Mercy Hospital was dying. Now the staff and rescue workers scrambled to make sure no patients died with her.

Mark and Lars scuffled onto the landing.

"Watch the rail," Mark said.

His pager went off.

Lars froze. "Is that the disconnect alarm?"

"Nope. Beeper."

Lars grunted. "You want me to get that while you carry this yourself?"

"Very funny, Jensen. Lift."

"Why would anybody buzz you, anyway? You're already here."

Good question. Sweat snaked down his spine. The downside of having somebody to wave goodbye was you had to worry about them the whole time you were gone. How was Danny? Where was Nicole?

"It's probably my sister calling me back."

"Everything okay at home?"

"That's what I called to find out."

And as soon as they stowed their patient, he called her again.

She answered on the first ring. "Tess DeLucca."

She sounded distracted. That was okay. That didn't mean there was anything wrong. She could be working on her story.

"How's Danny?"

"Danny's fine. Mom gave both the kids dinner. How are—"

"You okay?"

"I'm fine, too. Jarek—well, he's up to his eyeballs rescuing motorists and diverting traffic, but he's safe so far. Are you—"

"What about Nicole?"

Silence.

Fear slid along Mark's ribs like a knife. "Tess? Did you reach Nicole?"

"The phone lines are down."

"That's why I gave you her cell number."

"I know. Look, I just haven't been able to get through yet. I'm sure she's all right. Jarek says the lake is large enough to absorb most of the runoff. Most of the flooding is on the west side of town."

"I thought Harbor Street was closed."

"Because of sewer backups. Not the lake levels."

"What about Front Street?"

"Evacuated. But—"

Mark swore.

"Mark, a lot of folks have chosen not to leave."

"Because they're afraid of looters," Mark said grimly.

"Jarek's entire department is out on patrol."

"Six men? One woman? Yeah, that'll stop the bad guys. Keep trying, okay?"

"You know I will."

"Tell Danny I said good-night."

"Absolutely."

"And ask Jarek if he can get an officer to check on the Blue Moon."

Lars touched his shoulder, signaling silently for him to get off the phone and hit the stairs. Teams continued to arrive in the E.R. One backboard went by carried by four men with two nurses in attendance, one to ventilate the patient and one keeping the IVs running.

"Got to go," Mark said.

"Mark...are you all right?"

"Fine," he said.

Oh, yeah. Filthy, exhausted, chafed and sore, but fine. His apartment was in an evacuation zone, his boat could have floated into a tree, his son was spending the night with his sister, and the only woman who could make him feel better about it all was lost in the flood and not answering her damn phone.

"Just fine."

Nicole owned copies of *The Dating Survival Guide, The Breakup Survival Guide,* and *The Single Woman's Survival Guide for the New Millennium.* She didn't have a *What To Do When You're Trapped Alone by Floodwater in a Deserted Bar Survival Guide.*

But she was managing pretty well without it. She had raided the restaurant kitchen for food. There was a danger she could get tired of snack mix if the waters didn't recede in a day or two, but she wouldn't go hungry. And the dog was happy with raw meat.

She had plenty to drink, cans of soda and bottled water from the bar and a tub of water for washing and flushing the toilet.

Shelter? Well, her apartment was dry. But the lake had seeped into the downstairs, overrunning the makeshift dam of bar towels she'd stuffed under the door. Standing on the stairs, she could see the water shining in the beam of her flashlight, covering the floor. She couldn't gauge its depth in the darkness, but it hadn't cleared the tabletops yet.

Something else slithered and gleamed in the darkness. The dog pressed closer to her leg and growled.

The growl surprised Nicole. She didn't think the dog had it in him. Her, she corrected herself. She'd rescued a girl dog. She tried to take power from the thought: *all girls together,* but at that moment she would have welcomed a strong, fearless male with a really big flashlight.

I'll be back, Mark had promised, but that was hours ago.

Ten hours and twenty-eight minutes ago, to be precise. Not that she was counting.

Nicole played the puny beam of her flashlight over the darkness again. And there was—oh, God, were those *eyes,* tiny eyes, close together, glowing at her from the tangle of tables?

Rats? Snakes. Icky things in the dark. Her heart hammered. Her gorge rose.

The dog shivered and growled again.

"I agree," Nicole said. Her voice shook. "What do you say we go back upstairs?"

They retreated one step at a time, Nicole keeping careful watch on the floor in all directions.

She closed and locked her apartment door. Shadows jumped away from her light. In the center of her living room, the stacked chairs and piled cartons created a lumpy landscape.

"Well," she said, making an effort to keep her voice bright, "this is cozy."

The dog sat and looked at her. Patient. Expectant.

"Are you still hungry?" Nicole asked. The dog stared. "Food?"

Its tail thumped once, but she suspected it was merely being polite. What she really needed was a book on dog care.

The apartment was very quiet. The rain had stopped. Which was a good thing, she knew that, but the silence left in the wake of the storm was a lonely thing. No traffic. Only the wind, the groan of wood and the lap of water.

It was going to be a long night. In the burst for the bar, she had stupidly left her cell phone on the passenger seat of the car. However hungry she was for the sound of a human voice—ten hours and forty-seven minutes since Mark had left her—she certainly wasn't braving whatever lurked or plopped or floated downstairs to retrieve it. But she still had her computer, at least until the battery died.

She unearthed her laptop from the pyramid of boxes. The screen glowed reassuringly in the darkened living room, crisp white cards against a still, green backdrop. Nicole clicked on an ace of spades and flicked it to the upper right-hand corner.

The dog sighed and laid its head at her feet.

Seventeen games later, the grumble of a motor broke the hush. The dog stiffened. Nicole strained to listen. A car? No, she decided. A boat. A single engine tooling quietly along the water-filled streets. She heard something scrape and someone swear, a man's voice, low.

And a new fear leaped in her like a candle flame, sudden and bright.

Some snakes driven by the flood were human.

She sat paralyzed as a powerful light pierced the window and bounced across her ceiling. Stay or move? Scream or be silent?

The engine clattered and choked.

And then the voice called, "Nicole! Babe, are you there?"

Joy flashed through her. "Mark!"

She scrambled to her feet and lunged for the window. The dog scuttled after her, yapping.

Boat. Searchlight. Men. Mark. There, riding the waters of what had been her parking lot, were two rain-slickered figures in a boat, one dark and tall and one dim yellow with reflective stripes.

Nicole struggled with the swollen sash.

The yellow slicker called, "Miss Reed? Nicole Reed?"

"Yes!" Nicole banged the window open. "Up here!"

The light swung crazily, blinding her. The dog barked and yipped.

"Why the hell don't you answer your phone?" the dark figure exploded.

"I—" Now didn't seem a very good time to explain she'd left it in her car. Thankfully, her companion was providing a distraction. Nicole bent to pat and shush her. "It's okay. Good dog."

The good dog announced that it was not okay, there were strange men out there in a boat, with lights and nasty engine sounds, and it was her duty to scare them off.

"What is that?" Mark demanded.

Nicole smiled in the direction of the light. "It's a dog," she said. "For Danny."

"Oh, God." The boat rocked as the dark figure sat down abruptly. The shoulders of the yellow slicker appeared to be shaking, but it could have been a trick of the light or the bobbing of the water.

"I found her," Nicole explained. Her heart raced. Did he remember? Would he understand? *And then I could stay, and we'd be a real family with a dog and everything.*

But Mark seemed perfectly willing to drop the subject of the dog. "How is the downstairs? Can you reach the door?"

Nicole sighed. But she didn't really want to discuss their possible future in front of the yellow slicker. And she was still awfully glad to see him.

"Nicole." Mark's voice was tight with control. "We're attempting a rescue here. Can you get downstairs to the door?"

Downstairs. Little eyes close together, glowing in the darkness. Nicole shivered. "I'm not sure. I don't think so."

"How deep is it? Because—"

"It's not the water," Nicole interrupted him. "There are…*things*…in it."

There was a brief silence. "Okay," Mark said calmly. "Then I'll carry you."

"And the dog," Nicole said.

Mark swore.

"No dog," the yellow slicker said regretfully.

"Excuse me?" said Nicole.

"Sorry, ma'am. No pets. We're a small department. And this is a small boat. We have to set priorities."

"It's a very little dog."

"Ma'am, we still have all of Front Street to cover. There may be people stuck in these buildings who need help to leave their homes. I cannot make room in the boat for a dog. Even a little one."

The boat pitched as Mark dropped over the side. Nicole squeaked, but the water only came up to his thighs. He waded forward, his slicker dragging on the black surface.

The dog barked once.

Nicole looked down. "I can't just leave her."

"I'm sure it will be fine alone overnight," the young patrol officer assured her.

"Is the water still rising?"

"We still have some runoff. But there's no more rain in the forecast. As long as you leave it closed up upstairs with plenty of food and water, it will be perfectly safe for your pet to stay."

"How safe?" Nicole asked.

"Oh, no," said Mark. His voice was directly below her now. "You're leaving with us."

"Why? If there's not enough room in the boat—"

"For animals. There's no room for animals." He grunted. "What did you do to this door?"

"Did you forget your key?"

"No, I did not forget my key. It's stuck on something."

"Oh. When the water first started coming in, I stuffed bar towels under the door."

"Right. I'll have to break a window."

"No!"

"Nicole, it's the only way I'm going to get in."

"But you don't have to get in. I'm fine. The officer said so."

"You can't stay here."

His order rankled. Not that she was crazy about the idea of spending the night alone above her water-logged and rat-infested bar. But now that Mark had come back for her, the way he'd promised, she no longer felt so scared and alone.

Anyway, it was important she meet him as an equal, not a victim. Maybe she wasn't out saving the town. But she had rescued a dog. She could keep an eye on her own property. And she could give up her place in the boat to someone who was actually suffering.

"I have food and water and a flashlight and a dog," she said. "Go rescue somebody who needs it."

Mark drew a sharp breath.

"We do have other calls to answer," the young cop said hastily. "And the chief wants us to check out Liberty Sporting Goods, make sure the grill is down over the window."

Mark sloshed back toward the boat until he was in her line of sight. He looked up at her window, his face harsh in the glare of the search light, his voice grim. "We'll be in the area all night," he told her. "You have a problem, you yell."

"I will," she said.

"And I'm coming back."

She smiled. "That's a promise," she told him.

The vibration woke her before the noise. Nicole blinked bleary eyes in the dark room. It was…okay, it was the dog. She was growling, her small, furry body shaking with warning, her head raised from the bed she had shared with Nicole.

"It's all right," Nicole whispered, although she wasn't sure it was yet, not really. She threw back the covers and slid out of bed, still wearing her T-shirt and slacks.

A knock sounded from the front of the apartment. That was good, Nicole thought as she armed herself with the flashlight and hurried down the hall. The dog's toenails clicked beside her. Burglars wouldn't knock. Would they?

"Nicole?" It was a man's voice. Mark's.

The dog yipped once. Nicole sighed in relief and pleasure and moved to let him in.

"It's about time you showed up," she said, opening the door. "What is it, two o'clock? Three?"

He slouched through the doorway. "Four-thirty. Call off your beast."

Nicole bent to shush the dog. "You must be exhausted," she said, straightening. Her heart pattered in her chest. "Come to bed."

He stopped in the middle of her living room floor among the cartons and the stacked chairs. "I'm not coming to bed with you. I'm wet and I smell."

She wrinkled her nose. Now that he mentioned it... "Yes, you do. Why don't you take your clothes off?"

He didn't move. "Too tired."

She might have felt rejected, except he had been up all night with the rescue effort.

"Then I guess I'll have to do it for you," she said, and reached to take hold of his slicker.

He made a halfhearted effort to fend her off. "You'll get all dirty."

She ignored the jerky motion of his hands to tug the slicker down his arms.

"Then you'll get to undress me," she said. "I don't see this as a problem."

He stood there then, as she concentrated on snaps and buttons, as she wrestled with wet and wrinkled fabric. Under the stink of the floodwaters, he smelled of male and exhaustion. She uncovered him, his leanness and his manliness and his strength, the black hair that grew on his chest and his thighs, his olive skin still cold from the water, and an enormous tenderness flowed in her and filled her.

It was such a small, intimate service, undressing him. So personal, so practical, so...subservient, almost. She could have felt used. Maybe with another man, at another time, she would have felt used. But now she was only happy to be able to do this one thing for him.

She let his clothes fall in a heap to the floor, where the dog nosed at them. Taking his hand, she started to lead him down the hall to her room.

"I'm useless to you, babe. I'm too tired to start anything."

She shut the door on the dog and held open the covers for him. "You could try sleeping."

He smiled crookedly. "Yeah, I could try that."

He folded his long limbs onto the bed. She tucked him in, her hands lingering on his shoulders as she pulled the covers up and then crawled in beside him. He rolled toward her and hooked an arm around her waist, pulling her into him. His naked chest was a wall against her back, his naked thighs cradled her rear. She could feel the heaviness of his limbs and the tension in his muscles.

He had pushed his body past mere tiredness into sleepless fatigue. But for long minutes he lay very still, careful not to disturb her.

Nicole held her breath, willing him to relax, wanting him to sleep, wanting...

She exhaled noisily. "So, how was your day?"

His silent laughter stirred her hair. "It was all right. Power's back up at the hospital. Water's receding. Jarek's doing a good job. Only found one broken window on the whole street."

"Would that be my window?" she asked wryly.

"Is that a problem?"

"No." She smiled against his arm. "I'll just deduct it from your next paycheck."

He bit her neck gently, making a nerve there kick and tickling other nerves, lower down. "I wouldn't have had to break in if you'd left here when the flood started."

"Really? And where should I have gone?"

"Away. Chicago. Your parents' house, maybe."

She shook her head, enjoying the texture of his skin against her cheek. "'Hi, Mother, can I move back home? My new business venture is about to be swept away by floodwaters.' No."

"You should talk to them." He sounded serious. Too serious.

"Oh, like you talk to your mother," she mocked.

"I do. At least, I did today."

She turned in his arms, genuinely pleased. "Mark! Really?"

"Mmm." Their knees brushed. Their legs tangled. He dropped a kiss on her nose. "She ended up watching Danny for me."

"That's good." Nicole bit her lip; studied his face. "Is it good?"

"It was okay."

"Only okay?" she probed.

He shrugged, making the blanket slide from his shoulder. "I'm still not sure how much I trust her. I mean, in my head I do. She's been dry a long time. But I can't help feeling—" He broke off.

"Angry?" Nicole suggested.

"No. Why would I be angry?"

She traced the outline of his lips with her finger. "Because she's your mother and she didn't take care of you?"

His mouth tightened. "That was a long time ago. I was a kid."

"Exactly. And now that you're a compassionate and caring man with a child of your own to consider…" She kissed him softly until she felt his lips relax under hers. "You don't have to be angry with her anymore."

"Is that something else you got out of a book?" But he didn't sound upset.

She raised her head. "Is that bad?"

"Only if you're trying to change the subject."

The heat in his eyes made her heart pound. "What was the subject?"

"We were talking about you leaving. You should have gotten out when the flood warning was announced."

Okay, obviously they were thinking about different subjects. She tried not to mind. He was very tired.

"You didn't leave," she said.

He scowled. "I had work here."

"So did I. I have my business here. My home."

"Your life is worth more than this damn place."

His sudden fierceness startled her. And gave her hope.

"Well—" She tried smiling at him. "If I hadn't stayed, I might not have rescued the dog."

"Yeah, and that was another stupid risk."

Her smile came more naturally this time. "You'll just have to trust my judgment about the dog."

"Trust your judgment?"

"Yes," she said firmly.

"Yeah? And if the owner comes looking for it?"

"Then we'll deal with that." She wiggled closer, partly because he felt so good and partly because he was naked and warm and apparently oblivious to the fact that she was naked, too, and totally available.

When she was sure she had his attention—*Hello…naked. Yes, I've got that*—she said, "Pets don't come with a guarantee. But sometimes the risks are worth taking anyway."

"We still talking about the dog here?" he asked huskily.

She swallowed. "We could be."

She wouldn't ask for promises he was not prepared to give. What they had now would be enough. She would make it be enough. Even if he broke her heart, she would never regret loving him.

He was silent so long she was afraid he had fallen asleep. Her chest tightened with love and disappointment. She held him close in the darkness, absorbing his heat, sharing his breath.

"So. You ready to take a risk?" he asked abruptly.

She raised her head. "Didn't you bring a condom? Because I bought—"

"Not that kind of risk." He rubbed his face with his hand. "Jeez. I'm too tired to do this right."

"That's all right," she assured him, although she wanted him, wanted the comfort and connection of sex. "We can wait until morning."

"Wait for what?"

"Well, to—" make love "—have sex."

"Babe, I'm not talking about sex."

"Okay." She waited, bewildered.

He exhaled. "Marriage," he said. "I'm talking marriage."

Marriage. The possibilities crashed over her in a wave, leaving her breathless and sputtering. Her chest was too tight. Her mind spun.

"You want to marry me?"

"Yeah. Well, I want to have sex with you, too, but I figured this was a good time for a proposal."

Joy welled inside her. She opened her mouth to say yes, a hundred times yes, but a tiny habit of doubt remained.

She narrowed her eyes at him. "We're tired, we're filthy, we're lying above a snake-infested bar in the middle of a flood, and you think now would be a good time for a proposal?"

He lifted his hand and smoothed a strand of hair away from her temple. The simple tenderness of the gesture melted her heart.

"How else am I going to convince you I want you for yourself?" he asked, and kissed her. His warm breath skated across her face. His warm mouth glided along her upper lip and rubbed her lower one.

But even as she sighed and opened for him, she wanted more. He had so much love to give, such a need to give it. And she wanted it all.

"You could try telling me," she suggested breathlessly when at last he raised his head.

"Tell you what?"

"Why we should get married."

Mark rolled so that he was on top of her, all that lovely heat and weight pressing her into the mattress. "You want reasons?" He rocked into her suggestively. "I can give you reasons."

She sucked in her breath, feeling the length of him all along her body. Oh, my. Oh, yes, he could. But this time she wasn't going to settle. This time she was going to get everything she wanted and give everything she had in return.

"I only need one. If it's the right one."

"Babe, this is the only one I've got."

She was hot with embarrassment, warm with laughter and desire. "The right *reason*."

"Okay." He frowned, considering. "You need me to fix your window."

"That doesn't count. You're the one who broke it in the first place."

"Right. All right." He nuzzled her neck, making the pulse there go wild. "You need me to walk the dog."

"Wrong. I'm giving you the dog. You and Danny. Try again."

"Well, you might not think so," he said, the words muffled against her throat, "but I've got a lot of pay saved up. You could use it to fix the flood damage."

His careless offer stunned her. She grabbed a handful of his hair and pulled so she could look into his face. "You would give your savings to me?"

"Sure." He smiled crookedly, making her breath catch. "I would give you anything you wanted."

"I don't want your money. Anyway, I have flood insurance. I need a personal reason. An *emotional* reason."

There. Her heart pounded. She couldn't be plainer than that.

"Like, 'Marry me, it will drive your mother crazy'?"

Disappointment made her mouth droop. "No. That's not good enough. Besides, everything I do drives my mother crazy."

"You could marry me for Danny," he suggested, his voice teasing.

"For—"

He held her gaze. "You like boys. You said so."

"I do. Oh, I do. But—"

"Or…" His voice deepened. His eyes darkened. "You could marry me because I love you. I love you, Nicole. Nobody will ever love you the way that I do."

Joy and relief swept through her in a flood. She hugged him to her, closing her eyes in gratitude.

"That's all I need to hear. That's all I need." She took a deep breath. "But I won't marry you because of that."

His body tensed against hers. "Right. Well, there isn't anything left to say, then, is there?"

A great tenderness filled her heart. "Yes, there is. The reason. The only reason I could marry you."

"What reason, damn it?"

"Because I love you back the same way."

He went very still. In the dim light that came through her window, his face was as hard and beautiful as an angel's.

"That's a good reason," he whispered, and held her tight until the dawn broke over the water.

Epilogue

The morning of Teresa DeLucca's marriage to police chief Jarek Denko dawned bright and clear.

Half of Eden turned out to see their hometown reporter wed their chief of police. After the week's storms and floods, most people were eager to put aside the cleanup of their homes and businesses to rejoice and give thanks.

At the back of the church, the bride's tiny blond attendant bent to twitch her train into perfect folds. To the surprise of everyone except those who knew her very well, Tess had chosen a traditional gown and veil.

Even to a brother's eyes, she looked beautiful.

Mark waited as Faye straightened from fussing with his sister's dress.

"There," she said with satisfaction. "All set."

"Thank you," Tess said.

Faye flashed a smile. "I'm counting on you doing the same for me." The little blonde was engaged to be married to Jarek's brother Aleksy two months from now.

Mark stepped into the foyer, having just delivered their mother to the pew.

"You ready?" he asked his sister.

Tess nodded, her golden eyes glowing. Up in the choir loft, Shirley Mulroney started something on the old pipe organ that shivered through the church like a fanfare.

"There's my cue," Faye announced and grabbed her bouquet—deep pink roses to match her dress—from Jarek's dark-haired daughter, Allie.

At the edge of the white runner, Allie paused and looked over her shoulder. Not so much for permission to start forward, Mark thought, as to make sure Tess stayed in line behind her.

Tess blew her a kiss. Allie grinned, suddenly ten again, and stepped out in her new high-heeled shoes.

Tess tightened her hold on Mark's arm.

"This is it," he said. "The DeLuccas' last charge. Unless you want to borrow my Jeep."

She took a deep breath. "Nope."

He shrugged. "Probably just as well. Jarek would come after you anyway. After he broke my nose."

So she was smiling when he led her into the church.

The Denko brothers stood at the altar, shoulder to shoulder beside the priest, tall and dark and formidable. Mark hoped like hell his sister knew what she was getting into. He leveled a look at the groom—*Be good to her or you're a dead man*—but Jarek only had eyes for Tess, walking up the aisle toward him. Next to him, tough cop Aleksy watched Faye with the hopeful, stunned expression of an outfielder seeing a pop fly drop into his mitt.

So maybe it was okay. Maybe everything was going to be okay.

Stolid Eric and dark-eyed Mary Denko beamed from their position across the aisle from Isadora DeLucca. His mother's slight figure blocked Mark's view of her pew, but he knew Danny was sitting beside her.

And beside him…

Tess's manicured nails dug into the sleeve of Mark's rented tux. The priest stepped forward to meet them. They were there. It was time to let go.

"Well," she whispered shakily, "we made it."

He leaned down to kiss her cheek. When he stepped back, her golden eyes were bright with tears and happiness.

"Nothing but fair winds and smooth sailing from now on," he told her.

Jarek took her hand. The look on Tess's face was enough to make anybody believe she'd found her own safe harbor.

Isadora sobbed happily behind them. Well, hell, Mark's own throat was a little tight.

Turning, he walked along the front of the pew until he reached the open end on the far side. His mother sat on the aisle. Danny was beside her, interested and uncomfortable in a white shirt and a navy blazer. And next to his son, wearing pale blue silk and a welcoming smile, stood Nicole.

It was like staring at his future and knowing it was going to be good. Better than good. Outstanding. Everything he wanted was right there, with her.

She watched him slide along the pew toward her, the look in her blue, blue eyes only for him. Always for him. His heart swelled like a sail. With her love behind him, he could go anywhere. Do anything. Be the man he was always meant to be.

Reaching them, he lifted Danny in his arms and then turned back to her. Hopeful. Happy. And his.

"Looking for someone?" he murmured.

Nicole smiled back with complete confidence and tucked her hand in the crook of his arm. "Not anymore."

* * * * *

There could be more TROUBLE IN EDEN *next year, but first watch out for Virginia's thrilling story in the* FEMME FATALE *single title available this August wherever Silhouette Books are sold. And then October brings us* THE ASSASSIN, *part of the* FAMILY SECRETS *continuity!*

Don't miss the latest miniseries from award-winning author Marie Ferrarella:

The MOM SQUAD

Meet...

Sherry Campbell—ambitious newswoman who makes headlines when a handsome billionaire arrives to sweep her off her feet...and shepherd her new son into the world!
A BILLIONAIRE AND A BABY, SE#1528,
available March 2003

Joanna Prescott—Nine months after her visit to the sperm bank, her old love rescues her from a burning house—then delivers her baby....
A BACHELOR AND A BABY, SD#1503,
available April 2003

Chris "C.J." Jones—FBI agent, expectant mother and always on the case. When the baby comes, will her irresistible partner be by her side?
THE BABY MISSION, IM#1220, available May 2003

Lori O'Neill—A forbidden attraction blows down this pregnant Lamaze teacher's tough-woman facade and makes her consider the love of a lifetime!
BEAUTY AND THE BABY, SR#1668,
available June 2003

The Mom Squad—these single mothers-to-be are ready for labor...and true love!

If you enjoyed what you just read,
then we've got an offer you can't resist!

Take 2 bestselling
love stories FREE!
Plus get a FREE surprise gift!

Clip this page and mail it to Silhouette Reader Service™

IN U.S.A.	**IN CANADA**
3010 Walden Ave.	P.O. Box 609
P.O. Box 1867	Fort Erie, Ontario
Buffalo, N.Y. 14240-1867	L2A 5X3

YES! Please send me 2 free Silhouette Intimate Moments® novels and my free surprise gift. After receiving them, if I don't wish to receive anymore, I can return the shipping statement marked cancel. If I don't cancel, I will receive 6 brand-new novels every month, before they're available in stores! In the U.S.A., bill me at the bargain price of $3.99 plus 25¢ shipping and handling per book and applicable sales tax, if any*. In Canada, bill me at the bargain price of $4.74 plus 25¢ shipping and handling per book and applicable taxes**. That's the complete price and a savings of at least 10% off the cover prices—what a great deal! I understand that accepting the 2 free books and gift places me under no obligation ever to buy any books. I can always return a shipment and cancel at any time. Even if I never buy another book from Silhouette, the 2 free books and gift are mine to keep forever.

245 SDN DNUV
345 SDN DNUW

Name	(PLEASE PRINT)	
Address	Apt.#	
City	State/Prov.	Zip/Postal Code

* Terms and prices subject to change without notice. Sales tax applicable in N.Y.
** Canadian residents will be charged applicable provincial taxes and GST.
   All orders subject to approval. Offer limited to one per household and not valid to current Silhouette Intimate Moments® subscribers.
   ® are registered trademarks of Harlequin Books S.A., used under license.

INMOM02   ©1998 Harlequin Enterprises Limited

Coming in April 2003

baby and all

Three brand-new stories about the trials and triumphs of motherhood.

"Somebody Else's Baby"
by *USA TODAY* bestselling author Candace Camp

Widow Cassie Weeks had turned away from the world—until her stepdaughter's baby turned up on her doorstep. This tiny new life—and her gorgeous new neighbor—would teach Cassie she had a lot more living…and loving to do….

"The Baby Bombshell" by Victoria Pade

Robin Maguire knew nothing about babies or romance. But lucky for her, when she suddenly inherited an infant, the sexy single father across the hall was more than happy to teach her about both.

"Lights, Camera…Baby!" by Myrna Mackenzie

When Eve Carpenter and her sexy boss were entrusted with caring for their CEO's toddler, the formerly baby-wary executive found herself wanting to be a real-life mother—and her boss's real-life wife.

Silhouette®

Where love comes alive™

COMING NEXT MONTH

#1219 GABRIEL WEST: STILL THE ONE—Fiona Brand
Gabriel West would do anything to win back his wife,
Dr. Tyler Laine—even quit his high-risk career with the SAS.
Then he discovered that *she* was the one in danger. A stalker had
framed her for a priceless jewel theft, and now he wanted her dead.
Gabriel had lost Tyler once before, and no matter what, he wouldn't
let anyone take her away again.

#1220 THE BABY MISSION—Marie Ferrarella
The Mom Squad
Alone and eight months pregnant, FBI agent C. J. Jones
should have been taking it easy, but when an elusive serial
killer resurfaced, she couldn't ignore the case. Nor could she
ignore the feelings growing between her and her longtime partner,
Byron Warrick—a relationship that was strictly forbidden. But when
C.J.'s life was threatened, Warrick would break *any* rule to save her.

#1221 ENTRAPMENT—Kylie Brant
The Tremaine Tradition
For two years, CIA agent Sam Tremaine had followed
a criminal mastermind across the globe. Now, to finally apprehend
him, Sam needed help from an unlikely source: Juliette Morrow, an
international thief with a hunger for revenge and a weakness for sexy
special agents. Could Sam stick to his plan, or would the beautiful
thief steal his heart?

#1222 AT CLOSE RANGE—Marilyn Tracy
Corrie Stratton opened her heart to the many orphans she took in at
Rancho Milagro, but she had never been able to open herself to love.
Until she encountered Mack Dorsey, the ranch's intense new teacher.
She needed his help to solve an ancient mystery that threatened her
kids, but could he also discover the passion Corrie kept hidden
inside?

#1223 THE LAST HONORABLE MAN—Vickie Taylor
An innocent man was dead, his pregnant fiancée, Elisa Reyes, was
alone and Texas Ranger Del Cooper blamed himself. Due to Elisa's
dangerous past, the government wanted to deport her—an act that
would equal a death sentence. To save her, Del proposed, risking his
hard-earned career. But when she was kidnapped, he realized he was
willing to lose anything—except her.

#1224 McIVER'S MISSION—Brenda Harlen
Despite her undeniable attraction to attorney Shaun McIver,
Arden Doherty refused to let him into her life. But when a madman
targeted her, Shaun rushed to her rescue. As he investigated her
case, he uncovered painful secrets from Arden's past. But could he
convince her that she could count on him? And could he find her
killer before the killer found her?

SIMCNM0403